"I've had four years of celibacy."

Grace made the confession with the air of pride that commitment deserved.

"You mean you've gone four years without sex," Mac scoffed.

She sat up a little straighter, stuck her chest out a little more. "Four years, three months and five days to be exact."

"I don't believe you."

"What? Why?"

"Because nobody with a body like yours could go four years without sex," he said bluntly.

"I'm not sure I know what you mean by that."

He didn't say a word as his gaze slid down. "Yeah, you do," he said finally.

Grace was unbearably aware of the brush of her clothes against her skin. Her nipples had hardened, and she squeezed her knees together in a vain attempt to quell the slow ache growing between her thighs.

Images flashed across her mind: Mac's superbly muscled chest, the firm perfection of his butt in jeans.... As much as she didn't want to admit it, she wanted him. Now.

Blaze™

Dear Reader,

Welcome to Grace's story. I must confess to a serious case of living vicariously through this book. Grace and Mac each drive one of the most beautiful cars ever made. If you're not familiar with what a '57 Corvette looks like, check it out on the Internet—it's a lovely beast and a must for any romantic heroine.

I also had a lot of fun researching Grace's vintage wardrobe. I know what you're thinking—no one can actually *see* what she's wearing. But when I write, it's a little like watching a movie in my mind, and Grace's wardrobe was spectacular. My hearty thanks go to www.vintageous.com, a great online retailer of vintage clothing. This is a fabulous place to waste a few hours!

Of course, the story isn't really about the clothes and the car—it's about the people. Mac and Grace are both flawed, cynical people who battle to the death to see who can out-cool the other. We all have our reasons for needing to protect ourselves. I hope you enjoy discovering theirs.

Hearing from readers makes my day. You can contact me via my Web site—www.sarahmayberryauthor.com—or c/o Harlequin Books, 225 Duncan Mill Road, Don Mills, Ontario M3B 3K9, Canada. Keep an eye out for the last installment in the SECRET LIVES OF DAYTIME DIVAS miniseries, *Hot for Him,* due out in May 2007.

Happy reading!

Sarah Mayberry

ALL OVER YOU
Sarah Mayberry

HARLEQUIN®

TORONTO • NEW YORK • LONDON
AMSTERDAM • PARIS • SYDNEY • HAMBURG
STOCKHOLM • ATHENS • TOKYO • MILAN • MADRID
PRAGUE • WARSAW • BUDAPEST • AUCKLAND

ISBN-13: 978-0-373-79324-2
ISBN-10:   0-373-79324-3

ALL OVER YOU

www.eHarlequin.com

Printed in U.S.A.

ABOUT THE AUTHOR

Sarah Mayberry lives in Melbourne, Australia, with her partner, Chris. In addition to writing romance novels, she also writes scripts for television shows. While she has never even shaken hands with a star on any of the shows she works on, she has a rich fantasy life and a vivid imagination, and she has definitely written her share of shirtless scenes for hunky male actors.

Books by Sarah Mayberry
HARLEQUIN BLAZE
211—CAN'T GET ENOUGH
251—CRUISE CONTROL*
278—ANYTHING FOR YOU*
314—TAKE ON ME†

*It's All About Attitude
†Secret Lives of Daytime Divas

This book was a battle, and I wouldn't have survived it without chief medic Kirsty, my great friend and writing partner, and Chris, my own personal hero. Without his patience, ideas, soothing arms, tissue passing, massages, chocolate therapy and sounding board, this book would not exist. You're the best. And, as always, thanks to Wanda, super-editor, for lifting my game.

1

GRACE WELLINGTON slid into a chair at her favorite Santa Monica café, arranged her shopping bags beside her and glanced at her watch. Sadie Post and Claudia Dostis, her two best friends, were meeting her for lunch but neither of them had arrived yet.

Might as well use the time to gloat over her latest find. Sliding a hand into the brown-paper shopping bag propped against her chair leg, her fingers encountered the sensuous softness of angora. Unable to resist a full gloat, Grace tugged the sweater out and spread it across her lap. A soft cream color, the sweater had embroidered flowers garnished with sequins above one breast and three-quarter sleeves. Best of all, it bore the label of a prestigious 1950s knitware manufacturer. Genuine vintage, and she'd picked it up for a song.

Resisting the urge to purr like a contented cat, she folded the sweater and put it back in its bag. Feeling every inch the satisfied, smug shopper, she glanced at her watch once again and picked up the menu. Would it be terribly wrong to have a cocktail in the middle of a Sunday afternoon? Some people would think so, but Grace had never been too worried about what other people thought.

She ran her finger down the list until she found something fresh and bright to suit her mood. The sun was shining, she'd just cruised all her favorite vintage-clothing boutiques, and she was about to have lunch with her two best friends. Did life get any better?

The sound of a motorcycle engine roaring to a stop drew her attention to the street outside and she smiled, bracing herself for her daily exposure to love's young dream. Crossing one leg over the other, she sat back and crossed her arms, prepared to indulge her cynical side.

There were two riders on the bike—a male driver and a woman clinging to his back. Only the woman dismounted, unfolding legs that seemed to go on forever as she pulled off her helmet and shook out a mane of honey-blond hair. Having slid his own helmet off, the man watched her appreciatively. He said something, then pulled the woman close and kissed her so thoroughly that Grace actually felt a blush stealing into her cheeks. Feeling distinctly like a voyeur, she glanced away.

Sadie and Dylan were so happy, so in love. So perfect together. If they weren't her friends, she'd be making gagging noises right now and telling them to get a room. But even though she didn't believe in monogamy and marriage and all that other hoopla for herself anymore, she absolutely respected Sadie's joy. Each to her own, right?

She risked another look and saw the coast was clear—they were just talking now, smiling goofily at each other, their fingers intertwined.

Watching their interplay, noting the teasing glint in Dylan's eyes, the gentleness in their hands as they caressed each other almost unconsciously, an odd yearning sensation spread out from the region of Grace's heart, sneaking up the back of her throat and triggering the hot sting of tears behind her eyes.

Whoa! What the hell was that *about?*

Blinking furiously, Grace reached for her sunglasses and

sniffed surreptitiously. Trying to shake off the moment, she shifted in her chair and frowned at the tabletop. Maybe she was allergic or something. Maybe the angora sweater would have to go back.

She snorted at her lack of belief in her own excuses and forced herself to look at her friends again. What she saw made her swallow, hard. Dylan had cupped Sadie's face, and he was talking intently as he stared into her eyes. Grace didn't need to hear him to know what he was saying—he was telling Sadie he loved her, how important she was to him, how he was going to miss her even though she would only be lunching with her friends for a few measly hours. It was written all over his face and, as his thumb caressed Sadie's cheekbone, Grace felt such a stab of longing in her belly that she actually pressed her hands to her stomach.

Tearing her eyes away from the scene outside, she stared unseeingly in front of her.

She wasn't jealous of Sadie and Dylan.

Was she?

It was a ridiculous idea. Absurd. It had been four years since she'd let a man into her bedroom and her life, and they had been the happiest, most productive and content years of her life.

Even discounting her ex-boyfriend, Owen, and his spectacular contribution to her lack of faith in human nature, life had taught Grace plenty of salutary lessons about what to expect from the male of the species—not much, was what it boiled down to. Once she'd accepted that concept, her life had become so much easier. She'd become mistress of her own domain, so to speak.

So what was the whole yearning-pain-in-chest thing about?

Out of the corner of her eye, she saw that Sadie and Dylan were kissing again. She was just marveling at their endurance and the fact that they hadn't been arrested for indecent happiness or something similar when the penny dropped—it was the sex.

Of course.

It had been a long time since she'd felt the warmth of another body against her own, a long time since she'd found release in a man's arms. That was all. Who wouldn't look at Sadie and Dylan's obvious passion and feel a little…empty?

She shifted uncomfortably as she registered her own choice of words. *Empty.* Did she really feel empty? Her lips firmed. No, she did not. Definitely, she did not.

"Gracie, sorry I'm late." It was Claudia, dressed in her signature black, her small frame vibrating with energy as always. Her Greek-American heritage was evident in the sparkle of her near-black eyes, the olive tone of her skin and the take-no-shit attitude in her straight shoulders.

"You're not late, I was early," Grace said.

As one, their gazes drifted to the front window where Sadie and Dylan were *still* kissing each other goodbye.

"How long has that been going on?" Claudia asked.

Grace sighed. "About five minutes. I figure one of them will need oxygen any second now."

"We could turn a hose on them," Claudia mused.

"Shame to ruin those nice leather jackets."

"I guess."

Claudia met Grace's gaze across the table and laughed.

"Listen to us—envy dripping from every word."

Grace shook her head, her claret-colored hair swishing around her shoulders.

"Not guilty, sorry."

"Really?" Claudia sighed, eyes on Sadie and Dylan again. "Not even a little bit? Even though I'm way too busy to think about men at the moment, I still can't help looking at them and feeling a little I-want-what-she's-having."

"Nope," Grace said, ignoring the odd feeling she'd experienced mere minutes earlier. "Unless I can stuff a man and turn him into an umbrella stand, there's no place for one in my home."

Claudia choked out a laugh.

"Sorry, guys. Dylan and I just had some last-minute things to sort out." Sadie was pink-faced and faintly breathless as she slid into the last chair at their table.

"Like whose tongue belongs to who, that kind of thing?" Claudia asked wryly.

"Yeah," Sadie said, grinning unrepentantly.

All three of them smiled at each other and Grace registered how great it was to have some quality time with her friends. It was one thing to see each other every day in the production offices of *Ocean Boulevard,* the daytime soap where they all worked—Claudia as producer, Sadie as script producer and Grace as script editor—but it wasn't quite the same as having time to laugh and talk without the pressures of work interfering.

"Cocktail time, ladies," Grace said, passing around the menu.

"Excellent. I could slaughter something sweet and creamy," Sadie said, smacking her lips together.

"Martini for me. Dirty," Claudia said, wiggling her eyebrows suggestively.

"Now there's a surprise," Grace said.

Twisting in her seat, Grace made eye contact with the waiter. He shot to their table as though he'd been pulled on a string, his eyes lighting up as his gaze slid from Sadie to Claudia and back again.

That Sadie was many men's idea of the perfect woman hadn't escaped Grace's notice over the years. And if men didn't go for Sadie's tall, blond, leggy good looks, they were usually pretty damn partial to Claudia's petite perfection. Mentally resigning herself to being ignored, Grace adopted her best Bette Davis demeanor. Bette was a take-no-prisoners kind of woman, the type who didn't give a snap of her fingers if men were attracted to her or not. It helped that Grace was wearing one of her favorite Bette Davis-era dresses, a 1940s dark-green crepe sundress with cap sleeves, a sailor collar and a short white tie.

Arching one eyebrow, she tapped a varnished nail on the menu to get the waiter's attention. He managed to drag his gaze from Sadie and Claudia's cleavage, only for his eyes to widen as he took in Grace's substantial twin endowments. Grace growled low in the back of her throat. Just her luck, their waiter was a breast man. If there was one thing she hated more than being ignored, it was being ogled. Inevitably, his gaze would make it up to her face and she'd see the same old disappointment there as always. She was used to being the odd one out, the ugly duckling among the swans—but for four years now she'd opted to skip the part where men tried to weigh up the relative merits of her stupendous bosom versus her plain-Jane face—she much preferred to cut straight to the bit where she froze them in their tracks. It had become something of a hobby, in fact.

"Hey, up here," she said, waving her fingers in his sight-line and directing his attention to her face.

He blushed and she tapped the menu again.

"One dirty martini, a Fluffy Duck—that's right, isn't it, Sadie?" she asked, checking with her friend even though she knew it was Sadie's favorite cocktail. Sadie nodded and Grace eyed their waiter steadily as she delivered her own order, daring him to maintain eye contact with her and not check out her breasts again. "And I'll have a Mojito."

"Sure. Any meals?"

"We're not ready yet. We'll let you know when we are," she said, waggling her fingers dismissively.

He nodded obediently and shot toward the bar to put their order in.

Claudia was shaking her head when Grace turned her attention back to the table.

"The way you treat men is almost a form of cruelty," Claudia said. "Almost."

"I know. I can never decide whether to be appalled or amused," Sadie agreed.

"He deserved it." Grace shrugged. "Imagine if women went around staring at men's packages the way they stare at our boobs."

"You *do* have a great rack, Gracie," Claudia said, eyeing Grace's chest impartially.

"Then he needs to learn to be more subtle and I've just taught him a powerful lesson," Grace said.

"Sometimes I think you really hate men," Sadie said sadly.

"Oh, I don't care enough to hate them," Grace drawled.

Sadie leaned forward, her expression earnest.

"Not everyone is a rat like Owen."

"I know that."

"I wonder if you do," Sadie mused. "When was the last time you went on a date?"

"I honestly can't remember. But do I look like a woman who's pining for a man?" Grace asked, gesturing toward herself.

Sadie's gaze traveled over Grace, obviously assessing her dead-straight burgundy-colored hairstyle, her severely straight bangs, her lush, full mouth outlined in deep-red lipstick, her ever-present chunky black-framed glasses and the smooth creaminess of her skin—her one acknowledged vanity.

"No. As always, you look fabulous. Except for the glasses."

"There we go, then. And I love these glasses," Grace said.

"Those glasses are ugly. And I'm not pining for a man, but I miss the sex. Don't you miss sex? I miss sex a lot," Claudia said. "I so need to call Harry or Simon and set up a date."

Claudia had been so busy working her butt off as the newly installed producer on *Ocean Boulevard* that she hadn't had a man in her life for months and months—but Harry and Simon were ex-boyfriends who were happy to provide essential services on demand.

"I have sex." Grace shrugged.

"I meant with a man," Claudia said dryly.

"Now why would I ruin something so good by inviting a man along?" Grace asked.

Sadie looked so outraged that Grace ruined the whole Bette Davis thing by laughing. Sadie threw a napkin at her.

"So, what date is the wedding?" Claudia asked, masterfully changing subjects.

Sadie sat up a little straighter. "How did you know we'd set a date?"

Grace snorted with laughter. "Hello! We thought we were going to have to pry you guys apart with a crowbar out there."

Sadie blushed, then shrugged a shoulder. "End of August. Is two months enough time to get our shit together?" Sadie asked worriedly.

"Hell yeah," Grace said.

"The dress won't be a big deal, since I'm going off-the-rack this time. And it's all going to be very low-key… But I still want you guys to be my bridesmaids. What do you say—are you up for a second shot?" Sadie asked, referring to her first, failed wedding to her former fiancé, Greg.

"Try and keep us away," Grace said.

"The bridesmaids' dresses are my shout this time around," Sadie said. "I don't want anything to be the same again, but you guys shouldn't have to pay twice."

"Forget it," Grace said firmly. "There's no way we're letting you pay for our dresses."

"Yeah. How are we supposed to argue with you when you're paying?" Claudia asked.

"And, this time, I get a vote," Grace said. "Something with straps would be nice for the fuller-figured members of the wedding party."

"You looked hot in that strapless red sheath and you know it," Sadie scoffed.

The rest of their lunch slipped quickly away as they hammered out the broad strokes of Sadie and Dylan's wedding, argued over dress styles and laughingly suggested flowery wedding vows to personalize the ceremony. After two hours, they'd moved from cocktails to coffee and had filled the backs of innumerable napkins.

"Why do writers never have paper on them?" Grace asked as she gathered the napkins together.

"Or pens," Claudia added, counting out her share of the bill. "What's with that?"

Sadie shrugged. "Don't want to take our work home with us?"

As if that particular strategy ever worked.

Later that evening, Grace sat down to a gourmet-meal-for-one at her small drop-leaf dining table. She'd bought a crisp sauvignon blanc to accompany her salmon with baby vegetables and garlic mash, and she slathered her bread roll with proper butter, damning her curvy hips and thighs to hell.

Consigning the washing up to tomorrow—one of the joys of living alone—she slipped into a satin gown she wore to bed and flopped onto the couch. When a quick flick through the offerings on TV drew no interest, she resorted to her movie collection. She was about to dust off an old *Indiana Jones* DVD when her eye fell on the DVD she'd brought home from work. She hesitated a moment, then gave in to temptation.

Sliding the disc into her player, she made a fortress of cushions for herself on the couch and settled in for the evening. The *Ocean Boulevard* theme song came on and the credits flickered across the screen. Her heartbeat picked up and her body tensed a little in anticipation…. And then Mac Harrison's tall body filled the screen and every nerve ending in her body went on hyper-alert.

It was part of her job to keep up-to-date with how the scripts she edited translated on-screen—but she'd be kidding herself if she pretended watching the show was anything other than a chance to spend some time with the only man she'd allowed into her life in the past four years.

He was so hot. Six-foot-three-inches of sexy, hard male. Gorgeous. Dynamic. Charismatic. And all hers for the next few hours.

She narrowed her eyes, trying to define exactly what it was about Mac that had captured her imagination and led her to cast him as the star of her most intimate fantasies. It wasn't as though she'd been looking for a man to play the role. She'd always spread her favors, so to speak, across a broad spectrum of hunks—George Clooney, Jude Law and Johnny Depp. And even if she had been looking for inspiration closer to home, there were plenty of attractive men on the show—eye candy galore, in fact—who could have fit the bill equally well. But none of them had the power to turn her insides to mush the way Mac did.

Of its own accord, her finger pressed the pause button, the better to complete her appraisal.

He was wearing only a pair of worn jeans, exposing most of the good stuff to her roving eye. She scanned his broad shoulders appreciatively—well-muscled but not too Arnold Schwarzenegger chunky, they were just about perfect. Then her eyes dropped to his trim, toned waist. Also pretty damned fine. And his butt—the perkiest, most grabbable, most I-want-to-take-a-bite butt she'd ever seen. As if all of the above wasn't enough, her gaze slid to his long, strong legs. Firm thigh muscles hinted at speed and strength and stamina and a whole lot of other *S* words that were making her feel decidedly...*warm* as she lay stretched on the couch.

God, he was hot. With a capital *H*.

Biting her lip, Grace pressed the play button and watched as he swung back into action. He had an amazing walk—almost a swagger, really. Like a modern-day cowboy. It screamed masculinity and confidence, and combined with his sans-shirt condition, was almost enough to make her hyperventilate.

"Oh, yeah," she groaned as he turned toward camera, revealing superbly toned abdominal muscles and a chest covered with exactly the right amount of darkened caramel curls.

The camera zoomed in tight for a close-up and she was treated to the full force of his cerulean-blue gaze as he stared down the barrel. He had a strong brow, cheekbones and jaw line, with a straight, very masculine nose. His lips were chiseled and generous, and his dirty-blond hair flopped over his forehead enticingly. The preferred media comparison was to Paul Newman as a young man. Personally, Grace thought his face was all his own.

"I trusted you," his character, Kirk, said on-screen, his voice a low, gravely husk. "I believed every word you said."

"I didn't know how to tell you," his on-screen wife, Loni, said.

"Haven't we always been honest with each other?" he asked.

"Too honest sometimes," Loni admitted.

A long silence as they eyed each other. Mac lifted a hand, running it through his already tousled hair. Grace squeezed her knees together as she watched his muscles ripple.

On-screen, Loni crossed the space between them and laid a hand on his bare chest.

You lucky witch, Grace thought, imagining how hot and hard his skin must feel.

"I've ruined everything, haven't I?" Loni asked in a small voice.

As though he couldn't stand her pain, Mac ducked his head to press a quick kiss to her cheek. Loni started to cry. Mac groaned and cupped her face.

"Don't," Mac said, torn.

Loni shook her head, inarticulate, and he ducked his head again to kiss her tears away. This time their noses bumped and within seconds their lips had found each other. Loni clutched at him, desperately trying to hold onto him. Mac hesitated a moment, then angled her head back, deepening the kiss. Her hands splayed down over his neck, across his back. He pulled her closer, absolutely intent on getting what he wanted.

Heart banging against her rib cage, Grace reached for the pause button on the remote.

She was turned on. There was no denying it. She'd been

fantasizing about Mac for so long now that all she had to do was look at him and her body responded. Briefly she considered inviting Mr. Buzzy out from her bedroom drawer to join the party, but she was too far gone already. Closing her eyes and giving herself over to the desire pulsing through her veins, she slid a hand over her breasts and down her belly to between her thighs. She knew the sets on the show like her own home and the scene she'd just watched sprang to life behind her closed eyelids in full Technicolor. Only, instead of Loni standing in front of a half-naked Mac, it was her.

He was so close she could smell his aftershave—something dark and spicy, hinting at open fires and warm bodies and sex. In the bedroom of her mind, she stepped closer to him. He was staring at her, his expression unreadable, but she could see the banked passion in his eyes.

"What are you doing?" he asked.

"What we both want," she replied. She reached out and ran her finger down his chest, sliding over the hardened nub of one nipple before tracing her way down into the tidy arrow of curls that disappeared beneath his waistband. He swallowed, hard, and she licked her lips.

"Tell me to stop and I will," she said. She dropped her gaze for half a second, just long enough to take in the rigid length of the erection straining against his jeans.

He remained silent, although she could see a battle going on inside him. She wanted him to resist a little—enough for her to prove to him how pointless it was to deny the attraction between them. Flattening her hand, she slid her palm down along the hard bar of his erection, then curled her fingers around it through his jeans.

He shivered and she smiled a secretive, confident smile. Her hand slid back up, and she grasped the stud at the top of his fly. Still he didn't say anything, and she popped the stud free with a deft twist of her hand. Her fingers found the tab of his zipper and she opened it with one smooth move. Then she stepped close and pressed a kiss to his hard, hot chest even as she slid a hand inside his boxers and grabbed a handful of rock-hard masculinity.

"Grace," he groaned. Then his hands were all over her, smoothing down her back, cupping her butt, sliding up and around her rib cage to massage her breasts. She panted and continued to work his hard shaft, unable to let go, as he pushed her top down over her breasts and sucked a nipple into his mouth. Her knees went weak as he tongued each hardened tip in turn, his mouth rough, his hands gentle, the combination sending her spiraling toward her climax.

As though he sensed how close she was, Mac pushed her back against the wall. A hand shoved her skirt up and she moaned low in her throat as his fingers slid between her thighs. He murmured his approval as he discovered her panty-less state, his knowing hands dipping between her folds to find her slick and ready for him. Whispering words of praise and promise in her ear, he slid a finger inside her. She clenched around him, so close, so close—but she wanted more, she wanted it all, and she pushed his hands away and worked feverishly on his jeans.

He knew exactly what she needed. Lifting one of her legs up and hooking it around his hip, he slid his hands up the backs of her thighs until he cupped her backside. Then he hoisted her up and slid inside her with one powerful stroke.

She came instantly, her head falling back, her cries echoing in the room. Sensation rippled through her body, a tsunami of pleasure that swamped her entire being.

For a long beat, she simply existed as she floated on the afterglow of her orgasm.

Then, as always, she forced herself back to reality. She was in her apartment, alone, the TV screen frozen on an image of Mac Harrison, bare-chested and gorgeous.

With a press of her finger, the screen went to black and the DVD player shut down. It was time to go to bed. She made her way to the bathroom, frowning as she squeezed toothpaste onto her toothbrush. She couldn't help wondering how Sadie and Claudia would react if she confessed her little secret to them: that ever since Mac Harrison had returned to reprise his role on *Ocean Boulevard* after a six-year absence, she'd had a lust crush on him a mile wide.

Claudia would fall about laughing. Probably Sadie would, as well. Not *at* her, but at the irony of the situation—Grace Wellington, founding member of the Nothing But Contempt For Men Club, had a soft spot for the show's biggest horn-dog.

It was too, too ironic. And faintly embarrassing, really. She should know better, she really should. The man was a known womanizer, he was paid to play make-believe and he lived a frivolous, pointless life. In short, he represented about a million of the things she liked least in men. There really wasn't anything admirable about him at all, in fact, apart from his superb body and gorgeous face. Her crush was ab-solutely a manifestation of lust. But, somehow, some way, no matter how many times she chastised herself for her bad taste in virtual lovers, he kept on sliding into her fantasy bed and taking her in his arms. Which was why she'd never confided in her friends. And, after all, it wasn't as though she knew everything about Sadie and Claudia's sex lives, right? It was nobody's business but her own. It was utterly harmless, a private indulgence that affected no one save herself.

It helped that she'd never met the man. Sure, she'd passed

him in the corridors when she'd been across town at the studios for meetings, but she'd never exchanged actual words with him. There was an unspoken divide between the writing team and the cast and crew—it wasn't just about being in different locations, it had been the same on every show Grace had worked on—so it wasn't particularly notable that they'd never been introduced. But she didn't need to meet him to know what he was like—she knew his type.

Yep, Sadie and Claudia would definitely lose a lung laughing if they knew.

Sliding between the sheets, Grace set the alarm and switched the light off. Her body was humming with satisfaction. As usual, virtual Mac had been the perfect lover: flawless technique, intuitive, voracious. Best of all, he came with absolutely no strings attached and she didn't have to wonder when he'd call again or listen to his lame-ass excuses for why he couldn't stay the night.

And he would never, ever cheat on her.

The perfect man, indeed.

Smiling smugly, she fell asleep.

MAC HARRISON GRUNTED with disgust as he threw the script he'd been reading across the room.

Drivel, absolute drivel. How anyone expected him to say those lines of dialogue with any sincerity was beyond him. Reaching for his beer bottle, he realized it was empty. He was about to push himself off the couch to grab another brewski from the fridge when he registered that there were another three empty bottles lined up on his coffee table. Four beers. And he was alone. And it was midnight on a Sunday evening. Not quite time to check into the Betty Ford center, but still… Perhaps it was time to switch to soda water.

He sank back onto the couch and ran a hand through his hair. He felt like crap. He'd been sleeping way too much lately and spending too much time on his own—probably because his libido was nonexistent. Depression tended to do that to a guy. His gym routine was about the only thing keeping him sane at the moment.

He stared at the discarded script where it lay crumpled on the ground a few feet away. He had five scenes he needed to memorize for tomorrow's shoot, but he couldn't make himself pick it up again.

Jesus, he needed another beer. Which was a pretty good reason not to have one. Mac had seen his fair share of actors succumb to drug and alcohol addictions over the years. He didn't plan on becoming one of them. But he also knew he had to do something because he couldn't continue living his life the way he was.

It had been a mistake coming back to *Ocean Boulevard*. The moment he'd gotten over his relief at having a regular paycheck again he'd known it. He'd been greeted like a returning king by the producers when he walked back on set twelve months ago and the show's loyal fan base had gone wild. The soap magazines had splashed him across covers and he'd smiled, answered all their questions and basically acted his butt off to look as though he was exactly where he wanted to be.

But he so wasn't.

He'd come to Hollywood from Seattle as a determined eighteen-year-old and hadn't been able to believe his luck when he'd scored a role on a new soap. He'd only intended to stay with the show a year, two max. But each year his paycheck got fatter as the show's ratings rose and his character became more and more popular. At the same time, the older actors on the show were constantly telling him how good he had it, how lean it was Out There, how he'd never have it better. By the time he'd been with the show for eight years, he'd crossed the line from complacency to boredom and frustration. Finally, he made the leap.

And failed spectacularly.

Hollywood had swallowed him in one easy gulp, with barely a ripple to mark his passing. He'd been on the soap for too long, his agent had told him, he was tainted by the association.

On a good day, he didn't hate *Boulevard*. It had bought his house, his car, fed him, clothed him, got him laid for many of the past fifteen years. It was a fun, entertaining, sometimes even moving show. It just didn't feed his soul. And how pretentious was that, anyway, wanting a career that made you proud, made you want to jump out of bed in the morning? Most people settled for three square meals and a roof over their heads, smiles on their kids' faces and backyard barbecues. He was a spoiled bastard. He knew it, but it didn't stop him from feeling as though a giant hand was slowly grinding him into the ground.

The reality was, he should have had the courage to walk away altogether, to pursue something completely outside of the industry. Instead, he'd succumbed to the lure of money and security. And it was slowly killing him.

"Boo-goddamn-hoo," he sneered at himself, launching himself to his feet.

The only thing worse than a worn-out has-been was a self-pitying worn-out has-been. Prowling around the house, he picked up books and put them down again, shuffled through his CD collection looking for something—anything—he could bear to listen to, and generally behaved like a lost soul.

Inevitably, he wound up in his study, staring at the calendar on his wall. Tomorrow's date was circled in red, and he shook his head as he acknowledged his own desperation. Tomorrow he found out if the *Boulevard*'s new producer was willing to continue what her predecessor had started and hand over a block of the show for him to direct.

Originally, he'd floated the idea of directing some blocks of the show to his agent half as a joke—he'd figured the producers would say no, or that if they said yes it would be an entertaining diversion from the usual. To his surprise, they'd given him the nod. Twice now he'd been allowed to step behind the camera and direct the show. It had been challenging work both times, but it had also been the most alive he'd felt in a long time.

Then there had been a regime change, a fairly regular occurrence in television. Heads had rolled and new heads had taken their places. He'd been waiting for nearly two months since then to find out if the new producer, Claudia Dostis, was willing to continue what her predecessor had started. There was a high chance she wouldn't—many producers would have said no simply because he'd been a pet project of the guy whose seat they were now warming. But tomorrow was the day of truth, the day she was handing out the new directors' roster.

And he wanted his name to be on it, bad. He needed his name to be on it, if he was being honest with himself.

There had to be something more out there. Didn't there?

It was mid-morning when Claudia called Grace into her office the next day.

"I wanted to talk to you about Mac Harrison," Claudia said by way of kicking off the conversation.

Grace started in her seat and tried to will away the blush that she could feel rising into her cheeks. There was no way that Claudia was about to tell her to stop using him as her convenient virtual stud. No one could know what she'd been doing in the privacy of her apartment last night. No one.

It didn't stop her from blushing, however. Ducking her head, she pretended to have an itchy nose.

"Right, Mac Harrison. The actor who plays Kirk on the show," she said, fumbling for time.

Claudia gave her an odd look and Grace winced mentally. Probably pretending to not be familiar with one of the show's biggest stars was not the smartest way to appear natural.

"Yes. That Mac Harrison," Claudia said dryly. "What did you think of the blocks he directed recently?"

Grace blinked a few times, trying to work out where this conversation was going. Mac had directed two five-episode blocks since he'd put up his hand to step behind the camera. Both had been good—inventive, interesting, tight.

"Does he want to do more?" she hedged.

"His agent has approached me. You still haven't answered my question."

Grace fiddled with the hem of her 1950s-era sundress. "They were good, strong. He brought a lot of energy to it," she said honestly.

Claudia smiled. "I'm glad you liked his work. He's a big fan of your scripts, too. It'll make the whole process much smoother."

Grace frowned, feeling as though she'd just missed something very important.

"Um, what process?" she asked hesitantly.

"Well, you're writing the script for our feature-length wedding episode," Claudia explained.

"Yessss," Grace said slowly, beginning to see the yawning chasm that loomed before her.

"And he's going to direct it."

Grace's whole body went hot, then cold.

"You'll have to work closely with each other—he'll be on light duties on-set and we'll get in an extra body to take over some of your usual workload so you can do reconnaissance with him for location shoots and anything else that's necessary. I want this to be the best wedding the *Boulevard* has ever done," Claudia said with determination.

"Right. The best," Grace repeated numbly.

She felt blindsided. For twelve months, she'd used Mac Harrison as the personification of all her sexual desires. She'd had sex with him in her mind a hundred different ways, cried his name out as she climaxed, gone to sleep with his image in her mind. All despite never having met the man.

And now they were about to become each other's shadows.

Why did she feel as though she'd set herself up for the fall of a lifetime?

2

MAC PULLED INTO the visitors parking slot at the *Boulevard*'s Santa Monica office and switched his ignition off. Instead of getting out of his car, however, he sat for a moment listening to the tick-tick-tick of his engine cooling.

He was nervous. He felt like an idiot as soon as he admitted it to himself. It had been a long time since he'd felt the peculiar mix of adrenaline and expectation that was pumping its way around his body right now. He'd stopped being nervous about auditions roughly three years after he'd left his cushy, high-paying role on the show—that was about how long it had taken Hollywood to suck his hopes and dreams out of him. It was hard to feel nervous about something when you knew you didn't have a snowball's chance in hell of achieving it.

He forced himself to acknowledge his feelings. Claudia Dostis was entrusting him with the most important episode of the year—a feature-length, stand-alone wedding episode that was supposed to knock everyone's socks off. And she'd chosen him, a still-wet-behind-the-ears novice to direct it. When she'd called to tell him her decision a week ago, he'd thanked her, written down the appropriate details and discussed his studio schedule with the production manager to ensure they could work his shooting schedule around these new directing commitments.

He'd read through the story line they sent him, made notes, come up with some ideas of his own. But it was only now that he was sitting here, about to commit himself wholly to the project, that he could admit to himself there was a very real chance he wasn't up to the challenge she'd offered him.

He was a novice. He'd directed ten episodes, and now they wanted him to make their big special shine. Frankly, he thought they were crazy handing their baby to him.

Of course, he could always say no. He could tell Claudia that he didn't want or need the hassle. This whole directing thing had only ever been a diversion, after all, something to stop him from banging his head against the wall in frustration.

He could start the car up and drive away from it all. If that was what he wanted.

The door of his '57 Corvette complained with a metallic squeal as he stepped out. If he sat around contemplating his navel much longer, he was going to be late. Grabbing his notebook, he headed toward the building entrance.

With the decision made, some of his nervousness dropped away and he realized that underneath his uncharacteristic adolescent self-doubt there was a buzz of anticipation, the yin to the yang of his nervousness. He didn't have to look far for the source—he was about to meet Grace Wellington.

He'd been reading Grace's work for the past year and every time he picked up a script with her name on it his curiosity and his respect for her had grown. She was the best writer on the show, hands down. She only penned one every now and then—she was obviously absorbed with her duties as script editor—but when she did, it was like a beacon in the night. The dialogue sparkled, emotions ran deep, laughs were sincere. She could write.

He'd whiled away a lot of long, boring hours in his dressing room wondering what she was like, the woman who put down words with so much energy and life and power. It was hard to get a bead on her, since there were so many different facets to her writing.

For starters, there was the sexy, sizzling, witty banter that delighted an actor. That Grace Wellington struck him as savvy and confident, a man-eater in red silk garters and stilettos.

Then there was the wry humor that she managed to inject into every episode. When he dwelt on that aspect of her writing, he thought of messy hair, big smiles, hot cocoa and woolly sweaters.

Then there was the wrenching emotional content of her scenes. She always managed to strike a chord, helping him dig deep to find the humanity in any story, no matter how soapy or silly. That woman he imagined as razor sharp, dressed in minimalist black with a bent for double-shot espressos and books by dead Russian authors.

He was looking forward to meeting her, to satisfying his curiosity about the mystery woman behind the scripts. He also figured that if he was going to have to jump headfirst into the unknown on this project, it would help to have the show's best writer by his side.

For the first time in a long time, he was looking forward to something. He wasn't sure if that was a good thing or not. In his experience, wanting something only made failure more painful.

He smiled grimly as he stepped over the threshold. Ready or not, he was already free-falling.

GRACE WIPED her sweaty palms on the sides of her dress, angry with herself for being nervous. Mac Harrison was just a person.

No, he was less than that—he was an actor. A man who

traded on his good looks and sex appeal to live in the lap of luxury. All his life, doors had opened for him, women had thrown themselves at his feet and he'd sat back and lapped it all up because he'd been lucky enough to be born with a body and face that the world worshipped.

He was like her sisters. Just as he was the epitome of male good looks, her sisters were stunning, each in her own way a different version of perfection. Felicity, Serena and Hope had also parlayed their looks into careers—Felicity as a weather girl, Serena as an actress and Hope as a model. Growing up as the ugly sister among three beauties had given Grace a front-row appreciation of how the other half lived. She loved her sisters, but she wouldn't have been human if she hadn't resented the number of boyfriends she'd had over the years who'd looked distinctly ripped off when they walked into her family home and saw Felicity, Serena and Hope lounging around. Their expressions said it all: *How come I got the dud sister?* It was no fun being the booby prize, so she'd opted to fight on her own terms. She dressed differently, lived her life differently, had separate dreams from her sisters. And it had worked for her, it really had. She had a great career. And until Owen had betrayed her, she'd thought she'd found the one man who valued her heart and soul more than he valued long legs, perfect features and shampoo-commercial hair.

Ha.

He'd sure shown her. But in doing so he'd shattered her last illusion. She lived in L.A., possibly the most appearance-obsessed city in the world, and she worked in the television industry. Perhaps that distorted her perception, but she knew that for many, many people, what was outside a person was more important than what was inside them.

Her lust-crush on Mac Harrison was a perfect example. All

those times she'd pleasured herself and imagined it was him touching her, licking her, tasting her, had she once thought about what kind of man he was? Had she fantasized that he cared for animals, was nice to old people, that he stopped to give money to the homeless? No. She'd fixated on his amazing eyes and his hot body and how hard and ready he'd be.

She was as bad as everyone else. Absolutely guilty as charged.

And when she had more time to chastise herself for her superficial values and blatant hypocrisy, she'd do it.

But right now, she was concentrating on surviving the next hour or so. Very foolishly, she had eroticized Mac to the point where the mere sound of his voice turned her on. She'd practically made him her fetish—and she was about to step into an intimate meeting with him that would lead to an intimate working relationship for the next few months.

She'd set herself up to be vulnerable. And she didn't do vulnerable, not any more.

Put simply, she would rather shave her head than let him know in any way, shape or form that she was attracted to him. He had women falling all over him all the time, she knew that. Probably he expected her to do the same. But he was so wrong. She would never, ever let him laugh at her or give him the opportunity to reject her. She'd had enough of that, thank you very much.

She checked her watch. He was late for their first meeting— a brilliant start and typical actor behavior. Brick by brick she built a wall of disdain around herself.

He'd probably had a Pilates session or a pedicure that he simply couldn't miss, and had neglected to pass on this vital information to Claudia or herself. She pictured him swaggering in a couple of hours late, all shiny teeth and bronzed skin.

Claudia would lose it, and that would be the end of Mr. Harrison's short-lived dalliance with directing.

She basked in the surge of relief this vision inspired, but her hope died a quick death when she heard a hush fall over the outer office, closely followed by the excited murmur of feminine speculation.

Mac Harrison had entered the building. There was no other explanation for it.

She gathered her notes together, shaking her head over the secretarial staff's behavior. It wasn't as though they were all greenhorns—they should be beyond gushing over one of their own actors by now. The man played dress-up for a living— it wasn't as if he was a Nobel Prize winner or anything.

You screaming hypocrite, she chastised herself.

If Mac Harrison was so contemptuous, why was sweat prickling her underarms, and why was she flicking her hair over her shoulder and rubbing a finger over her teeth to ensure none of her crimson-warrior lipstick had transferred itself?

She gave herself a stern talking to as she marched toward the conference room. She had been thinking about this moment ever since Claudia had handed down her sentence last week. A whole seven days of dwelling on this scenario, shooting it from every angle with her mental camera, playing both leads, considering all possibilities.

She was not going to gush or simper or blush or ogle or flirt. She was simply going to walk into that meeting room and greet him coolly and professionally. Not by the flicker of an eyelid was she going to reveal that just a week ago she had imagined him pressed against her, his body buried deep inside hers. Hell no. They were going to discuss the upcoming project intelligently, then they would go their separate ways. All very business-like and orderly. All very dignified.

Then she entered the room and lost the power to think.

Claudia was sitting to one side, a smile on her face as she talked to Mac. But all Grace could register was *him:* his scent, his presence, his height, his breadth, his charisma. She felt as though someone had just driven over her with a silk and velvet steamroller, then punched her in the stomach for good measure.

Then he actually looked at her and it was like standing under a million-watt klieg light. Her knees literally gave out on her—fortunately she was close enough to grab the back of one of the chairs and she held on with a white-knuckled grip as her body went up in flames.

He was, quite simply, too good-looking to be fully human. Everything was perfect—the small screen didn't do him justice. He was taller. His eyes were clearer, bluer. His jaw was stronger, his nose prouder. He was more graceful, as well as more powerful-looking. He was simply…*more*.

"Mac, you and Grace have met before, right?" Claudia said.

He extended his hand, his smile broadening. "Actually, believe it not, we haven't," he said.

Grace stared stupidly at his outstretched hand for a full, agonizing ten seconds. He wanted her to actually *touch* him? To lay her skin against his and not expire on the spot?

Swallowing, she slowly extended her own hand. There was no choice, right? Claudia was already staring at her as though she was an escapee from planet loopy and the smile on his face had lost most of its spontaneity. Gritting her teeth, she clasped his hand in hers.

Sensation skittered up her nerve endings and danced around her body. His hand was large and warm, strong. His skin was smooth but firm. She stared at his well-tended nails and perfectly shaped fingers, remembering how many times she'd imagined him cupping her breasts, thumbing her nipples, sliding her underwear down….

She snatched her hand away and took a jerky step backward.

"S-static electricity," she blurted when Claudia and Mac stared at her.

He frowned and she busied herself with settling into a chair and arranging her notes and pencils in front of her on the glass-topped table.

Where had her game plan gone? What about dignity and coolness and professionalism? She'd never felt less digni-fied or professional in her life. She felt exactly like a star-struck teenager, complete with a mouth full of braces, bad acne and baby fat.

"Might as well get started, I guess," Claudia said, shooting Grace a questioning glance. Grace got the distinct feeling she'd be having an intense interrogation session with her friend later. Her toes curled in her shoes at the very thought.

"Grace, you're still working on the first draft of the script, I know, but I really want this wedding feature to rate off the graph. I'm kicking in extra money for location shoots, what-ever it takes. As far as venues go, Mac, the scouts have narrowed it down to two locations—a vineyard in the Santa Clarita valley, just north of L.A., and the Malibu West Beach Club. I want you to take a look at both of them with Grace and see what kind of ideas they suggest. Once we've decided on a location, we'll swing the team into action."

Grace concentrated on scribbling down Claudia's words verbatim—it gave her something to do and it meant that she didn't have to try to comprehend what her friend was saying until afterward. As much as it galled her, while Mac was in the room, she was hard pressed to simply master the whole inhale-exhale thing.

"Any questions, guys?" Claudia asked, looking from Grace to Mac and back again.

"Yeah. It's for Grace, actually. I've gone over the story line for the episode, but is there any chance of getting a look at your script while it's a work-in-progress? Just so we can start thinking on the same page?" Mac asked.

Grace just managed to stifle the instinctive scoff of rejection that rose in her throat. The thought of him looking at her half-assed, half-finished work was enough to make her break into a sweat again. Writing was her thing, the thing she did better than anything else in her life. There was no way she was letting this man see her at anything less than her best.

"Um… Let me take a look at it, see what kind of shape it's in," she hedged. She couldn't say no outright in front of Claudia, but Mac Harrison would have to pry her half-finished script from her cold, dead hands if she had any say in the matter.

She shot him a quick look to see how he handled her answer, waiting for the inevitable star's tantrum. But it was impossible to read his expression. Probably because she was too busy staring at his sexy mouth. He was a drug for her and every time she looked at him she took a hit.

"Right, well, I guess there's not much more for me to do here. I'll leave it up to you guys to work out a time to do reconnaissance on both locations and anything else that needs to be done before we move forward."

Claudia was standing, moving toward the door. Grace jerked upright in her seat, panicking. Claudia was leaving her alone with Mac? No way!

But before she could launch herself out of her chair, grab onto one of her friend's ankles and hold on for dear life, Claudia was gone.

By definition, leaving her alone with Mac Harrison. Her most secret fantasy—and her worst nightmare. Her heart was pumping like mad. Her breasts felt heavy and sensitive in her bra. And she would *kill* for a glass of water right now. He was sitting opposite her, exuding sex appeal as if he'd bought it in bulk and she didn't know how to handle the situation or what to say or do to protect herself.

How she resented him for making her feel this way!

She ducked her head, trying to pull herself together. Which was when she caught sight of her reflection in the glass table. Her features were indistinct, distorted by the bad lighting and the angle, but she could see the expression in her own eyes. She looked utterly lost, like a scared child. She had a sudden out-of-body flash of how she must appear, sitting head down, knees pressed together—the shy spinster in front of the golden hunk.

She didn't like it very much. She didn't like it at all, in fact.

For four years, she'd built her life alone. And she'd been happy and successful. She didn't measure her happiness by whether she had a man in her life anymore. Certainly she didn't measure it by whether a man like Mac Harrison was attracted to her or not. She was her own woman.

Her mind defaulted to her usual touchstone for feminine power and confidence. What would Bette do in this situation, she asked herself?

Instantly she felt her spine straighten. Bette Davis wouldn't feel intimidated by anyone—especially by someone like Mac. Who the hell was he, after all? A fake-tanned slice of beefcake with a bleached smile and the ability to be insincere on cue. Yes, there was a pleasing symmetry to his features, a certain robust physicality to his body that spoke to some primitive feminine instinct in her. But his appeal was only skin deep.

He was an *actor,* her personal definition of the word *vapid*. He probably spent more time working out than she spent sleeping or eating. When he wasn't working out, she bet he accessorized himself with the latest leggy blonde and made sure he was seen in all the right places, because those were the things that mattered to him. He was an empty Christmastree bauble of a man.

He was nothing special. And she was determined to treat him that way.

MAC FROWNED over his notes as Claudia exited the room. Was it just him, or was Grace Wellington less-than-thrilled to be working with him?

She'd barely looked at him since she walked into the room. He couldn't work out if she was shy, embarrassed or angry. She was definitely *something*—the air around her was practically vibrating with suppressed emotion.

She was nothing like he'd expected. None of his feeble imaginings came even close to the real Grace Wellington. She was…totally original. Her hair was a deep claret, her bangs cut severely straight across her creamy forehead, the rest falling thick and straight down her back. A memory teased at his mind, and he plucked a sepia image from his mental filing cabinet—a voluptuous siren posed provocatively on a beach towel. Bettie Page, the famous 1950s pinup—that was who she reminded him of. Except she wasn't as traditionally beautiful as Bettie. Grace's green eyes, almost hidden behind heavy-framed black glasses, had a slight exotic tilt. Her nose was bigger, her mouth wider. Each feature taken alone was perfect, but together the effect was too strong for her ever to be labeled as conventionally beautiful. She was, however, strikingly attractive. Her skin glowed like freshwater pearls, and it was hard to keep his gaze from straying to her full crimson lips or dwelling on her exotically tilted eyes.

Fortunately, there was plenty of action down south to keep him fully occupied. The smooth, creamy skin of her face gave way to an expanse of smooth, creamy neck and chest that finished in a crescendo of bosom—two firm, proud breasts that strained at the confines of the floral sundress she was wearing. Hollywood being Hollywood, there was every chance they were the work of the men at Dow Corning, but his baser self hoped they were the real deal. They looked warm and soft and silky, and he caught himself wondering if her nipples were a dusky pink to match her pale skin tone.

The air in the room shifted, and his tingling man senses told him that not only had Ms Wellington finally decided to make eye contact with him, she'd also busted him ogling her chest like a horny teen.

He met her gaze as openly as he could, reasoning with himself that anyone with such spectacular assets was used to having them admired. She stared back at him coldly.

"Look, sorry if I stepped on your toes before, asking to see the script before it's finished. Guess I must have broken some secret writer's rule, huh?" he asked lightly.

He was used to making people like him. It was his stock in trade. He threw in a smile for good measure.

Her lips pursed slightly, and she leaned back in her chair, looking over her glasses at him like a disapproving librarian. The schoolmarm effect was dissipated somewhat, however, by those red, red lips and those amazing— Well, he'd already gotten in enough trouble in that direction already.

"There's no rule, as such. It's just that handing over a rough draft for a writer is the equivalent of you leaving the house without your massage, wax and facial. No one wants to be caught with pillow-face, do they?" she said.

His back stiffened. Where the hell had that come from?

It had been a long time since Mac hadn't been liked by someone—or at least since someone had stopped sucking up to him long enough to let him know it. He was surprised by how much it annoyed him. To his knowledge, he'd never done anything to merit the dagger-eyes she was currently sending him.

He wondered what her problem was. Was she one of those precious people who resented actors moving into other areas of production? They were out there, he knew— writers and directors and producers who figured actors who were trying to parlay their time in the limelight to time behind the camera were asking for more than their fair share of pie.

He'd already copped a few sideways glances from a few of the other *Boulevard* directors. He even suspected a couple of the long-term regulars on the cast weren't too thrilled to see him dabbling with direction. The same thing had happened when he'd been trying to break out of soap acting. People had wanted to keep him in a clearly defined box. But Mac knew now that if he didn't get out of that box, he'd be buried in it.

"Given the time constraints we're under, I think the best thing to do is to set a deadline for viewing the two prospective sites," Grace said briskly, flicking through a diary. "What if we both agree to have looked over the two options by the end of the week? Then we can reconvene and discuss things."

She glanced up at him, her face set, impassive.

"I was under the impression that Claudia wanted us to go out together. It being a collaborative thing and all," he said.

She shrugged one shoulder. "I was planning on checking out the vineyard this afternoon since I'm ahead on edits, but that probably won't suit you."

She flicked at a piece of invisible lint on her dress. He didn't have to be a genius to read the subtext of her body language—*be gone, pesky man, be gone.*

He'd never taken well to being dismissed.

"You know, it must be our lucky day—I've got the afternoon free as well," he said easily. In reality, he had a swathe of lines to learn for tomorrow's rehearsals—but that was what late nights and strong coffee were for.

She didn't look pleased. Which only confirmed his suspicions about her. She didn't think he was up to the job. All his earlier doubts about taking on such an important project evaporated. There was no way he was walking away now. Flashing another one of his red-carpet smiles, he leaned back in his chair and put his feet up on the boardroom table—just because he knew it would piss her off. Her gaze flickered to his legs and back again and she sat a little straighter in her chair.

"Why don't you go grab your bag and we'll get going?" he suggested.

Her full lips compressed into a thin, ungenerous line.

"I have some things to take care of first. Why don't I meet you out there?" she countered.

His moment of amusement faded as he had a sudden vision of how the next few months were going to be if he was fighting against this woman every step of the way—it would be a bloody battle for each square foot gained. He was a straight-up kind of guy at the end of the day. As amusing as it was to egg Grace on, he figured it was better to call her on her attitude now, get whatever it was out of the way and sorted before it affected the show.

Then she stood up.

Hubba hubba.

It was the only coherent thought that came to mind as he took in the rest of the package that was Grace Wellington. He'd been too busy talking to Claudia to get a full head-to-toe on Grace when she walked in, but now his eyes tracked from the fullness of her breasts to her tiny waist and out again to her curvy hips and butt, all of it showcased by a dress that would have looked right at home on Doris Day in her heyday.

She had an old-fashioned pinup girl's body, that was for sure. And she dressed in an old-fashioned style that accentuated all the good bits in a really, really...*good* way.

He frowned as she gathered her notes, trying to piece together the different signals he was getting from this woman. She didn't like him, seemed uptight, but dressed in a fun, flamboyant, sexy style that belied the cool little voice and condemning glances over the top of her ugly glasses.

Realizing she was about to walk off, he dragged his gaze from her va-voom curves and concentrated on winning this first battle of wills.

"I can hang around. Doesn't make sense to take separate cars all that way," he said.

She blinked, her back stiffening.

"I might be a while," she countered.

He shrugged. She stared at him. He stared back. He wasn't going to back off just because she did a good line in bitch. Finally, after a long, tense silence, she tossed her hair over her shoulder and turned on her heel.

He watched her butt all the way out of the room, only letting out the breath he hadn't noticed he'd been holding when she stepped out of sight. It was also when he registered the tightness in his jeans. He stared down at his straining boner.

Great. Just what he needed—the return of his libido at the most inappropriate time possible.

GRACE LINGERED. Then she loitered. She even lurked a bit. She went to the bathroom twice. She sorted through her in-tray. She made a couple of pointless phone calls to freelance script writers. She cleared out her junk e-mail folder.

And still Mac sat there. He'd taken up position in one of the random chairs placed throughout the open-plan outer-office and was just waiting her out. She swung between being irritated with him for being such a stubborn bastard and feeling stupidly breathless and dizzy at his proximity.

Every time she glanced up from her "work" and caught sight of his tall, powerful body sitting outside *her* office, waiting for *her,* she had to fight the urge to melt into a puddle beneath her desk.

It made her feel so weak and stupid. Which in turn made her angry with herself—and Mac Harrison for having won the genetic sweepstakes that made him so irresistible to her.

Finally, however, she was out of tricks. It was already more than evident that she'd been stalling and, after an hour of time-wasting, she gave in, snatching up her handbag and notepad and stalking out of her office.

"I'm ready. Unless something else has come up…?" she suggested hopefully.

He eyed her steadily and pushed himself to his feet. She suppressed a shiver as he loomed over her. He was so close— just like in her fantasy the other night. If she took a step forward, she'd be able to reach out and run a finger down his chest. She'd need to rip his shirt off first, of course, for it to be an accurate re-enactment of her fantasy, but she had strong hands….

The jangle of car keys snapped her out of the pheromone-induced daze she'd sunk into.

God, she was so pitiful. Lips pressed together, she marched toward the exit. She could feel him following her, and she felt absurdly conscious of the wiggle of her hips. He probably hadn't seen real hips for years, living in Hollywood. All the actresses on the show had visible ribs and chicken wings sticking out of their backs from their no-carb, no-fat, no-life diets. He probably thought she was obese by comparison. The thought spurred her to put a little extra sass in her walk.

"Over here," Mac directed as they exited the building, and she turned toward the guest parking. And stopped abruptly.

"That is not your car," she said disbelievingly, her eyes caressing the pristine curves of a Venetian-red-and-white 1957 Corvette soft-top with whitewall tires and red leather upholstery.

He shrugged. "We can put the roof up if you're worried about your hair."

She stared at him, then resolutely resisted the urge to glance toward the far corner of the lot where her own parking space was located. The last—the very, very last—thing she needed was for him to see her car. She'd been restoring her own '57 Corvette for nearly two years, but it was a long, slow process. Compared to his shiny, showroom-condition dream machine, her baby looked like a very tired, very ugly duckling.

The story of her life.

It was almost enough to make her hate his car, too. But that would be taking things too far.

Wordless, she slid into the passenger seat and reached for the scarf and sunglasses she habitually carried in the side pocket of her handbag.

"The seat-belt catch is a little tricky…" Mac began to explain, but Grace had already snapped hers shut.

While he occupied himself with starting the car, Grace deftly tied the scarf over her hair and swapped her office frames for the cat's-eye sunglasses she'd inherited from her grandmother.

Then she turned her face away from him, signaling her absolute lack of interest in any conversational gambits he might choose to throw her way.

For the hour and a half it took them to drive to Santa Clarita, it appeared he didn't choose to throw anything her way at all. After the first five minutes of silence, he simply reached across and flicked on the stereo. She noted out of the corner of her eye that he'd had a suitably low-key CD player installed so as not to destroy the original dash. It was the same model she'd been eyeing for herself for the past six months, trying to justify the expenditure when there were other, more mundane things to fix on her car.

Damn him.

Her irritation only grew when she recognized the track he'd put on. Nina Simone's "Sinner Man." One of her favorites.

It was no wonder that she was feeling particularly snippy by the time she stepped out of the car at the winery. So far, he'd managed to subvert all of her preconceptions about him, and she was finding it very disconcerting. She was also quiveringly aware of him. Every breath he took, every shift of his hands or body—she was blindsided by how attractive she found him…and how vulnerable that made her.

Shedding her scarf but keeping her sunglasses, she didn't bother looking behind herself to see if he was following as she headed for the front doors of the winery. Let him keep up, if he could.

She realized instantly that he wasn't—she'd become so damned attuned to him so quickly that the absence of his presence behind her was like the sun disappearing behind a cloud. She paused in the shadows of the entranceway to check on him discreetly and saw that he had stopped to take shots of the location with a small camera.

Humph. A good idea, she supposed. Maybe he was more than just a life-support system for a whole lot of muscle.

Determined to get the inspection over and done with, she stepped into the coolness of the interior and began to look around. The entrance hall was attractive but small. She couldn't help but wonder how it would translate on-camera. Following the signs, she walked through to the main tasting room and gift shop. Again, it was pleasant, but she wondered whether the art department would be able to dress it to the level of glamour required for the special.

She knew the moment Mac joined her and watched him survey the space out of the corners of her eyes. He snapped off a couple of shots, and she tensed as he moved toward her.

"What do you think?" he asked.

"It's nice. Homey and cozy," she said.

He nodded neutrally and looked around some more. He had such a great profile. She wanted to reach out and run her finger along his nose, rub her palm against his five o'clock shadow, run her tongue along the full curve of his lower lip.

"What's wrong—not enough bling for your liking?" she asked coolly, furious at herself for staring at him.

He took his time answering, his blue gaze pinning her for a long beat. She had no idea what he was thinking.

"It's cozy, like you said. But Gabe comes from money. The wedding needs to be lavish, over the top," he said, turning to study the room again.

Even though she agreed with everything he was saying—or perhaps, because of it—Grace found herself defending the location.

"I know it's probably not up to your own personal high standards, but I'm sure we can get a hot tub installed and borrow some of the bunnies from the Playboy mansion," she said sweetly.

He raised an eyebrow, then shot her a slow, appraising look.

"I'm going to go look at the grounds," he said, "and then you're going to tell me exactly what stick you have up your ass."

Grace spluttered angrily but he just walked away. She glared after him, unable to resist the lure of that perfect butt, even though he'd spoken so rudely to her.

Kind of the same way she'd been speaking to him. She was painfully aware of the fact that she'd regressed to elementary-school sexual politics to cope with her stupid awareness of this man: be mean to the handsome boy and he wouldn't guess that she liked him. It was petty and immature.

But it was all she had—and by God, she was clinging to it.

MAC TOOK DEEP BREATHS of the fresh, earth-scented air. It had taken all his willpower not to tear into her back there. He'd hoped to disarm her, befriend her, find some common ground during their drive. Instead, she'd given him the silent treatment. And now she was taking shots at him again.

He didn't consider himself a hot-tempered kind of a guy, but he had his limits. And she was straining at them.

What really pissed him off was the fact that he still found her attractive. He didn't kid himself—while his face was on national TV, he was never going to have a problem getting laid. But it had been a long time since he'd gotten any buzz out of that aspect of his fame. He'd had his share of relationships and flings with women in the business—mostly actresses, although his only long-term relationship had been with a makeup artist, Kerry, with whom he'd lived for several years. Keeping a relationship alive was tough enough at the best of times, but when the shifting sands of Hollywood vagaries were added into the mix, Mac figured it was pretty much impossible. Most of the women he met were beautiful, with tanned, sculpted bodies. They all wanted fame in some way—be it through notoriety, association or their own achievements. Why live in L.A. otherwise? Not even a dyed-in-the-wool L.A.-lover would claim it was a beautiful city. Nope, L.A. was a city where dreams and ambition came first and love a pale, sickly second.

He didn't even know if he believed in love any more. He'd seen so much greed and ugliness over the past few years that cynicism was practically a religion for him. He had a couple of regular lovers who he saw on and off—more off than on lately, if he was being honest with himself. His sex-drive was at an all-time low. Yet, here he was, faced with the obvious disdain and contempt of a rude, sharp-tongued shrew and his gonads were trying to get in on the action. How goddamned contrary was that?

Running a hand through his hair, Mac squinted off into the distance and forced his mind to the matter at hand. Pulling his slim-line digital camera from his pocket, he fired off a few shots, but his heart wasn't in it. His gut told him this was not the location to make the episode sing. He might not be the most experienced director in the world, but as an actor he'd played his part in innumerable soap weddings. This place just wasn't right.

The sound of full-throated feminine laughter cut through the silence, and he looked over his shoulder to see Grace approaching, arm in arm with a gray-haired guy who looked to be in his late fifties. Grace was laughing up into his face, her cheeks rosy, hips wiggling as she walked with him.

It was like getting a peek behind the curtain during an audience with the Great and Powerful Oz. The hard-nosed witch he'd been dealing with all day was gone and in her place was a sparkling eyed, fun-loving woman who radiated charm.

So why was *he* getting the Alexis Carrington treatment?

As though on cue, Grace's smile slid from her face as she spotted him and her body stiffened.

Mac grit his teeth. He was getting a little sick of feeling as though he had a personal-hygiene problem.

"I've just been talking to your lady friend," the older man said. "Name's Rusty. I'm the winemaker here."

"Rusty took me on a tour of the winemaking shed," Grace said coolly.

"Great," Mac said. "You've got a lovely place here."

"Oh, I'm not the owner. I just work here," Rusty explained.

Grace patted Rusty's arm confidingly.

"Don't worry about Mac—he figures that because his life is like a game of Monopoly, the rest of us are all land barons and heiresses."

Mac's nostrils flared and he shot her a hard look. She gazed off over the marching rows of vines as though she'd done nothing more contentious than comment on the weather.

"Actually, the wife's a big fan, Mr. Harrison," Rusty said, ruddy color staining his cheeks. "Do you think you'd mind…?"

Mac smiled, ignoring the hyena on Rusty's arm. It wasn't the winemaker's fault that Grace was a bitch.

"Not a problem, it'd be my pleasure."

Rusty pulled a small diary from his pocket and offered up an empty page.

"What's your wife's name?" he asked.

"Alison," Rusty said, craning his head to see what Mac was writing.

Finishing his inscription, Mac signed his name neatly.

"There you go."

"And, also…?" Rusty asked, producing his cell phone with built-in camera.

Signaling his agreement, Mac waited while Rusty handed the phone over to Grace so he could pose with Mac. A smile, a click and Rusty was offering up his sheepish thanks before heading back to his work.

As one, he and Grace began walking back toward the car. They hadn't taken two steps before she tilted her head slightly as though she was contemplating a difficult riddle.

"I'm surprised you don't keep head shots on you," she drawled. "You're taking an awful risk—what if someone snaps you on a bad-hair day?"

The sunlight glinted off her dark cat's-eye sunglasses and the last shreds of Mac's patience evaporated.

"Right, that's it," he said tightly, grabbing her arm and hauling her the last few feet to the Corvette.

"Do you mind? Get your hands off me!" Grace said, outraged. She twisted her arm in his grasp, trying to escape.

He just tightened his grip.

"You're not going anywhere until you tell me why you're being such a grade-A bitch. And before you say 'bite me,' you might want to think about how long a walk it is back to L.A."

Finally she succeeded in pulling her arm loose.

"Would you like me to shine your shoes after I've finished kissing them? That's what you're used to, isn't it?" she sniped.

"Have it your way."

Without another word, Mac got into his car, gunned the engine and left her for dust.

3

THE THING ABOUT STILETTOS was that they looked great. They elongated the leg, transformed the calf muscle and gave a girl an extra few inches in height. They were sexy, stylish fashion must-haves, essential additions to any woman's arsenal.

And they were totally unsuitable for a two mile trek on a gravel road.

Pride was a terrible, terrible thing Grace admitted after the first blister had burst on her heel. She could have walked the handful of steps required to take her back into the winery so she could use their phone, having discovered she'd left her own cell phone at work. Even now she could be lounging in shady comfort, chatting with Rusty over a nice glass of red while she waited for a taxi. But pride had dictated that she instead make her way down the long driveway to the main road and then traverse the apparently short distance to the craft shop she'd remembered passing on the way in so that no one at the winery knew that her handsome, famous escort had blown her off and driven away without her.

The first blister blossomed halfway down the drive. By the time she'd reached the main road, it had burst and been replaced by brothers and sisters on both feet.

Striking out to her left, she made it another hundred feet before the spike heel on her left shoe snapped off in an ant hole. Swearing like a trooper, Grace whipped off her shoe to examine the damage. It was a clean break, and she heaved a sigh of relief. She knew a shoe wizard who would be able to resuscitate her prized vintage Roger Vivier green-suede peep-toes—some solace, at least.

Tugging off her other shoe, she let out a gasp of pure ecstasy as she flexed her overheated foot. Her relief was short lived—by the time she'd traversed another fifty feet she was hobbling from walking on the sharp gravel.

The worst thing was, she had no one to blame but herself. She wanted to blame Mac—oh, how she wanted to—but she knew that she was the only one responsible for her current situation. She'd been a sniping, vitriolic, sarcastic cow all day and the man had copped her abuse like a gentleman. But even gentlemen had their limits, and now she knew Mac's.

After ten more minutes of cursing and pain, Grace shook her head. There was no way she was going to make it to the shop. It wasn't even a speck on the horizon—it was obviously miles off. She looked toward the vineyard, biting her lip. There really was nothing for it but to walk back and eat a large slice of humble pie before asking Rusty to call her a cab. But before she went anywhere, she was giving her poor, tortured feet a break. A rail fence separated the road from the open pastureland that fed into the rows of vines, and she stepped over a drainage ditch and climbed between the top and bottom rails so she could sink her feet into the cool grass. It felt so good that she rested her butt on the bottom rail and closed her eyes, relishing the sensation.

But as much as she wanted to concentrate on only the cool of the grass on her sore, hot feet, she couldn't stop her mind from picking at the tangled mess she'd made today. She'd gone a little overboard on the protecting-herself thing. She'd been unprofessional. She'd been stupid. She'd been the queen bitch from hell, basically. And she wasn't particularly proud of herself.

She had a lot of excuses lined up: he pushed all her buttons, reminding her of age-old resentments and ancient insecurities. He was the epitome of so many of the values she'd fought against all her life. And, to her everlasting embarrassment, she had a crush on him that she knew would never be reciprocated.

But none of it was good enough when put in the balance against her poor behavior. Beneath all the sass and the attitude and the Bette Davis drawl, she was a fair woman. She owed him an apology. Big time.

Her eyes were still closed when she heard the sound of a car approaching and slowing to a halt. Even if she hadn't recognized the distinct burble of the Corvette's engine, she would have known it was Mac by the way all the small hairs on her arms stood on end.

Secretly, she'd been hoping he'd relent and return for her. It had taken him nearly an hour, but he had. It didn't escape her attention that she'd kept him waiting for an hour back in the office, too. He hadn't looked as though he cared, but he had. He'd just bided his time and waited for an opportunity to serve her up some of her own medicine.

Clever.

Swiveling, she ducked her head beneath the top rail and peered at him.

"Ready to go home now?" he asked.

He'd pushed his sunglasses up into his hair and there was a distinct challenge in his gaze. Her eyes dropped to the Popsicle he was holding in one hand. While she'd been vandalizing her shoes, he'd been snacking.

A wry smile found its way to her mouth. He knew how to rub a woman's face in her wrongdoings, that was for sure.

"That would be very nice, thank you," she said, determined to show him she'd learned her lesson.

Crouching and easing through the rails, she stepped back over the drainage ditch. He pushed the passenger door open for her, but she hesitated before crossing the threshold.

"Before I get in—I owe you an apology," she said uncomfortably. She was eternally grateful for her sunglasses—at least they afforded her a tiny skerrick of protection from his bright, hawkish gaze.

"I'm listening," he said.

She took a deep breath. "I have been beyond rude all day. I'm sorry. It was entirely my problem—nothing to do with you—and I took my bad mood out on you," she said, fudging the last part but figuring he really didn't need to know that the reason she'd been such a harpy all day was because she hated herself for finding him almost irresistibly attractive.

There was a long pause before he reached across to the glove compartment and pulled out a second Popsicle, still in its wrapper.

Offering it to her, he jerked his head. "Get in," he said.

He'd bought her a treat. Bewildered, she slid into the car, unconsciously wincing as one of her blisters brushed the carpet. He frowned.

"Did you hurt yourself?" he asked.

"Blisters," she explained, too busy tearing the wrapper off her Popsicle to elaborate.

His glance dropped to her broken shoe, lying on the floor.

"And you broke your shoe?" he said.

"It's repairable." She shrugged, taking a big, deliciously cool bite of tangy raspberry ice.

He gave her an intent look before signaling and pulling back out onto the road.

She polished off her treat and he silently passed her a travel pack of tissues to wipe her sticky hands.

"Thank you." She hesitated a moment, then reminded herself that she still had some ground to make up. "Does this mean I'm forgiven?" she asked, forcing herself to be light.

He shrugged. "It depends."

"On what?"

"On whether you'll have dinner with me tonight."

Grace jerked her head around to look at him. "You're kidding."

"That's my price for pretending today never happened," he said, eyes hidden behind his own sunglasses now.

"Why would you want to have dinner with me when I've been a total bitch all day?" she asked honestly.

He didn't take his attention off the road. "We need to have a decent working relationship," he said.

"Okay, I agree with that. But dinner really isn't necessary, is it?" she asked. The thought of spending more time with him—of sitting opposite him for a meal, being unable to avoid looking into that stunning, unforgettable face—was too, too overwhelming.

"I think it is."

She could hear the determination in his tone. He'd offered his deal—forgiveness for dinner. She closed her eyes. Why-oh-why hadn't she picked someone completely outside her world to be her fantasy lover? Hell, why hadn't she picked someone really safe, like Elvis or Jim Morrison?

She opened her eyes again. "Okay. Where do you want to meet?"

"I'll pick you up," he said.

This time, she didn't even bother trying to argue.

GRACE WELLINGTON was a revelation. The thought crossed his mind somewhere between their appetizers and main courses that evening.

By the time he'd arrived at her low-rise art deco apartment block to collect her, he'd had two hours to regret his impulsive invitation. Why prolong the misery of a genuinely shitty day by extending it into dinner? But he'd always been unable to refuse a challenge—and Grace was definitely challenging.

The moment she'd opened her door to him, most of his doubts had turned to dust. Somehow, in the time between dropping her off at the production offices and navigating his way to her Venice Beach apartment, he'd forgotten how striking she was. The smell of her heavy, musky perfume smacked him in the nose even as his eyeballs boggled at all the delights they were being offered. Her breasts looked incredible in a fitted, high-necked-but-still-sexy pale-yellow dress featuring about a million little buttons down the bodice. Her hips got their fair share of attention, too, since her skirt hugged her curves like nobody's business. Her toes peeped out from between the straps of a pair of elegant red-suede stilettos and he'd felt an instant surge of desire as she brushed past him.

The feeling had only intensified when she'd slid into his car and run an unconsciously sensual hand along the upholstery. It wasn't until they were halfway to the intimate little restaurant he'd chosen in Malibu that he'd realized she was half lit. Not actually drunk, but definitely…relaxed. At first he'd been annoyed, but then she'd started to let her guard down. And now he was officially intrigued.

The cold-eyed, hard-nosed sourpuss of earlier in the day had been replaced by a lighthearted woman with a quick wit and a ready laugh. It was as though the earlier Grace had been sketched in black and white and at last he was being treated to the Technicolor version.

"I love mushrooms," she purred now as her main course was delivered. "They've got everything—aroma, texture, taste. Don't you think?"

He wondered if she was aware that she was running her fingers up and down the stem of her glass. And if she knew what it was doing to him.

"I'm a big fan of the pea, myself," he countered.

"The pea?" She smiled, ready to be amused. He liked that about her.

"Why not? It's small, it's green, it rolls. Design, color, movement—the pea has a lot to offer."

She shook her head and looked vaguely annoyed. "There you go again, surprising me."

"Let me guess, you had me pegged as a potato kind of guy?" he asked.

She took a slug of her wine and shook her head for the second time. One of her elbows found its way onto the table and she leaned forward to accentuate her point.

"You're an actor. You're supposed to be one-dimensional. We're supposed to be talking about how great you are," she said.

There was just the slightest slur in her words, enough to make him shake his head subtly when the waiter approached, wine list in hand, hoping to secure an order for a second bottle.

"But, instead, we're talking about vegetables. And music. And architecture. And our favorite movies," she said.

She sounded put out.

"This bothers you?" he asked, slicing into his panfried snapper.

"Yeah, it bothers me. The way I figure it is this—some people in life get the looks, others get the smarts. You can't have both."

"Why not?"

She looked genuinely outraged. "It's not fair. Good looks *and* smarts—there's no defense against that," she said.

He raised his eyebrows and reached for the lemon wedge on the edge of his plate.

"Defense? Is there some kind of war going on that I don't know about?" he asked, squeezing lemon juice over his fish.

"Oh!" she said suddenly, jerking back.

He glanced up and realized that his lemon wedge had misfired and squirted her in the eye.

"I'm sorry—are you all right?" he asked, half standing and leaning forward.

She pulled her glasses off and blinked a few times. Then she smiled.

"Nice shot," she said, tongue in cheek.

Smooth, really smooth, he chastised himself. The only time she'd unwound with him all day, and he tried to blind her. Feeling guilty, he plucked the heavy black frames from her fingers.

Her eyes widened. "It's okay, I can clean them myself," she said when he began drying them on his pristine napkin.

"At least allow me to exorcise my guilt," he said, caught in the unobscured magic of her green gaze.

He'd noticed her eyes before—their exotic tilt, their color—but her glasses had always provided a chunky barrier to her thoughts. Now he felt as though he could see straight through to her soul.

"What's wrong?" she asked, tugging at the neckline of her dress uncomfortably.

"You have amazing eyes," he said, staring into them intently. "What color is that? Like sea foam. But greener."

"Moldy green," she said dismissively. "That's what my sisters used to call it."

"Jealousy is a curse," he said.

"Oh no, they're not jealous of me," Grace quickly corrected him, reaching for her wineglass again. "They're stunning, all of them."

He shrugged, unconvinced. In his experience, brothers and sisters only took shots at the qualities they most envied in their siblings.

"They are," Grace defended. Her long earrings brushed the creamy skin of her neck. "They even get paid to be beautiful—Felicity's a weather girl, Serena is an actress and Hope's a model. So there's nothing for them to be jealous about where I'm concerned."

For the first time, he sensed vulnerability beneath her tough-broad demeanor. First she was sexy and amusing, now she was vulnerable. He felt as though he was being treated to the dance of the seven veils, except it was Grace's disguises that were dropping away instead of veils.

"Felicity, Serena, Hope and Grace. Let me guess—your Mom's Catholic?" he asked. He'd long since finished cleaning her glasses, but her eyes were too beautiful to hide. He set the frames on the table. If she wanted them, she could ask for them—in the meantime he was going to enjoy the view.

"As Catholic as it gets," Grace said, rolling her eyes. "I still blame Dad for not stopping her with the names."

"Are you close to your sisters?" he asked, knowing he was pushing it. Grace had already proven she was a very private person.

She shrugged, looked away. "Sure."

He saw a flash of unhappiness in her eyes and wondered.

"What about you? Do you have a big family?" she asked.

"Two younger brothers," Mac said. "Both of them happy-as-pigs-in-mud married with kids."

She cocked her head to one side. "Now *you* sound jealous."

"Absolutely. They're the smart ones—knew what they wanted, went out and got it, and now they're in clover. Why wouldn't I be jealous?"

For a long time, he'd viewed his brothers as having mundane lives full of routine and obligation. Only lately had he begun to realize that they were content, even fulfilled, in a way that he'd never been.

She made a disbelieving raspberry noise. Quite a loud one, thanks to whatever she'd had to drink before he picked her up and the lion's share of the bottle of wine they'd been enjoying. The couple at the next table looked across with a frown. Mac hid a smile behind his napkin.

"What have I done wrong now?" he asked, responding to her derision.

"You're rich, famous and last year you were voted one of the sexiest men in America. And you're jealous of them?" she asked disbelievingly.

"Guess it just depends on what you think is important in life. Do *you* think being on the cover of *People* magazine is the be-all and end-all?"

The waiter began clearing their plates and Grace eyed Mac assessingly.

"Why are you interested in directing?"

He blinked at the direct question. He remembered his earlier suspicion that she resented his moving into a second career. Not that he was doing that. He was just…dabbling.

"Change of scenery. Something a bit different." He shrugged.

"Huh," she said, her eyes narrowing. "You're a terrible liar for an actor."

He spread his hands wide to signal his complete honesty.

"It's the truth, I swear. You're welcome to pat me down and see if I'm concealing a single lie."

Her gaze flicked up and down his body, then she studied him over the rim of her wineglass. "Maybe you're lying to yourself, too," she said. "Either way, you're still too good to be true."

He raised an eyebrow. "Am I?"

Why did he get the feeling he was about to feel the sting in the tail?

"Too good-looking. That body. Now you're smart and nice and funny and modest, too. Something's wrong," she said.

"Wow. I should feel flattered, but somehow I'm not. That's a real gift you've got there," he said. He let his gaze drop to her breasts. Man, he hoped they were real. Was it possible he was going to get a chance to find out?

She shrugged a shoulder, the movement languid and relaxed. Her breasts swayed hypnotically.

"Four years of celibacy," she said, as though that explained everything. "You make the preemptive strike early on, guys back off and you never have to fight with temptation. I've got a black belt in verbal self-defense."

That got his attention.

"Four years without sex. Now who's bullshitting," he scoffed.

She sat up a little straighter, stuck her chest out a little more. "Four years, three months and five days, to be exact," she said.

"I don't believe you," he said.

"What? Why?"

"Because nobody with a body like yours could go four years without sex," he said bluntly.

She shifted in her chair, made a huffing noise, frowned and then blinked.

"I'm not sure I know what you mean by that," she finally admitted.

He didn't say a word, just let his gaze roam, from her tilted green eyes to her lush, ripe mouth to her even lusher breasts and her tiny waist.

She blushed.

"Yeah, you do," he said, unable to stop a slow smile from curving his lips. He was enjoying himself more than he had in a long time. She was prickly as hell, but he had a hard-on that desperately wanted to make her closer acquaintance.

"There's no need to look so pleased with yourself."

"Am I looking pleased with myself?" And there he was, thinking he was looking horny. For the first time in a long time.

"It's not a skill test," she said.

"Sorry?"

"Me being celibate. It's not a challenge to you to try to get me into bed. It's just a lifestyle choice I've made. End of story."

"Believe me, rising to the challenge would be last on my list of reasons to get you into bed," he said.

She froze, then her eyelids dropped to half-mast. "There's a list?"

"A long one. Getting longer by the second."

"What's at the top?"

His eyes dropped to her mouth, then to her breasts again. He smiled. He caught a brief glimpse of her tongue as she bit her bottom lip.

"Let's just say there are a number of…items jostling for position," he said.

Across the table, he could see her pupils dilate. The temperature at their table rose about ten degrees. Her breasts rose and fell as she took a deep, sudden breath. He felt as though he was witnessing something momentous—like standing on the brink of a volcano that was about to erupt.

"Dessert, sir? Madam?" the waiter asked, offering two slim, leather-bound menus.

Grace broke eye contact. Mac turned to the waiter, mentally raining down a million curses on the guy's head. Did the man not realize that he was performing delicate work here, coaxing a self-confessed celibate back into the land of the living?

"Not for me, thanks."

When he glanced across at Grace, he saw that she'd rescued her glasses from the table and that she was once more ensconced behind them.

Damn. The moment was gone. Possibly never to return.

"Not for me, either," she said. "In fact, I've got an early start tomorrow...."

He could take a hint, even if it meant his boner was flying solo tonight. It was probably the smarter course, anyway. They had to work with each other. The wedding special was a big deal and she'd already shown she could be obstructive. No point in making things messier by crossing the line.

He shot one last regretful look at her breasts before turning back to the waiter. If only...

"Just the check, thanks," he said resignedly.

THE FULL HORROR of her behavior struck Grace as she walked out into the cool night air. The brisk ocean breeze was like a bucket of cold water—brutal and highly effective in cutting through the fuzzy shroud of alcoholic courage she'd woven around herself in an attempt to survive the evening.

She'd told him she was celibate.

Mac Harrison. A walking god.

And she'd told him he was gorgeous. Even that he had a hot body. God, he must think she was gagging for it.

And he would be right—she was.

The two glasses of wine she'd had before he arrived to pick her up had been supposed to keep her calm, in control. But she'd underestimated the power of nerves and a good Californian chardonnay on an empty stomach. By the time he'd appeared on her doorstep, she'd been feeling no pain at all.

Which had given her the *illusion* of being calm and in control. But the moment she stepped outside the restaurant and the chill night air rushed across her overheated skin, she saw the flaw in her strategy.

She'd made a fool of herself. She'd confessed her born-again-virgin status to him and she'd flirted shamelessly. Now she felt like the biggest moron to ever walk the earth. What must he be thinking? She'd really stuffed up spectacularly. First, her utter bitchiness during the day, now her inappropriate—drunken—fumblings over dinner. Talk about from one extreme to the other.

"Lord, please take me now," she mumbled as she stared up at the starry sky.

"Did you say something?" Mac asked, turning away from his conversation with the valet.

"No," she said quietly, feeling utterly miserable. She just wanted to be home, in her bed with the covers over her head and her eyes tightly shut. Then this would all be a dream, a horrible nightmare, and she wouldn't have to endure the selected highlights that would no doubt be flashing across her mind for the next few months.

She shivered, rubbing her hands along her arms.

"Cold?" Mac asked. Before she could shake her head, he'd

shrugged out of his designer denim jacket and was holding it out for her to slide her arms into.

Because it was easier to comply than to explain that it had been more a shiver of self-recrimination than actual cold, Grace poked her arms into the proffered sleeves. Immediately, he settled the jacket on her shoulders and she was enveloped in his warmth and his scent.

"Better?"

She forced a smile. "Thanks."

It wasn't his fault that she found him attractive. Well, not completely, anyway. He'd been born good-looking, so that part wasn't his fault. But the working-out-to-achieve-a-perfect-body thing—that was definitely something she could lay at his door. And the good fashion sense—that was his fault, too, even if his taste came via a stylist. Then there was the witty dinner conversation, his taste in cars, his laugh and the mesmerizing intensity of his blue eyes. They were all definitely, definitely his fault. He could have been a cocky, egotistical jerk, like all the other stars she'd met. But no, he'd chosen to be charming. The irresistible bastard.

The Corvette burbled to a halt in front of them, valet behind the wheel, and Mac rested his hand on the small of her back as he guided her toward the passenger seat. Heat slithered along her veins from the brief contact.

So stupid, she told herself. *So, so stupid.*

But it was useless. She'd fantasized about having Mac Harrison and now here he was, sitting beside her, driving her home. Her body didn't know the difference between fantasy and reality. She'd trained it too well.

Even though she knew nothing would happen, even though she knew it was insane to even consider that something might happen, her body was off and running.

She could feel her heart clamoring against her ribs. Staring out the side window, she was unbearably aware of the brush of her clothes against her skin. Beneath the protection of Mac's coat, her nipples had hardened into two urgent peaks and she squeezed her knees together in a vain attempt to quell the slow ache that was growing between her thighs.

Images flashed across her mind: Mac's superbly muscled chest, the firm perfection of his butt in jeans, the strength of his thighs.

God, she wanted him.

And she was *so* never going to have him.

"You okay? Not still cold?" Mac asked, shooting a look across at her as they stopped at a red light.

Cold? She'd never been hotter. If he took off too fast, she was liable to slide off the seat.

"I'm fine," she lied.

Surreptitiously, she snuck a peek at his thighs flexing and relaxing as he clutched to change gears, then accelerated away from the light.

Biting her lip, she focused her eyes higher, toward the substantial bulge in his crotch. She'd wondered about him so many times, how thick he was, how long, what it would feel like to have him inside her….

The screech of brakes behind them brought her back to reality and she tore her gaze away.

"Moron," Mac said, glaring at the rearview mirror.

He might as well have been talking to her. Eyes fixed straight ahead, she spent the rest of the drive reciting the times tables in her head. Anything to distract her libido from the object of its persistent desire. But she felt as though she'd let the genie out of the bottle. It had been years since she'd flirted with a man, exchanged loaded glances, laughed knowingly at risqué jokes. She didn't know how to backpedal, how to shove the genie back down where he belonged.

The genie wanted to get busy. And the chances of that happening were about a million to one.

She practically sprang from the car the moment it stopped in front of her apartment block.

"Thanks for dinner," she blurted, but she saw with a sinking heart that Mac was getting out of the car.

Just her luck—she'd eroticized the only Hollywood hunk with old-fashioned manners.

Gritting her teeth, she scampered up the single flight of exterior stairs to her entrance porch. If they were teenagers, or even two normal people home after a night out together, she'd feel slightly nervous about the whole good-night-kiss thing. But she had no expectations where Mac was concerned. He was a star. She was…well, she was what she was—early thirties, too curvy, too busty, not pretty enough, veteran of too many dumpings to count. He may have flirted with her over dinner, but only because she'd been so tipsy that he hadn't had much choice.

Desperately, she tried to call on her Bette Davis demeanor, but she was too rattled to pull it off.

"Okay. Thanks for dinner," she said as she pushed her door open with trembling hands. "And, again, I'm sorry about today."

And tonight, she added mentally. God, how was she going to recover from tonight?

"Already forgotten," he said. She couldn't see his face properly in the dim light in the entrance porch.

"Well. That's good," she said stupidly. "Anyway, I'm dying to get into bed."

She closed her eyes briefly as she heard her own words. She truly was not fit to be out without adult supervision.

"I mean, alone. Get into bed alone," she clarified.

Offering a feeble wave of her hand, she stepped hastily toward her open door.

"Grace," Mac said from behind her.

She froze. Despite all the common-sense lectures she'd given herself, despite all rational thought, she couldn't help hoping against hope that he was about to say something incredibly sexy and romantic. Something straight out of one of her fantasies—maybe that he'd been unable to stop thinking about her all day. Or that he'd tried to fight it, but the attraction between them was undeniable. She'd even settle for "Yo, hottie"—anything that matched the unbearable desire-filled ache inside her.

"My jacket," he said.

"Oh. Right," she said.

It was ridiculous to feel disappointed. Crazy, even.

Turning toward him, she began to shrug out of his jacket, then winced as her long, dangling earring got caught on the collar. In vain she twisted her head and tried to free the snag.

"Sorry, stupid earring," she explained as she continued to struggle.

"Here, hold still for a moment," Mac said, stepping close.

She held her breath as he loomed over her, grabbing her shoulders and spinning her toward the warm golden light spilling out from the lamp in her hallway.

Stepping closer, he reached for the tangle of earring and denim and hair that she'd created. She could feel the heat radiating from his body, the brush of his fingers on the sensitive skin of her neck, even the hush of his breath on her cheek.

It was too much. She'd craved him too long.

She whimpered.

A completely, utterly revealing whimper that spoke of desire and want and need.

At the same time, she felt her earring come free as he unsnagged it.

She wanted to die. Right then. Even if it hurt, a lot. Because nothing could be worse than whimpering with need in front of a man like Mac Harrison. Four long years of self-esteem building went out the window. Why had she just exposed herself like that?

After a long moment, she dared a glance up at him, convinced she'd see pity or surprise or indifference on his face.

Instead, she saw desire.

It was the last thing she'd expected, the absolute last. A roaring sound filled her head as she realized that she had her ultimate fantasy man standing in front of her, and—miracle of miracles—he wanted her.

What happened next was totally beyond her control. It was almost like watching some other woman reach out and wrap a hand around the back of Mac's head and pull it down toward her—except it was her mouth that was parting in anticipation, her eyes that were closing.

There was nothing gentle or tentative about their first kiss. Mouth met mouth, tongues clashed, hands grabbed at body parts as they strained toward one another. Grace flattened her length against his and gave a mew of pleasure when she felt his erection pressing against her belly. He grabbed her hips and ground himself into her softness, all the while devouring her mouth with his own.

His mouth left hers and he trailed kisses across to her ear. She met the shockingly hot, wet invasion of his tongue in her ear with a moan, running her hands down his back and, finally, after all her nights of wondering and imagining, onto his butt.

"Perfect," she whispered, hauling him as close as she could and rubbing herself against his hardness.

He responded by sliding a hand up onto her breasts. She felt his gust of satisfaction as his palm took the full weight of her, his thumb finding her nipple unerringly.

Her knees trembled as his other hand slid down her hip and thigh, searching for the hem of her skirt.

A sudden urgency gripped her. As soon as he touched her *there,* she was going up in flames and nothing was going to stop her taking what she wanted. And they were still standing outside her apartment in the entrance porch she shared with the place next door.

Fuelled by need, she pushed on his chest, unwilling to break contact, but urging him toward her open doorway nonetheless. He wasn't a stupid man. Together, they stumbled backward, his hands still torturing her breasts, hers sliding around his hips now and seeking out the ridge of his erection.

He felt big. And hard. And very much exactly what she needed to stop the throbbing ache between her thighs.

A crash sounded as they bumped into her hall table and a pile of books hit the floor. She murmured her lack of concern and pushed him into her living room. Fumbling with his fly, she swore as she got the teeth caught in the fabric of his boxers.

"Damn thing," she muttered, trying to concentrate on the pleasurable pain of his hands on her breasts and his mouth on her neck while simultaneously freeing his erection from the prison of his jeans.

She felt him smile against her neck.

"Here," he said, ducking his head so he could get a look at the scene of the crime. She lifted her head at the same time and cracked him in the jaw.

"Yow!"

His head jerked up and back, she winced.

"Sorry, sorry," she said, reaching up a soothing hand.

"Doesn't matter," he said, kissing her hand away. She heard the beautiful sound of his fly hissing open, and forgot everything else as she zeroed in on his erection.

Sliding her hand into the warmth of his jeans, she first stroked his length, then wrapped her hand around him.

"Grace," he breathed raggedly as she stroked more confidently up and down his shaft.

"I know," she gasped.

They were wearing too much clothing. She'd never wanted to be naked more in her life. On fire, she shoved him backward into the armless chair beside her fireplace. No sooner was he seated than she had his erection free from his jeans, sitting up proudly and begging for her attention.

It didn't have to beg—she was Mac's for the asking. Lifting her skirt up with no finesse but plenty of alacrity, she hooked her thumbs into her panties and whipped them down her legs. He watched with an approving glint in his eyes, his hands reaching out to slide beneath her dress as she straddled him. The feel of his hands on her thighs and backside was her every wish come true and she rubbed herself against the hardness of his erection with a fierce abandon.

"This has to come off," Mac said, starting to tackle the first of the dozens of tiny buttons down the front of her dress. Imagining his mouth on her breasts was too much, and she was too greedy to wait. Grabbing both sides of the slightly opened neckline, she tugged, hard. Buttons pinged everywhere, one hitting Mac near the eye, but within seconds she'd bared her dusky-peach lace bra to his eyes and he was pushing it out of the way and sucking a nipple into the moist heat of his mouth.

Gasping, Grace writhed. She was about to come, but she wanted him inside her.

Tangling her fingers in his hair, she gripped tight and pulled him away from his very important work on her breasts.

"Condom," she panted when he frowned at her.

His frown cleared. "Back pocket," he said, tilting up on one hip so she could slide her fingers around to retrieve his wallet.

A single, beautiful condom resided in a credit-card slot and she pulled it free and ripped it open in one smooth move. Tossing his wallet to one side, she stood for the brief time it took to protect them both. Then she slid a hand between their bodies, positioned the head of his erection between her slick inner lips, and began the slow slide to ecstasy.

He groaned and dropped his head back as he penetrated her, even as his hands slid over her breasts and began to massage them rhythmically. Grace's eyes narrowed to slits as she stretched to accommodate him, every nerve ending on fire, her orgasm just a hair's breadth away. Slowly, savoring every hard, thick inch, she began to ride him.

She felt overwhelmed with sensation. The scratch of his stubble on her breasts. The fullness of his hardness inside her. Then, almost too much, the smooth caress as one of his hands moved around her hip to delve into the moist curls between her legs. He found the swollen nub of her clitoris with his thumb and she shuddered as he began to massage it firmly.

"Mac, oh, Mac," she cried out, as she had a hundred times before. But this time, he was here, a real man, not a figment of her imagination.

As though he sensed her imminent climax, Mac's head came up and she found herself matching his wide, reckless grin. Her body began to shudder and he leaned forward, pulling an already-taut nipple into his mouth as everything converged within her. She ground herself against him as she came explosively, back arching, breasts thrusting forward, hands digging into his shoulders as she shouted out her release. A few seconds later, he grabbed her hips and she felt the powerful, instinctive thrust of his hips up into her as he joined her in ecstasy.

Panting, a bead of sweat trickling between her breasts, Grace flopped forward, her face resting against the side of Mac's neck.

Four years. Four long, lonely, horny years since she'd had sex.

And, oh boy, had it been worth the wait.

4

GRACE WOKE to the smell of Mac's aftershave in her bed. The instant she recognized the smoky mix of cloves and sandalwood, a big smile stretched across her face. She stretched languorously, her eyes still closed as she savored the deliciousness of it all.

God, he'd been insatiable. So had she. She hadn't known her body was capable of feeling so good. Rolling onto her side, she stretched out an arm, hoping that they would have time to replay a few selected highlights before Mac had to race off to work.

When her hand encountered nothing but cold sheets, her eyes popped open.

The bed was empty. Apart from an indentation in the spare pillow, there was nothing to indicate that last night had been any more real than the many fantasies she'd had about Mac over the past year.

She felt a lurch of disappointment, then her brain kicked into gear and she remembered Mac explaining he had to be out at the studio early today. That had been some time in between condom number two and condom number three.

Which meant no recaps. Bummer. Snorting at her own greed, she rolled to the edge of the bed. Small muscles that she hadn't used in a *loooooong* time protested as she stood.

She caught sight of her naked body in her dressing table mirror and stopped to stare. She had the suggestion of whisker burn on her breasts and a definite hickey low on her neck. Her hair was tousled, her eyes heavy and slumberous. She oozed smug, languorous, satisfied woman.

Another big smile curled her lips. If she were a cat, she'd be purring.

The caress of her silk robe over her skin brought a host of sensual memories cascading into her mind. Mac had been so intense, so utterly absorbed in the here and now of their sexual play. The way he'd smoothed his hands over her body, the low sound of satisfaction he'd made when he touched her breasts, the knowing movement of his fingers inside her.... Her nipples tightened and a distinct warmth began to throb between her legs.

She shook her head at her own voraciousness. Four bouts of soul-searing sex and still she wanted more. She'd thought Mr. Buzzy had been ample compensation for missing out on having a love life, but last night had taught her that there was nothing that could even come close to real contact with another human being. Skin on skin, the smells, the tastes, the sounds—the whole experience had been one big sensory feast.

She realized now that for four years she'd been depriving herself. She needed to take a leaf out of Claudia's book and find herself a reliable lover or two. Nothing permanent or emotional, just someone to take the edge off every now and then. For a second she allowed herself to imagine what it would be like to have Mac as her real-life convenient lover. It was a dangerously attractive prospect, but she pushed the fantasy away. She wasn't stupid—last night had been a one-off. She'd had one amazing experience with him and it had opened her eyes to what she'd been missing out on. That would have to be enough.

Yawning, she padded into her living room, then stopped with a frown when she felt something small and hard beneath her bare foot. She looked down to see she was walking in a sea of tiny pearl buttons.

A flash of memory: her tearing her dress open so Mac could tongue her breasts last night. She laughed out loud.

God, she'd forgotten how good sex could be. How much fun. How liquid and sensuous and powerful it made her feel.

Maybe a man wouldn't have to be stuffed and turned into an umbrella stand to find a place in her home. Maybe she could consider bending her no-fraternizing-with-the-enemy rule, after all, if it meant occasional access to a real, live penis.

She was still musing on the subject when the phone rang. It took her three rings to find it, since the receiver was hidden beneath her discarded dress.

"Hello?"

"Grace. You're up." It was Mac. She felt breathless suddenly and she sank onto the arm of her couch.

"Yes," she said.

"Listen, I don't suppose you've found my wallet anywhere?"

She frowned. There was something wrong with his voice. He sounded stilted, distant.

"Um, no. Let me check. Any idea where it might be?" she asked, her mind ticking away furiously. Why did he sound so awkward?

"You took it out of my pocket. For the condom," he reminded her.

"Right. Give me a moment."

She put the phone down and stared at it for a moment. She felt agitated, uncertain all of a sudden. What had seemed sensuous and decadent and delicious just seconds before suddenly felt faintly sordid. Why was that?

Forcing herself to the matter at hand, she scanned the room. Nothing. Dropping to her knees, she checked under the couches and the armchair. A black leather square lay beneath the closest couch, cheek by jowl with two enormous dust bunnies. She collected it and pushed herself to her feet.

"Found it," she said when she'd picked up the phone again.

"Great. Great. That's a load off," he said. He sounded as though he was talking to his dentist.

A slow anger was building inside her. What did this jerk think she was going to do, turn up at his place and boil his rabbit or something? She could practically hear him trying to work out how to get his hands on the wallet without having to commit to a second date with her. Just as well she hadn't been under the delusion that last night had been the beginning of something instead of the sum total of her personal relationship with Mac Harrison.

"Listen, my schedule is hell for the next few days, so maybe you could give my wallet to one of the production runners. When things clear up, I'll give you a call and we can catch up some time…?" he said when the silence had stretched too long between them. He sounded about as thrilled as if he was booking in to have a prostate exam.

It was almost funny.

"You can stop having conniptions, Mac," she said dryly. "I know what last night was. I'm not over here picking out china patterns."

"Sure. I know that." He sounded embarrassed and relieved in equal measure. "I mean, we're both adults, right?"

"I'll give the wallet to the first runner I see when I get to the office, okay?" she said, keen to end the conversation. The gloss was fast wearing off her fantasy evening.

"Thanks. Oh, and Grace?"

"Yeah?" she asked, one hand on her hip. She had a feeling something really good was coming.

"I had a great time last night," he said. It sounded like he was reading it off a cue card. If she hadn't been there to share his four orgasms, she'd have thought she'd imagined the whole glorious, mad thing.

"Did you?" she said. And then she hung up.

What a jerk off. She paced her apartment for a few minutes, swearing and stomping her bare feet against the boards. Was it too much to ask for honesty and mutual respect? She wasn't angry because he didn't want to see her again, she assured herself. She was angry because for a full fifteen minutes there she'd been basking in the afterglow of their night together—then he'd come along and lobbed a pile of steaming doggy do all over it with his standoff tactics and rote compliments.

Men. Suddenly she remembered why Mr. Buzzy had looked so good for four years.

MAC STUDIED the blank display of his cell phone for a few beats.

Wow, wasn't he the old silver-tongued devil, really smoothing over the awkwardness there with Grace? He could just imagine the names she was calling him about now.

He shook his head at his own lack of finesse. This was the danger of acting on sensual impulse, of course. With Jen or Lisa, his regular bed-buddies, there was no question that they knew the score. Sex was sex was sex—no strings, no commitment. Perfect for a guy who had too many relationship carcasses rotting in his emotional backyard. But he'd been so utterly absorbed by Grace last night that he hadn't thought through the consequences of tumbling her into bed. He'd wanted her, he'd had her. Several times. And it had been great. But in the cold light of day, it had occurred to him that Grace had just broken a four-year run of no sex to do the horizontal mambo with him last night.

He was no Dr. Phil, but he figured that there was a fair chance that she might be looking for something more than a one-night-only performance out of the man she'd chosen to break the drought with. And as great as the sex had been, Mac was not the guy to deliver on that kind of expectation. Been there, done that. Had the scars to prove it.

Some people—most of them women with strong feminist leanings—might think that his inability to commit might be grounds enough for stepping away from temptation last night when Grace had looked up at him with raw hunger in her eyes.

Those people hadn't spent a day staring at Grace's stupendous breasts and bodacious ass and that teeny tiny waist that made both her other assets look so damn fine.

So, he'd been a hound dog. Not the first time. Probably not the last. But he definitely could have handled the phone call better. Thing was, he'd never really mastered the art of letting women down. Hence, again, the appeal of women who already knew the score.

The great thing—the really, really great thing—was that now he and Grace had to work with each other. He could just imagine how warm and welcoming she would be after his ineptitude. Another minor detail he hadn't factored in when he was busy burying himself inside her last night.

God, it had been good. All he had to do was think about Grace's lush, curvy body—how tight and wet and hot she'd been—and he was gone.

Glancing around to make sure he was unobserved, he reached down to adjust his suddenly crowded crotch.

For a second he regretted the phone call. If he hadn't given her the cold shoulder, he could go there again. Then he gave himself a mental kick. He'd made the smart move. There was no point starting something that was only going to end in disaster, after all. When you didn't believe in happily ever after, there weren't many places a relationship could go.

GRACE SLAMMED THE PHONE down for the fifth time that morning and swore pithily at her computer monitor.

"Grace Elizabeth Wellington. If I wasn't so impressed I'd be shocked," Sadie said as she lounged against Grace's office door frame. "You've been hanging out with those sailors again, haven't you?"

Grace dragged a small smile from her politeness reserves, but Sadie wasn't buying.

"What's up?" Sadie asked, dropping into the guest chair opposite Grace's desk and arranging her long, lean legs before her.

"Nothing. It's just I've been trying to get one of the production runners up here from the studio all morning, but they keep saying they won't be making a Santa Monica run until later today," Grace said, referring to the two gophers who looked after anything and everything on the show. "Have you ever heard of that? I can't remember the last time we didn't have runners in and out of here all day."

Sadie shrugged. "It varies. It's one of those things—when you need one, they're never around, but when you don't give a hoot, they've used the last of the milk and stolen your sandwich from the fridge on their way out the door."

Again, Grace mustered a smile for her friend, but her

thoughts were all for the wallet burning a hole in her desk drawer. She wanted it gone. She definitely didn't want to have to have another conversation with Mac. Not that he'd tried to contact her. She bet he'd prefer to stick hot forks in his eyeballs before he gave a woman the impression she might be more to him that a casual lay.

"What's the big deal, anyway? I thought we got the script alterations out to the studio yesterday?" Sadie asked.

"We did. I just had something I needed to send over," Grace said vaguely.

Too late, she realized that any hint of mystery would arouse Sadie's writer's antennae. Before Sadie could open her mouth to ask the next question, Grace beat her to it.

"Mac left his wallet at my place last night." She shrugged, keeping her voice carefully casual.

"*Mac*. As in Mac Harrison?" Sadie clarified. "Actor on our show, certified hottie, voted Most Beddable Soap Star by the women of America. That Mac?"

"We had a working dinner." *Then we went home and really got to work*. Grace just managed to bite her tongue on the confession. She did not need her friend speculating about her one-night stand with Mac. Her own thoughts were already doing her head in—and Sadie's would inevitably be tainted with the rose-colored zeal of a woman newly in love.

"Oh. You had me excited for a moment there, Gracie. If anyone could break down that fortress of solitude of yours, Mac is the man."

"Why do you say that?" Grace asked before she could stop herself.

"He's hot, he's funny, he's got that body," Sadie said, ticking the items off on her fingers. "Plus, he's a nice guy. I've had coffee with him a few times out at the studio and he's got some great ideas for the show. He's really into the whole directing thing, you know. Which is amazing, given how good an actor he is. He's got it all, basically."

Grace realized she was leaning forward, sucking up every morsel of information that Sadie was dispensing. She sat back and forced a bored wave of her hand.

"Yeah, but does he come with an off switch?" she asked.

Sadie snickered. "You're so bad. You could at least consider him."

"Celibate, in case you forgot," Grace said firmly. She wondered briefly if one night of sex in four years disqualified her from her self-appointed title.

"Chicken," Sadie countered.

Grace opened her mouth in surprise, stung by Sadie's words.

"Are you joking or do you really think I'm a chicken?" she asked.

Sadie hesitated a moment, then shook her head. "No. I remember Owen."

"So does my sister," Grace said. "Anyway, me being single has nothing to do with Owen."

She felt as though she'd been saying that a lot lately. Sadie and Claudia had never understood how she'd picked up and walked away from her five years with Owen without shedding a tear. They thought that because she hadn't slobbed around and worn the same pair of pajamas for a whole week that she hadn't moved on. She dealt with things differently, was all. The moment she'd seen that things were not going to work out with Owen, she'd made the decision that he wasn't going to have a second more of her time. And she'd stuck to that decision. He'd wasted enough of her years as it was, he wasn't getting any more.

Sadie reached out to grab Grace's hand.

"I gave Dylan a chance after what Greg did to me," she said. "Sometimes it's worth risking the hurt to get the big payoff."

Grace shook her head and threw her hands in the air in exasperation.

"Sadie, no offence, but not everyone sees the world the way you do. I love it that you and Dylan are happy together, but I'm just as happy the way I am. Being single is not a disease."

Sadie smiled a little sheepishly. "Sorry. I've turned into the romance pimp, haven't I?"

"More a romance pusher." Grace put on a mock-deep voice. "Hey, girls, pssst, take a look at this…. I got sexual love, romantic love, even a small stock of first love. You want a hit?"

Sadie laughed and pushed herself to her feet. "Next time I start pushing, you give me a slap upside the head, okay."

"Damned straight I will," Grace said.

"Right, and before I forget—we're still on for dinner tonight, right? That's why I came by. What can we bring? Dessert, bread, salad?"

Grace's eyes widened as she remembered that she'd invited her friends for dinner.

"You forgot, didn't you?" Sadie asked, amused. "God, Dylan and I are a boring married couple already, aren't we?"

"I'm a little distracted, that's all." A flash of Mac's stunning, naked body raced across her mind. Okay, she was a *lot* distracted.

"So we're still good?"

"Absolutely. I'll see you at seven, okay?"

"Done."

Grace sat back in her chair, trying to order her thoughts. It would be a lot easier if her body wasn't doing a continual happy dance after a night of intense stimulation.

Irritated with herself, she pushed all thoughts of Mac away. He'd served his purpose. And there were other men out there, after all, if she chose to give up celibacy and explore the idea of taking the occasional lover.

"GUYS, YOU WANT ANOTHER DRINK?" Grace hollered from the kitchen as she poured cream into a jug later that evening.

"We're fine," Sadie called back.

Sliding slices of caramel walnut cake onto plates, Grace balanced all three on one hand and forearm—classic waitress style—and grabbed the pitcher of cream with her free hand.

"Okay, here we go," she said, sailing into the living room.

She'd pulled her small drop-leaf dining table away from the wall and it was a tight squeeze as she slid past Sadie to arrange Dylan's plate in front of him.

"Yum, Gracie," Sadie said.

Dylan inhaled the scent of cinnamon and caramel appreciatively. "You are a goddess," he said in reverential tones.

Grace was about to reply when her doorbell sounded.

Sadie raised an eyebrow. "You expecting anyone?"

"No."

Frowning, Grace headed for the door. It was too late for Girl Scout cookies or a door-to-door collector, so who else…?

"Hey, I was in the neighborhood, thought I should just stop by and grab my wallet, since the runners were too busy today.…" Mac said. He was leaning on the door frame, his large body all but blocking the night out.

Once again, she cursed the runners to hell, even as she drank in the sight of him, her gaze running from one broad shoulder to the other, her body tingling from head to toe as she remembered how good last night had been.

Then she remembered she was pissed with him for his woeful morning-after technique.

"Wow, you're pretty brave turning up here. Aren't you worried I might be embroidering handkerchiefs for you by now?" she asked.

"Look, about this morning—" he said, but she held up a hand.

"You don't have to explain to me, Mac. I understand that a stud like you has to spread himself around."

He frowned. "That's not why I—" he said, but she spoke over him again.

"Sorry, but I really don't have time to chat. Too busy having a life of my own. I'll just go grab your wallet."

Feeling distinctly pleased with herself—it wasn't every day that a girl like her got to put a guy like Mac in his place—Grace made her way up the hallway toward her bedroom where Mac's wallet was in her handbag.

"Sorry, guys, won't be a minute," she told Dylan and Sadie in passing.

But Sadie's eyes were focused over her shoulder.

"Hey, Mac. What are you doing here?" Sadie said.

Grace swiveled on her heel, startled and appalled to see that Mac had followed her into her apartment. He looked equally startled as he registered that she had company.

Shit. So much for privacy. Sadie was already highly suspicious that something was going on with Mac. There was something vaguely humiliating about having to admit that after four years of celibacy and Bette Davis-inspired man-contempt, she'd given it up to a known horn dog.

Mac's eyes shot to her face and she tried to tell him without winking or scrunching up her face that her friends were not aware that they'd devoured each other whole last night.

"My wallet," Mac said after a slightly-too-long silence. "I accidentally left it behind when I dropped Grace off last night."

"That's right. Grace mentioned it at work," Sadie said, but she was looking back and forth between Grace and Mac speculatively. Grace frowned faintly and shook her head, trying to deter her friend from jumping to the right conclusion.

Sadie just smiled mysteriously, however, and turned to Dylan. "You guys know each other, right?" she asked.

Dylan stood and offered his hand. "Good to see you, Mac. I've been meaning to call and let you know how much I enjoyed that last block you directed."

Mac looked surprised. "Yeah? Thanks."

What was with him and the whole directing thing, anyway, Grace wondered. He'd told her last night that he was only doing it for a change of scenery, but she wasn't buying. She remembered the way he'd taken photos at the vineyard, the thoughtful way he'd assessed the main rooms, the way he'd insisted on checking out the whole site even though she was making his life hell. He seemed to care an awful lot for a man who was just killing time.

"Yeah, we were all thrilled when Claudia gave you the wedding special," Sadie said. "Knew we were in good hands."

A dull red crept over Mac's cheekbones beneath his tan and he shrugged uncomfortably. Grace narrowed her eyes. Now he was *embarrassed?*

"It's a great story you guys came up with. Can't wait to read Grace's script," Mac said.

Dylan grimaced self-consciously. "We're seconds away from a group hug here, aren't we?"

Sadie punched him in the arm lightly and laughed. Meanwhile Grace tried to think of a way to edge Mac out of her living room before someone guessed that he'd done more than lose his wallet at her place last night.

But Sadie and Dylan were already sinking into their seats and picking up their dessert spoons and Mac was leaning on the back of the spare chair, looking as if he was settling in.

She shot him a dirty look but he ignored it.

"I ran into a friend of yours at the gym the other day. Olly Jones," Mac said.

Dylan grimaced. "Okay, what dirt did he dish? Or does Sadie need to leave the room? I'm a soon-to-be-married man, you know," he said.

Mac laughed and Grace resigned herself to the fact that her dinner for three had morphed into dessert for four. Wordless, she traipsed into the kitchen and cut another slice of cake for Mac. Returning to the living room, she slid it in front of him. He gave her a surprised look and she indicated with a grudging jerk of her head that he should pull up a seat.

Conversation and laughs flowed thick and fast, and by the time she served coffee they'd all moved away from the table. Sadie and Dylan had taken position on one of her two-seater couches, while Mac sat opposite on the other. Which left her with the choice of sitting next to him or taking the slipper chair close to the fireplace.

The same chair on which she'd ravished him the previous evening.

No contest, really. There was no way she could sit where they'd so recently gotten busy and look him in the eye without blushing.

Perching primly on the edge of the two-seater, she handed out coffees. Why hadn't she told Mac to wait at the front door?

And why couldn't he and Dylan have hated each other? There was something disturbingly…comfortable about the whole arrangement and it made Grace's hand tremble as she spooned three sugars into her coffee.

"Three for me, too, thanks," Mac said, holding out his cup.

"You're kidding? I thought only Grace ruined good coffee with so much sugar," Sadie said.

"I have a sweet tooth, what can I say?" Mac shrugged. "So, have you guys set a date for the wedding yet?"

"August," Sadie said smugly.

"I wanted earlier, but she insisted she needed more time," Dylan said fondly, lifting Sadie's hand to kiss her knuckles.

Grace held up a hand in mock self-defense. "Please. Enough already. Aren't you guys worried about the wrinkles you're going to get from all that smiling?"

"Grace is a cynic," Sadie confided to Mac. "She doesn't believe in love."

"That's not exactly true. I just believe it's a lot rarer than people think."

She could feel Mac's blue gaze on her face. She met his eye and raised an eyebrow in response to his searching look.

"What about you, Mac?" Sadie asked.

Mac shrugged, his shoulder brushing Grace's in the process. Since when had her couches gotten so small? And why was she still so turned on by this man when he'd had her every way but hanging off the light fixtures last night? Surely some of his appeal should have worn off by now?

"It's a nice idea. In practice, it never seems to go the distance," Mac said.

Grace stared at him, surprised to hear him echoing her personal sentiments so exactly.

"Absolutely," she said. "It's all very well at the beginning when it's just about not being able to keep your hands off each other—"

"But then the daily grind sets in," Mac finished for her.

"And before you know it, you're shredding your ex's suits and putting sugar in his gas tank," Grace said.

"Or filing for a restraining order to stop the stalking," Mac added.

"Wow. Inspiring. Shouldn't you two be out telling pre-schoolers there's no Santa Claus?" Dylan asked.

Grace realized she and Mac were grinning at each other. She gave herself a mental slap reminding herself that this charming, gorgeous, grinning hunk was the same man who'd dumped her so inelegantly this morning, hours after crawling out of her bed. She hadn't been looking for anything from him, but there was such a thing as respect.

Grace returned her attention to her friends. "Live and let live, Dylan. You and Sadie are in love, and Mac and I are like those two grumpy old men in the balcony on *The Muppets*."

"Statler and Waldorf," Mac murmured helpfully.

"Thank you," she said, making the mistake of glancing at him and getting lost in his amazing eyes again.

While she had turned away, Sadie had wriggled along the couch and was now looping her legs over Dylan's knees. Toeing her sandals off and wiggling her toes with a forlorn expression on her face, she batted her eyelids at her fiancé.

"Please?" she begged.

Dylan shook his head adamantly. "No way."

"Just a little rub. I'd do it for you," Sadie said.

"Would you? At the end of a long, hot L.A. day, you'd put your pristine, lovely hands on my hot, smelly feet?" Dylan said.

Sadie pouted, looking utterly adorable and undeniable.

Grace wasn't the only person to think so. Out of the corner of her eye, she was aware of Mac watching her friend, and Dylan soon sighed heavily and put down his coffee cup.

"Now *this* is love," he said, smiling into Sadie's eyes as he picked up her left foot and started to massage.

That quickly, the yearning-heart, stomach-punch thing from the café hit Grace again. She ducked her head for a second and blinked like crazy fighting out-of-nowhere tears.

What was it with these guys and chest pain? Was it possible to be allergic to other people's happiness?

God, how miserable did that make her?

Suddenly, she became powerfully aware of the warmth of Mac's body pressing against her side and the sound of his low voice as he said something to Dylan. The odd discomfort she'd felt earlier about how cozy and domestic this little scene was came back in earnest.

What was she doing sitting beside Mac Harrison playing happy couples with Sadie and Dylan? Especially given what had happened between her and Mac last night and this morning?

Before she knew it, she was on her feet.

"I'd better get that wallet for you," she said.

Mac looked startled, as though he'd forgotten why he'd come in the first place.

"Right, of course," he said, following suit and standing.

Grace went into her bedroom and grabbed his wallet from her handbag. He was saying his goodbyes to Sadie and Dylan when she returned to the living room, then he led the way up the hallway to her front door.

Handing the wallet over, she crossed her arms over her chest.

"There you go," she said briskly.

"Thanks. And thanks for the coffee and cake."

"Humph," she said, already pushing the door shut.

"You make that cake yourself?" he asked.

She frowned. What the hell was he playing at?

"I sew, too. Why, you looking for a housekeeper?" she asked.

He grinned. "Okay, I admit it—I handled this morning really badly. What can I say? I'm hopeless at giving women the brush-off. But wouldn't it be more offensive if I was really slick? If I promised to call and sent flowers and you never heard from me again?"

"It's so hard for me to answer that, since I only got the shitty, low-rent version," she said.

"Here's the thing—you don't believe in commitment and love. You just said so five minutes ago. And neither do I. Might work for Sadie and Dylan—and for their sake, I hope it does—but I don't buy it anymore."

"Is this going somewhere?" she asked, making a show of being impatient and tapping her foot on the ground.

"Yeah. I'll be honest with you—this morning I was a little worried about what you would expect after what had happened between us. But now that I know we both feel the same way about relationships, I think we might be throwing away a good opportunity here," he said. "We both like sex and we both have no illusions about what it means. Now that you've broken the drought, I bet you're not so keen on going back to the whole celibacy thing, are you?"

"Wow. Thanks for that, and for your riveting, perspicacious insights into my psyche," she drawled, "but I can take care of my own sex life."

She started closing the door between them.

"You are such a pain in the ass," Mac said, then he stepped forward and hauled her into his arms.

Sensation raced through her body and all her blood rushed

south as his tongue danced into her mouth. She told herself the only reason she wasn't pushing him away was because she was giving him enough rope to hang himself. It was a theory that began to wear a little thin as her breasts tightened into two perky, demanding peaks and her thighs went up in flames.

By the time he broke their kiss and grinned down at her she had been reduced to speechless, quivering Jell-O.

It took her a couple of seconds to regain the power of thought. She realized Mac was looking very pleased with himself.

"We're good together, Grace. Why not make the most of it while it lasts?"

She ignored the fact that he was proposing the exact same arrangement she'd imagined having with some faceless convenient male just that morning. All she could remember was how stupid she'd felt when he'd been so cold and distant on the phone. She never, ever wanted to give him the opportunity to make her feel like that again.

She glanced up at him from under her lashes and lifted a finger to the corner of his mouth. She traced his full bottom lip, then trailed her finger down his chin and onto his chest, delving into the V of warm tanned skin exposed at the neck of his T-shirt. Licking her lips, she sighed lightly.

"I won't say I'm not tempted, Mac. Last night *was* fun. But to be honest, my tolerance for beefcake just isn't that high. Sorry," she said.

"Fun?" he said. *"Beefcake?"*

But she was already closing the door.

Hah, she thought, *take that, Mac Harrison. See how you like being on the receiving end of the brush-off for a change.*

SOME WOMEN WERE JUST too much trouble. Mac had met his
fair share in his lifetime. Grace Wellington, however, took the
cake. Every time he thought of the amused, superior light in
her eye as she shut the door in his face on Tuesday night, he
ground his teeth and started thinking up elaborate revenge
schemes, most of which somehow involved him getting her
naked again, having his way with her, *then* teaching her a
salutary lesson.

Even now, almost two whole days later on Thursday afternoon, he was still steaming over her rejection. He didn't
understand why she'd pissed him off so much.

It wasn't as though he'd invested anything in their relationship, after all. He'd just been looking for more of a good
time—and she'd mocked him.

That was what it was—the mocking thing. That look she'd
had on her face, as though she was the puppet master and he
her malleable toy. Just because certain parts of his body
craved certain parts of hers did not make him her patsy. And
first chance he got he was going to show her, too.

Leaning against the sun-warmed trunk of the Corvette in
the parking lot of the Malibu West Beach Club, he crossed
his arms over his chest and frowned. Now she was keeping
him waiting, too. No doubt more of her power games.

His frown deepened as he spotted a faded onyx-black '57
Corvette on the freeway. There weren't many around, so naturally it drew his attention. Seconds later, it turned into the
parking lot and he recognized Grace behind the wheel.

Didn't that just beat all.

Somehow he didn't think she'd rushed out and bought the
exact same car as his in the time since their last outing
together.

For some reason, the discovery that she'd chosen not to tell him that they drove the same car pissed him off even more. What was with this woman?

She had the roof down and her eyes were hidden behind the retro sunglasses she'd worn at the vineyard. An aquamarine scarf protected her hair. She looked like she'd driven straight out of a 1950s soda ad and he grudgingly admitted to himself that she suited the car perfectly.

She swung her Corvette into the space beside his. While he was formulating a suitably chill remark about their twin rides, he allowed himself one brief head-to-toe perusal as she locked up. Big mistake. She was wearing a halter-neck sundress in shades of hazelnut and chocolate. The bodice crossed over her breasts, accentuating their round fullness before diving into her waistline. The skirt flared out over her hips, ending at knee height to reveal two shapely, sensuous calves, showcased to perfection in a pair of chocolate-leather pumps.

He tore his gaze away and shoved his suddenly fisted hands into his jean pockets. What was it about her that made him want to touch her? Her skin was so creamy and smooth, and he knew now precisely how sensitive it was, could vividly recall the delicate flush of desire that had colored her breasts as he lavished attention on them. His hands literally itched with the urge to cinch themselves around that tiny waist. There was something about those breasts, and that waist and those hips…

Just like that, he was hard for her. He gave a grunt of self-disgust as he pushed himself away from the trunk of his car. The whole show-her-he-was-no-puppet thing was going really well, what with his boner and the fact that his eyes were practically hanging out of his head. Without looking back, he started toward the entrance to the beach club. Let her keep up with him if she wanted to.

The coolness of the air-conditioned members' lounge went

some way toward taking the edge off his frustration. He stopped in the doorway to allow for her to catch up. Her perfume wrapped itself around him as she joined him. Neither of them said a word for a long, drawn-out beat. Mac pretended it was because he was surveying the room, thinking of camera angles and lighting rigs. He wondered what lie she was telling herself, because he knew she was aware of him, too. No matter what bull she told herself, she wanted him. He could feel it.

"We should check the exteriors first," he said brusquely.

"Sure."

Her voice was subdued. He spared a glance for her as they followed the signs to the beach doors. She was pale and she was biting her full bottom lip.

The sight of her white teeth on that soft, crimson arc was highly erotic. Mac resigned himself to a day of illicit hard-ons and frustration. It seemed that it didn't matter that his head had written this woman off as too much trouble—his gonads were hot to trot.

Pushing through double glass doors, they found themselves in a paved courtyard that opened out to the beach on one side. Pristine sand swept down to the ocean and colorful recliners and umbrellas dotted the area. A tropical-themed bar filled one corner and an array of outdoor tables served as an alfresco eating zone for the restaurant inside. Toned, taut women lounged and chatted to one another, their miniscule bikinis set off by deep tans. By contrast, Grace's complexion was alabaster white and the severe boniness of the Beverly Hills set only accentuated her bombshell figure.

Gritting his teeth, Mac left her behind, stalking onto the sand and down to the water. Turning back, he raised his hand to shelter his gaze as he tried to imagine the shot. It was better than the vineyard, he decided. The space was a blank canvas; the art department would have no trouble making it exotic and lavish. The sea and sand more than made up for the lack of chandeliers and sweeping staircases. He imagined a barefoot bride, with lilies in her free-flowing hair.

Pulling his camera from his pocket, he snapped off a number of shots and made some notes. He'd been reading up on some of the great directors recently and watching their work each night, studying techniques, assessing ideas. He'd always been interested in telling stories. As an actor, he told them through emotional interpretation and representation. But a director had a much broader pallette. He got to choose locales, costumes, cast, shooting style. Hell, in Hollywood he even got to choose the weather. It was the thing that had really captured Mac's imagination when he'd first stepped into the directing role a few months ago—there were so many elements to thread together to create a coherent experience that would shock and move and involve the viewer.

He was aware of Grace waiting for him on the patio, but he deliberately took his time down by the shore, turning his back on her to gaze out to sea. Haze hovered on the horizon; whether a product of L.A.'s famous smog or some natural phenomenon he didn't know. A cool breeze ran its fingers through his hair, and he wished he could open his fly and cool off his unruly equipment just as easily. Why did she fascinate him so?

He heard the soft scuff of sand as she approached. She came to a halt beside him, her shoes dangling from one hand. Out of the corners of his eyes he watched her gaze out at the ocean.

"Nice car, by the way," he couldn't resist saying.

She smiled faintly.

"What did you think I was going to do, let you know I had the crap version of your car?"

It annoyed him that it was always about who had the upper hand with Grace.

"I didn't realize we were having a battle of the cars. Stupid me."

She sighed. "You're pissed because I said no to your little offer, aren't you?"

He blustered. "Yeah, right. Trust me, sister, I haven't even thought about it all week. I have more important things to do with my time." *Like stare at my never-say-die boner, damn your gorgeous tilted eyes.*

She stepped in front of him, forcing him to look at her.

"We have to work with each other, Mac. Don't you think this is all a little petty?"

He nearly choked on his own tongue. "You're calling me petty? After you shut your door in my face. After you called me *beefcake?*"

She couldn't hide the smirk that twisted her lips. He got in her face, and was pleased to see her lips part with surprise.

"And we didn't just have *fun* the other night, babe. You think I didn't notice how loud you were screaming? You want to see the scratch marks on my back? Huh?"

She blushed, then licked her lips. His gaze dropped to her glistening red mouth. He was almost positive she knew what she was doing to him, but he wasn't going to give her the satisfaction by giving into his urge to kiss her.

"All right. If I admit that the other night was good, can we move on?" she said.

"Good?"

"Okay, it was great."

He crossed his arms over his chest.

"What do you want from me?" she demanded, her arms gesticulating broadly.

He simply waited.

She sighed.

"Okay. I'm only saying this once, so pay attention. It was incredible. Happy? I've never felt like that before in my life. Satisfied?"

He should have been. He'd turned the tables on her, after all. But suddenly he'd been struck by a worrying realization. He'd never felt that way before, either. No wonder he hadn't been able to forget about her.

What the hell was that about?

"It doesn't make any difference, Mac. I'm not going to fall into bed with you again. I'm not interested in having a man in my life. And once your ego has recovered, you'll admit that you feel exactly the same about being single. You said so the other night," she said.

A few seconds ago, he would have agreed with her. But now he had the never-felt-like-this-before sensation bearing down on him.

"I'm going to go check the interiors," he said, brushing past her. If he stood looking at her a moment longer he wouldn't be answerable for his actions.

She swore and he could hear her following him across the sand. But he stopped in his tracks when he stepped up onto the patio. A copy of today's *Variety* had been left abandoned on the nearest table, and a headline caught his eye. He grabbed the paper and scanned the story quickly.

"What is it?" Grace asked from over his shoulder. He held the paper out so she could see the bold black heading: Rival Soaps in Wedding Shoot-out.

He watched as Grace's brow wrinkled as she read the lead-in paragraph.

"Jesus. Claudia is going to flip out. We'd better get back to the office," Grace said.

5

THE SOUND OF CLAUDIA'S RANTING reached them as soon as they walked into the reception area. Grace winced—Claudia in full steam was a pretty formidable phenomena.

She glanced at Mac. "Brace yourself."

They walked through into the open-plan office, Claudia's voice becoming clearer with every step.

"...that slimy, conniving weasel. He thinks he can show me up. He thinks he can just steal our great idea and turn it into his own and then beat us in the ratings. I am going to punch him in the face. Then I'm going to kick him in his tiny, microscopic balls."

Claudia was pacing in her office as she verbally pummeled her archrival, Leandro Mandalor, producer of *Heartlands,* the soap that screened opposite *Ocean Boulevard.* For years the two shows had been neck and neck in the ratings and there had always been a not-so-thinly-veiled rivalry between them. Claudia was about to take it to a new level, Grace suspected.

Sadie and Dylan were seated on the other side of Claudia's desk. Dylan looked pissed off, while Sadie's brow was creased with concern.

"Hi. We came back as soon as we saw the paper," Grace said.

Mac brought two extra chairs into Claudia's office so they could have a proper powwow.

"He claims they've been planning it for months, the lying piece of shit," Claudia seethed. "We have a leak, people. And now we have a ratings fight on our hands."

"It shouldn't be hard to work out who squealed. Not many people know about the special," Dylan said. "As long as I get first shot at the little sneak in a dark alleyway, I'm happy."

Grace remembered that the feature-length wedding special had been Dylan's idea from the get-go. No wonder he was pissed. And Sadie had worked with him on the plot, while Claudia had put her ass on the line as a newly installed producer and talked the higher-ups in both the production company and the network into supporting the idea. Grace herself was writing the script, Mac directing it. They all had a lot invested in this project.

And now *Heartlands* was piggybacking their creativity and trying to eclipse them.

"I cannot wait until I see that smug bastard at the next awards committee meeting," Claudia said, referring to the industry committee she sat on to help organize the annual People's Vote Awards. "I'm going to pull his scrotum over his head."

Claudia clenched her hand and jerked her fist skyward in demonstration. Mac winced and Dylan crossed his legs protectively.

"Okay, let's take the bodily harm toward Leandro Mandalor as a given. May his worm-riddled carcass rot in hell," Grace said briskly, pulling a notepad from her bag and placing her pen at the ready. "How are we going to blow them out of the water?"

Claudia flashed her an approving look. "Good question. Thank you, Grace. And nice visuals," she said. She was still striding back and forth behind her desk, but she was a little less frenzied and furious.

"What else do we know?" Dylan asked.

"I've tapped every source I have," Claudia said. "It's a pretty closed shop. You'd think it was the Manhattan Project, the amount of knock backs I got. But I do know they're shooting in Aspen. Apparently Leandro is calling it 'a white wedding in every sense of the word.'" Claudia pulled a mocking face and put on a squeaky, effeminate voice to quote her rival. Grace almost pitied the man—Claudia was going to tear strips off him at their next encounter.

"There's his first mistake," Mac said quietly. "Golden rule of soap—when it's winter, people want to see summer. When it's summer, bring on the snowmen."

Sadie nodded. "You're right. We've been looking at the beach club already—how did it check out today?"

"We can dress it, lift it up," Mac said. "It doesn't offer many opportunities for sweeping panoramic shots, but we can make it sexy."

"Forget Malibu. I'm tapping the contingency fund," Claudia said, finally taking a seat behind her desk. "I like this summer-in-winter idea. We're going to Hawaii."

This caused an excited buzz of conversation as Sadie, Grace, Dylan and Claudia discussed possible scenarios that could be altered from the original script to incorporate the newer, more exotic location. In the original story, Hannah was reluctant to marry Gabe because she felt he was still in love with his first wife, who had died tragically. She asked for a time-out to consider her decision, but Gabe followed her and proved himself to her. Hannah was unable to resist him, but she was thrown when a mysterious, sexy woman appeared in their world who was very much like Gabe's long-dead wife. Both she and Gabe were unaware that the mystery woman, Tania, had been hand-selected to try to destroy Gabe's happiness by his bitter ex-mother-in-law.

Everyone agreed that this basic scenario could be tweaked to accommodate a Hawaiian setting.

"Who are they marrying off? Do we know?" Mac asked, having been silent during the Hawaii excitement.

"Max and Emerald," Claudia said tersely.

Grace was surprised. Max and Emerald were two of *Heartlands'* most long-standing, popular characters, so the competition would be fierce.

"It doesn't matter. Gabe and Hannah are just as popular," Sadie said loyally. "Our viewers would never miss their wedding."

"I don't want only our viewers to watch—I want theirs as well," Claudia said, her chin jutting mulishly.

Mac leaned forward, intent. "Can we get the network to chip in with some promo time?"

Claudia nodded. "What are you thinking?"

"We run a PR campaign on Gabe and Hannah, starting now. Get the audience invested so they come with us on every step of the journey. By the time the special airs, they'll be glued to the screens."

"Great idea," Dylan nodded.

"We did something like it in the early years of the show," Mac said modestly.

Grace hated to admit it, but Mac had a good brain hidden beneath all that sexy blond hair. Perhaps it was his natural charisma, but when he spoke everybody stopped to listen, and he always had something useful to add. He was a valuable resource, having been with the show as long as he had—even taking his six-year absence into account. And he cared.

He'd also obviously thought about the wedding special a lot, despite the fact that she hadn't even handed in the script yet. He started sketching out ideas for shots on

Claudia's whiteboard, Sadie and Dylan getting more and more excited by the minute. Grace felt a clutch of nervousness about her own role as she listened to his ideas for the episode. He wanted to create something special, something outstanding and innovative. And she had to supply him with the raw material to help him realize that dream. As one of the show's most experienced writers, it had been a long time since she'd felt challenged in this capacity. It felt good, she noted.

By the time an hour had passed, they'd roughed out changes to the existing story line to incorporate the change of venue and canvassed a range of potential locations.

"Right, excellent," Claudia said as their discussions wound down. "New plan of attack. As of now, Grace and Mac are relieved of all duties for the next week. We'll shoot around your scenes, Mac, and pick them up when you get back. Grace, you can hand your current edits off to one of the other eds. I'm going to grab someone from the art department, and whichever cameraman you most trust, Mac, and I'm sending you all to Hawaii to find me the best damned shooting locations in the country."

Grace's eyes widened and she could see Mac stiffen with sudden tension. Neither of them said a word, but Grace knew exactly what he was thinking: a week stuck in Hawaii when they could barely exchange two civil words with each other.

Not exactly paradise.

She waited until the meeting was over and everyone was drifting back to their offices before she cornered Mac in the kitchen.

"We need to talk," she said in a hushed tone, shooting a glance over her shoulder. "This changes everything. No more bullshit, okay? From now on, we're strictly about business."

Mac raised an eyebrow at her. "I wasn't under the impression we were about anything else," he said.

She rolled her eyes. "Don't be a dick. You know what I mean. No more squabbling. We have to pull together. Claudia is one of my best friends and I want to come through for her."

It wasn't that she hadn't been doing her best before, she assured herself. She'd just been a little…distracted. But that had to end.

Mac studied her for a beat. "You and her and Sadie are pretty close, huh?"

"Yes. And I know how hard Claudia has had to fight to get into that producer's role. She works damned hard. She deserves it, and I want her to succeed."

"I've always hated *Heartlands,*" Mac said after a brief pause. "That hokey small town bull they try to trade off. No one lives like that anymore. And I really hate their sets. The walls move when someone slams the door."

A smile slowly curved her lips as she realized he was agreeing with her. "So it's a deal? No more monkey business?" She stuck her hand out.

He shook it, then pulled a wry face. "I don't suppose you'd consider wearing a hessian sack while we're in Hawaii?" he asked.

She shouldn't be thrilled that he'd just admitted he found her attractive, given what they'd just shaken hands on, but she was. Thrilled, and flattered. For a moment she didn't know what to say, how to react. Fortunately, she had four years of smart-mouthing men to call on and sarcastic words were already on her tongue.

"Suck it up, tiger," she said, patting his hand consolingly. "I know you're up to it."

She hoped she could say the same thing for herself. Mac

Harrison and Hawaii—if that wasn't a deadly combination she didn't know what was.

THE HEAT HIT MAC the moment they exited the air-conditioned comfort of the airport in Honolulu. Marla Campbell, the Art department stalwart who had been allocated to their little task force, and Frank Menski, one of the show's most experienced cameramen, both lifted their arms toward the sun and grinned unashamedly as they saw the clear-blue skies.

"No smog! Check it out. This is going to be so good," Frank predicted, hefting his equipment bag higher on his shoulder.

Marla nodded happily and Grace murmured her own agreement. Mac just grunted. He'd been up all night looking over maps and other materials for the trip, and he'd just spent five-and-a-half hours sitting on a plane being ignored by Grace. It shouldn't have bothered him—she meant nothing to him—but it did.

Tearing his gaze away from her, he saw that the smiling local who'd greeted them at the arrival gate was waving them forward.

"This way," he said, gesturing toward a white stretch-limo. "We'll take you straight to your hotel."

After half an hour of cruising through the high-rises of Honolulu, they hit the coast road. Twenty minutes later, they were pulling into the circular drive in front of the JW Marriott Ihilani Resort & Spa hotel. Exiting the car, Mac stood and stretched, taking in his surroundings. Clean, white buildings contrasted with verdant tropical vegetation. All around them, palm trees brushed the blue, blue sky and the sweet scent of frangipanis wafted in the breeze.

Turning toward the hotel entrance, he caught Grace watching him. She snapped her head around instantly, but he'd already busted her. He wondered what her cat's-eye sunglasses were hiding, whether she was as aware of him as he was of her.

He grunted in frustration. Could he please think about something else? Like the location scout, for example? He couldn't remember the last time a woman had got under his skin like this. It had to be because she'd turned him down. As pathetic a comment as that was on his ego, it made more sense than the alternative—that he was developing a thing for her.

His hotel room was classy and luxurious, with a huge spa bath for two. Straight away his director's brain took over and he began to think of honeymoon scenes—saucy moments in the spa, shots in the big bed. There was so much natural light in the place they'd barely have to light it. He made a mental note to talk to Frank and make sure he filmed one of the rooms before they left.

They'd agreed to meet by the pool for lunch before heading off to check out the first of the beach locations on their list. Mac changed into a pair of lightweight indigo linen pants and a white T-shirt, sliding his feet into a pair of leather thongs. After smoothing sunscreen onto his face, he made his way down to the café by the hotel's main pool. A perfect circle, the pool sat between the arms created by the hotel's graduated floors. The water looked cool and inviting—which was just as well, because he knew he was going to need some serious help as soon as he clapped eyes on Grace.

She'd changed into another one of her vintage outfits—a pair of figure-hugging black-and-white polka-dot Capri pants with a matching bandeau top that bared an expanse of trim, creamy torso. Her waist looked small, her breasts infinitely enticing. She wore a large-brimmed black straw hat on her head and her ever-present sunglasses. His gaze zeroed in on her hot-pink mouth and he actually licked his lips.

If he could convince her to go to bed with him one more time, he was sure he could bang this growing obsession out of his system. The thought popped into his head as though it had been hand-delivered by his gonads and he slapped it down again instantly.

For starters, even if every self-preserving instinct he had wasn't screaming against his urge to put such a suggestion to Grace, he'd agreed to the no-monkey-business rule. Try as he might, he couldn't redefine monkey business to exclude sex. Which left him back at square one—horny, frustrated, hot and feeling increasingly challenged by the responsibility he'd taken on when he agreed to direct the wedding special.

It had felt natural to wade into the trenches and work alongside the others back in Claudia's office when the news of *Heartlands'* sneakery had come to light, but it wasn't until afterward that he'd recognized *that* had been his opportunity to stand aside and let someone more experienced take the helm.

He hadn't, though. He'd dug in with the rest of the team, started outlining his vision to them. Whether it was the right vision or not, whether he could achieve it or not, only time would tell.

Belatedly he registered that Marla was talking, exclaiming over her room and the hotel's amenities.

"Just don't touch the minibar," Grace warned. "They want your first-born child for a Snickers bar."

"I knew I should have brought the kids with me," Marla said.

Grace flashed a warm smile at the other woman and Mac could feel the mood in their little group lift, despite the rigors of their early morning flight. He'd never consciously acknowledged it before, but Grace was always quick with a compliment or a joke or advice. It had been the same with the meeting yesterday in Claudia's office, he realized in retrospect—she'd been the one to calm Claudia down and start looking for solutions.

It was an attractive character trait. He'd also noticed how warm and friendly she'd been to the airline and hotel staff. For all her hard-as-nails tough-broad bull, she was actually a pussycat.

Except with him, of course. Then it was a battle to the death.

After a light lunch, they trooped out to the SUV Claudia had booked for the duration of their stay and Grace insisted on signing on as a driver as well as Mac.

"We can share the driving," she said when he assured her he was happy to do all the wheel work.

"Tell me this isn't about you not being able to stand being driven around by a man," he challenged her.

She just slanted a smile his way. "You know me so well."

He should have been annoyed instead of amused. When had he started being fond of her prickliness?

The first stop on their list was the Ko Olina Lagoons, one of which formed the beach the hotel sat on. It was only a few minutes by car to the neighboring lagoons and Frank started to get excited the moment he saw the stunning combination of water, white sand and green foliage.

"That outcropping, there," Frank said, pointing toward a finger of land that thrust out into the sea.

Mac had spotted it the moment they crested the rise to the beach, also. It was picture-perfect—green with grass, the blue ocean behind it, palm trees swaying all around—a little bit of everything tropical, all in one location. Narrowing his eyes, Mac scanned the area and noted that even at mid-afternoon in the middle of summer, the beach wasn't overly crowded. Cordoning it off for a shoot shouldn't pose too much of a problem.

"This is good," he said decisively. He turned to Grace, wordlessly waiting for her call.

"It's perfect," she said, one hand holding her hat down in the brisk ocean breeze.

"We can double it for another location if we shoot back along the beach," Mac mused, getting caught up in the work.

"Horse riding," Grace said suddenly. "I saw a brochure in the foyer."

Mac could already picture it—ethereally beautiful Hannah wearing a trailing white skirt, galloping up the beach with Gabe chasing her on a snorting stallion.

"Great. Can we write that into the script?" he asked.

"There's a perfect spot for it. In fact, it will make a great mood transition between their fight when Tania turns up in Hawaii and the romantic dinner Gabe arranges back at their hotel," Grace said. She'd pulled a notebook from her handbag and was jotting down key points as she spoke.

His gaze was drawn to the barely contained energy in her hand as it moved across the page. He glanced at her face and saw a far-off look in her eyes, a sort of intense absence as she imagined her way into the story. She looked beautiful, inspiring, intriguing.

Frowning, he turned away. More and more lately, he was finding things to admire about her beyond her bodacious, sexy body and the chemistry they shared.

They spent half an hour pacing the beach while Frank filmed the location to show Claudia back in L.A. Then, although everyone agreed the site was perfect, they pushed on to inspect another four beaches on the basis that they might all be as ideal as the Lagoons. As dusk was falling, they held a quick conference in the car before heading back to the hotel.

"Opinions, people," Mac invited, twisting around in the driver's seat to address Grace and Frank in the back.

"I vote the Lagoons," Frank said immediately. Since he'd been raving about them all afternoon, Mac wasn't surprised.

"Don't look at me—not much the art department has to do when Mother Nature's got it all covered," Marla said from the front passenger's seat. "For what it's worth, though, I vote the Lagoons, too."

"Okay, I guess it's unanimous then," Mac said, turning back toward the windshield.

Marla shot him a surprised look. "What about Grace— doesn't she get a say?"

"She likes the Lagoons," Mac said. He didn't need to ask. Whether through osmosis or sheer dint of time spent with one another, he was learning to read her.

He met her eyes in the rearview mirror. For once, she was without either pair of glasses and her tilted green eyes stared into his for a long moment before she glanced away. She didn't say a word and neither did he.

He was frowning again as he started the vehicle and drove off.

OAHU WAS BEAUTIFUL. It was an understatement, but Grace quickly stopped trying to find the words to describe the breathtaking sights that the team routinely saw over the next few days. Finding locations for all their key moments turned out to be a snap—each day they found something that exceeded all their expectations. The way they were going, the week they'd allowed for the reconnaissance trip was insanely generous. Checking their location list on Wednesday morning, Grace saw that they had only one item left to cross off and three more days to find it. Brushing her hair out, she wondered if it would be premature to call Claudia and suggest they change their flights and cut the trip short.

She didn't want to go home, though. She admitted as much to herself as she pulled her hair into a ponytail. As stupid and pointless as it was, she was enjoying this time with Mac.

Over the past few days, she'd seen more of the man behind the perfect face and body. Just yesterday, for example, they'd scouted a beach location and while Frank was filming, a little girl's wooden tugboat had been pulled into the surf and out into deeper water. The girl had been inconsolable. Her mother had been almost as upset, explaining to anyone willing to lend a sympathetic ear that the toy had been made by her father, who had recently died. There were plenty of people milling on the beach—paunchy middle-aged executives on family breaks, young boys trying to be cool for teen girls with budding breasts and tiny bikinis, sporty girls with snorkels and flippers. But it was Mac who squinted out to sea to spot the bobbing toy.

"It's not far out," he'd said, then he'd tugged his shirt over his head and shucked his three-quarter linen pants so that he was wearing nothing but a pair of butt-and-package-hugging boxer-briefs. Grace knew absolutely that she wasn't the only woman to nearly have a seizure as he turned toward the water, six-foot-three-inches of masculinity.

He should have looked stupid, wading into the shallows in his underwear.

But he hadn't. Not by a long shot.

When he returned, body glistening with moisture, his blond hair slicked back from his beautiful face, the sound of camera phones clicking resounded along the beach. Who wouldn't want to preserve the sight of a hot, wet god striding out of the water? He was utterly, utterly desirable.

But the bit that had really sent Grace's stupid body into overdrive had been when he dropped to one knee to offer the precious toy to the little girl. The open delight on his face as the little girl laughed and thanked him was a revelation.

He was a nice person.

At some point—possibly day two—Grace had admitted to herself that her original lust-crush was fast becoming something much more substantial and scary. She liked him. She hadn't liked a man that she was sexually attracted to for a long time. It scared her a great deal, but she kept telling herself that it didn't really matter—it wasn't as though she was ever going to be in a position to betray her feelings again. Sex was out of the question. Apart from the no-monkey-business rule, she figured she'd pretty much had her chance and lost it where Mac was concerned. It wasn't as though he wasn't spoiled for choice. The list of hotel staff alone who wanted to sleep with him would form a queue back to the mainland. She was pretty damn certain that Mac wasn't lying awake at night the way she was, going over certain little moments from the day, trying not to think about their one night together.

She loved his laugh and his cowboy-to-the-rescue walk made her thighs weak. Just the sight of his strong, long fingers on the steering wheel or on cutlery or on pretty much anything was enough to invoke an image of those same fingers plucking at her nipples or delving between her legs.

To say that, after five days in his company, she was turned on was putting it mildly. She felt like one big overstimulated nerve ending. One whiff of his aftershave and she had to hide her hardened nipples by crossing her arms over her chest. God forbid she should brush up against him accidentally—she simply wouldn't be answerable for her actions.

Grace ran a comb through her bangs, then rubbed on sunblock and slicked on a coat of very berry lip gloss. The hot weather dictated her wardrobe more than her mood, and she pulled on her black cherry-print hipster bikini, then topped it off with a fifties red-and-white gingham playsuit. Red plastic flip-flops, complete with a white silk daisy on each toe, completed her ensemble. She looked very Mary Ann from *Gilligan's Island,* but what the hey, she was in Hawaii.

She wandered downstairs to meet the others, but pulled up short when she found only Mac waiting for her in the foyer.

"Where are Marla and Frank?" she asked lightly.

"Food poisoning. Guess those fish cakes weren't such a great idea yesterday," Mac said.

Grace pulled a face, remembering the questionable hygiene of the beach vendor where Frank and Marla had insisted on lunching the previous day. She and Mac had turned up their noses at the offerings, electing to wait till they got back to the hotel to eat. In hindsight, a wise decision, it seemed.

"Are they both okay? Should we call a doctor or anything?" Grace asked.

"The desk staff are filled in and I took up extra water and sports drinks for them. I got the strong impression they'd both prefer to be left to their misery in private." Mac shrugged.

"Right."

There was an awkward pause as they both registered that this meant they would be alone for the day. Mac broke it by clearing his throat.

"I spoke to Claudia this morning, too. She's keen on the scuba-diving idea over the nature trek, so I thought we could go check out the operators and find someone suitable."

"Sure. That sounds…sensible," Grace said lamely.

She'd been hoping against hope that the nature trek would win out over the scuba. She had a thing about any situation where there was finite oxygen. If Mac had just announced they were going down in a submarine or were about to launch off into space in a rocket ship, she'd feel the same way. It wasn't exactly a phobia, as such. More a preference. A strong, persistent preference.

Forcing her worry down, Grace followed Mac out to the SUV. For the first time all week, she slid into the passenger seat next to him. Though they'd taken turns driving, there had been an unspoken agreement between them that either Marla or Frank took the front passenger seat to avoid exactly the kind of forced intimacy that enveloped them the moment the car doors thudded closed and Mac pulled away from the curb.

"Did the hotel have any suggestions?" Grace asked, hating the way her voice broke a little in the middle of her sentence.

"There's a tour group who does beginners scuba courses in Hanauma Bay. I grabbed some brochures."

Mac pulled a folded glossy pamphlet from his hip pocket and passed it over, his gaze remaining steady on the road.

"Wow. It looks great," she said. Even to her own ears, her voice sounded stiff and fake.

Mac shot her a look and she pretended great interest in the brochure.

"Are you actually going to dive?" she asked oh-so-casually a few minutes later.

"Yep."

Her buttocks clenched with fear. Damn him. If he dived, she had to go down, too. Why did she have so much stupid, stupid pride?

She stared at the brochure intently, trying to talk herself

into it. The coral looked vibrant, almost psychedelic, and the fish looked cute and appealing. Even the water was a clear, perfect aqua.

By the time they'd found the dock where the tour group operated, she'd worked up a head of steam. She was going to do it. She refused to go down in Mac's mental photo album as the girl who was afraid. Not that she imagined she was memorable enough to go down in his mental photo album at all, but just in case. And it wasn't as though she was deathly scared of scuba. It was more a matter of inclination than anything else, and if her inclination happened to change, so be it. It was no big deal.

So when Mac stepped up to the counter and requested one dive and one accompanying ticket, she found herself leaning forward.

"Make that two dives," she said firmly.

Mac raised his eyebrows.

"Thought you weren't interested," he said.

"What gave you that impression?" she asked airily.

Like many decisions in her life lately, she began to regret putting her hand up to dive almost as soon as the boat pulled away from the dock and started cruising out to sea. The wet suits, masks, flippers and tanks hanging on either side of the wide, open cabin looked utterly foreign and she gripped the edges of her wooden bench-seat as their guide, Sean, began instructing them on the basics.

"The important thing is never to panic," Sean said as he handed out masks and snorkels for them to practice with.

Too late.

She noted with trepidation that Sean appeared to be around thirteen years old. Surely she shouldn't be taking instruction from an adolescent? What could he know, after all?

She glanced around at the six other people who'd signed on for the beginner's dive, but they all looked excited and not in the least bit worried about the fact that Doogie Howser's younger brother was their instructor.

"I've been diving off Oahu for nearly twenty years and we've never had a serious incident. Scuba is very safe as long as you follow the golden rules—always listen to your dive leader, never leave your dive buddy and always, *always* go slowly to the surface. We won't be going down deep enough for anyone to be at risk of the bends today, but it's a good rule to learn early."

Sean made eye contact with everyone to stress his words of warning and Grace saw with relief that there were crows feet radiating out from around his brown eyes. Not a teenager then. Given his comment about twenty years of experience, maybe he was even a sensible, experienced adult.

She nearly jumped out of her skin when Mac leaned across and spoke in her ear.

"Relax. It's supposed to be fun."

She nodded, her determination to tough this out doubling. Squelching all her irrational fears into a corner, she concentrated intently on Sean's instructions, learning how to equalize the pressure in her ears as she descended, how to signal that she was okay, how to signal that she was distressed and how to clear her mask should it fill with water. Sean passed out the tanks next and Grace soon found herself breathing in bottled oxygen and battling to keep her heart rate down.

When the boat's chugging motors switched to an idle, she glanced up from inspecting the gauge on her tank and knew they had arrived. Smiling broadly, Sean distributed shorty wet suits.

"Okay, once we're all kitted up, I'll take you through the process of getting into the water," he said brightly.

Grace wasted a full five minutes plaiting her hair out of the way before struggling into her wet suit. Black, stiff and unwieldy, it seemed to grab at the fabric of her bikini and she was feeling distinctly hot and bothered by the time she'd worked the suit up to her waist.

"Here," Mac said from behind her. Before she knew it, he was guiding her arms into the suit and shifting the stiff rubber around to fit her frame. Despite the fact that his touch was impersonal and he never once made eye contact with her, Grace felt acutely self-conscious and overwhelmed by how close he was. When he grabbed the fabric above her breasts and gave it one last yank, she closed her eyes at the absurdity of the situation. In all her months of fantasizing about Mac, she'd never once imagined him adjusting her wet suit.

The hiss of the zipper running up her back and the increasing tightness around her chest told her he'd finished dressing her and she stepped away with what she hoped was a grateful smile.

"Thanks," she said, trying not to stare at how broad his shoulders looked encased in black neoprene. She'd never been into kinky stuff, but he sure made rubber look good.

"Let's get your tank on now, Grace," Sean said, and she realized that everyone else was ready to go.

Color stained her cheeks and she fumbled the clasps as she shrugged into the webbed harness for her tank.

"Great. My advice is to wait until we're in the water to secure your fins, so we're all ready to go," Sean said.

A lurch of fear shot through Grace's body and adrenaline tingled in her fingertips. Vaguely she wondered why her fight-or-flight instincts had decided to kick in now—where had they been when she'd signed on for this stupid course back at the ticket desk? *That* had been the time to choose safety and comfort over fear and risk. Instead her pride had been in charge of the good ship Grace Wellington and she suspected it had abandoned ship in the last few seconds, leaving her prey to every neurotic urging of her overactive imagination.

Shuffling to the back of the pack, Grace loitered as long as she could. Finally, it was down to just Mac, Sean and herself. Both men looked at her expectantly. Grace took her courage in both hands and did what had to be done.

"I can't do it," she admitted. "I'm sorry."

She could hardly look at Mac as she sank onto one of the bench seats lining the side of the boat. She hated failing at anything. A geyser of bad memories threatened to well up inside her and no matter how much she tried to push them away or scoff them out of existence, they persisted—coming home from school with her first *B* on a report card instead of the straight *A*s she'd always received. The shame of falling off the balance beam in the junior gymnastics final. The horror of flubbing her lines in the school play.

As a child, Grace had attended all her sisters' beauty pageants, sitting in the audience with her mother. She'd watched Felicity and Serena and Hope wow the judges time after time. And she'd seen the pity in other mothers' eyes when they'd caught sight of her with her beautiful sisters. Everyone felt sorry for the plain girl in such an attractive family. She'd told herself that she didn't care and she had chosen to compete in other arenas—using her brain and her strong, healthy body. And she'd always set high benchmarks for herself—if she was doing something, she had to be the best.

It was the same with her writing. She didn't do just one or two drafts of her scripts. She did four or five. She agonized, she labored, she sweated.

Scuba was the first time in a long time that Grace had

admitted defeat. And it was hard not to feel like that big-nosed, wide-mouthed ugly sister sitting on the sidelines again.

Such old, old stuff. She hated that it still had power over her. Was it never possible to outgrow your demons?

She could hear Mac and Sean talking, then she heard the splash of someone hitting the water. Bracing herself for the inevitable pep talk from her tour guide, she was surprised when Mac kneeled in front of her and took her icy hands in his own.

"Okay, Grace, what's up?" he asked matter-of-factly.

"Isn't it obvious? I'm scared rigid," Grace said miserably. No point pretending at this point, right?

"Okay. Is this a phobic, I'm-going-to-need-therapy-and-sedation kind of fear or one of those things you might be able to conquer with a little push in the right direction?"

He asked so nicely, so kindly, so good-naturedly that she actually found herself considering his question.

"Maybe I just need a little push," she admitted in a small voice.

Mac smiled. He was barely two feet away and the power of his charisma nearly drove her back in her seat.

"Okay. Good. What if I assure you that no matter what, I will not leave your side?" he suggested.

She considered the idea for a moment, then shook her head. "Not quite doing it for me," she said reluctantly.

He threaded his fingers through hers and squeezed gently. "What if I promise not to let go of your hand, then?" he offered.

Heat from his palm was radiating into her own cold fish of a hand and she wriggled a little. Her fear eased a notch as she looked into the stunning blue of Mac's eyes. For a moment there was nothing in the world but the two of them—the rise and fall of the boat beneath them, the squawk of gulls overhead, the warmth of the sun beating down on their rubber-clad bodies all faded away to nothing as she got lost in his eyes.

"Want to give it a shot?" he asked.

She found herself nodding. Then standing. Then easing her way awkwardly down the metal ladder at the back of the boat into the surprisingly cool water. Mac handed her the fins and she worked them on as he joined her in the water. It was only when he was helping her adjust her mouthpiece that she realized that he was supremely confident for a first timer.

"You've done this before," she guessed as Mac slid his own mouthpiece in.

He raised his eyebrows innocently, then indicated she should put her face beneath the water. Feeling a little conned, Grace did as instructed and was immediately lost in the underwater world. Her body seemed to sink of its own accord, but she was too busy staring at the darting fish and waving sea anemones and coral sculptures spread out beneath them to register it.

True to his word, Mac's hand remained firm around hers as they kicked their way down toward the ocean floor. She knew from Sean's talk on the boat that the floor of Hanauma Bay was actually the crater of an extinct volcano. Now she gazed reverently at the teeming microcosm the crater supported, all her nervousness forgotten as she marvelled at the hidden treasures of the sea. Just like in the photographs, the fish were bright neon streaks of yellow, pink, blue and orange. Mac pulled her closer to the coral formations nearby, pointing out the ebb and flow of the fronds of a pale-pink sea anemone as it pulsed in time with the underwater currents. A splash of orange caught her eye and she clutched at Mac's arm and pointed excitedly at a stunning bright-orange and electric-blue fish. Mac's eyes crinkled as he grinned at her, and Grace let go of the last faint traces of her nerves and gave herself over to the experience.

For nearly twenty minutes they combed the crater floor, being careful to always keep Sean and the rest of the group in sight. After a while, Sean made a point of contacting them briefly, indicating through sign language that only five more minutes remained of their dive. Grace was surprised to feel regret and she shot Mac a mournful look. He pulled a sad face to indicate his agreement, then his eyes widened as he caught sight of something over her shoulder. Immediately, her imagination went into overdrive, the theme music from *Jaws* sounding loud in her ears. Before she could succumb to full-fledged panic, however, Mac tugged her around and she saw that he'd been staring at a family of turtles. Bubbles erupted from her mouth as she gasped and she had to remind herself to inhale and exhale calmly.

Brown-and-green with speckled flippers and heads, the turtles were roughly the size of her looped arms. They were extraordinarily graceful beneath the water, a stark contrast to their slow and steady pace on land. Captivated, Grace paddled to maintain her place beside Mac and watch their antics. The rest of the dive group were likewise mesmerized, and Sean received more than one frustrated look when he signaled it was time to return to the boat.

Grace was filled with wonder as she clambered back onto the boat. She'd never imagined that something so perfect existed. Even though she had about a million observations she wanted to share, she found she was oddly loathe to talk. The rest of the group seemed to share the same feeling. Everyone peeled themselves out of their wet suits with the minimum of quiet conversation, then proceeded to bask in the heat and exchange wide smiles. Her plait dripping down her back and her face turned up to the sun, Grace felt more at peace than she had in a long time.

"Worth it?" Mac said near to her ear.

This time she didn't start. He was sitting so close to her, his thigh and shoulder pressed alongside hers, that she'd felt him lean in.

"Yes," she said simply, flashing him a smile. "Thank you. I wouldn't have had the courage to do it without you."

He shook his head as though he disagreed, but he didn't say anything out loud. Instead, he leaned back against the railing behind him and closed his eyes. For a second, she allowed herself the rare pleasure of watching him unobserved. The crisp curls on his chest were tightly coiled and darkened from the swim and she followed them down the muscled sculpture that was his stomach to the waistband of his board shorts. Resisting the temptation to get an eyeful of something that she had almost perfect sense-recall of, she continued her inspection down his legs to where they were crossed at his ankles.

He was delicious.

And, it turned out, kind.

Closing her eyes, she leaned against the rail beside him.

Later she could worry and fret over her growing feelings for this magnetically attractive man. For now, she wanted to enjoy the moment.

The comfortable haze of their dive extended to the drive to the hotel. As they collected their various belongings from the car, she mustered the energy to talk about work matters.

"The bay would look incredible on-screen," she said as they entered the hotel foyer.

"Without a doubt. And Sean would be perfect—he just has to be himself," Mac said.

"You're right. I'll make sure I write him in," she said.

Their hands collided as they both reached for the elevator button. She pulled back, indicating Mac should do the honors. The bell pinged almost instantly and they stepped into the otherwise empty car.

Suddenly very self-conscious, Grace pressed the floor for her room and waited for him to do the same. The elevator whisked them speedily skyward and she kept her eyes glued to the floor indicator, oddly reluctant for their day to be over.

Her room was a floor below Mac's and she turned to him with a smile as the doors opened.

"Again, thanks for today. It was…amazing," she said, widening her eyes to indicate her sincerity.

"Yeah, it was."

She stepped out. It felt wrong, walking away from him, but she didn't know what else to do. The doors started to slide shut, and she acted on impulse, thrusting her arm out to stop the elevator departing. The doors bounced open and Mac eyed her steadily as she stepped into the car with him.

"Have dinner with me tonight?" she asked breathlessly.

He stared at her for a long, drawn-out beat. She waited for him to bring up the stupid rule she'd imposed on them.

"Yes."

Something hot and molten unfurled in her belly at the look she saw in his eyes.

"I'll meet you in the foyer at seven," she said.

"Done."

Stepping back, she let the doors close completely this time. A spring in her step, she headed for her room. She was having dinner with Mac. It was probably a bad idea—but right now it was what she wanted more than anything in the world.

6

MAC WAITED FOR A FULL twenty minutes past their agreed meeting time before admitting to himself that she wasn't coming. She'd changed her mind. Probably once the buzz of the dive had worn off she remembered that she didn't want or need a man in her life. She was probably in her room polishing her copies of *The Female Eunuch* and *The Beauty Myth*. Thoroughly pissed off, he strode across to the reception desk on the off-chance that Grace had been courteous enough to offer an excuse for her no-show.

"Yes, Mr. Harrison, we have a message for you," the pretty woman behind the desk said. She smiled brilliantly and let him know with her eyes that he could have more than a message if he wanted. She had dark mahogany hair and sun-kissed skin, but he offered her nothing more than a slight smile as he took the envelope from her. He wasn't interested in a one-night stand. Wasn't that how he'd got into this situation in the first place, standing alone in the foyer of this hotel like a dork?

Tearing the envelope open, he narrowed his gaze as he read Grace's short message.

Mac, Sorry about dinner, coming down with migraine. Grace.

Migraine his ass. At the very least she owed him honesty. What was wrong with saying dinner was a bad idea? Or that she wasn't interested? She was the one who'd broken her own rule and asked him out, after all. It was just like last time when she'd denied their mutual desire to stick it to him. He was stalking toward the elevator bank before he could stop himself and within minutes he was knocking on her door, ready to let rip with a mouthful of home truths.

Except she didn't answer. His lips thinned. She was hiding out. Probably hoping he'd just go away if she didn't respond.

Not a chance.

Hand clenched, he rapped on the door. He didn't appreciate being played for a fool. In the back of his mind, it occurred to him that he was perhaps a little irrationally angry over being stood up. It even occurred to him that she might really be sick. But four days' worth of mounting sexual frustration was crowding to the front of his mind, begging for an outlet. What he really wanted was to have her again, but since that wasn't in the cards, a damned good yell-fest was a nice alternative.

He was raising his hand to knock again when he heard the sound of someone fumbling on the other side of the door. Bracing his arms on either side of the door frame, he prepared himself to go in hard.

The door opened a crack, and he caught a glimpse of pale skin, sleep-mussed hair and an oversize hotel bathrobe.

"What is it?" Grace croaked. Her hotel room was in complete darkness and she shielded her scrunched-up eyes as though her life depended on it.

He bit back the diatribe on the tip of his tongue.

Either she'd suddenly acquired Meryl Streep's acting talent or she really had a migraine

"You've got a migraine," he said stupidly.

"Mac. I'm so sorry…" she mumbled. She opened the door wider, then reeled away from the bright light in the corridor. "Ugh. I have to lie down," she said, disappearing into the darkness of the room.

Since she'd left her door open, he figured it was an invitation. Following her inside, he shut the door behind himself and blinked while he waited for his eyes to adjust to the lack of light. He could hear her stumbling into bed and he frowned as he made his way in that direction.

"Have you taken something?" he asked.

"Just some aspirin. I don't have anything stronger on me— I haven't had a migraine in years. I think it was all the stress today and the sun and maybe the chocolate I had when I got back to the room…" she muttered.

"Where's your room key? I'll go get you something stronger," he said quietly.

She pointed a finger at her bedside table where a key-card glowed white against the dark wood.

"Five minutes, I'll be back," he assured her.

It took ten, mostly because the hotel pharmacist gave Mac a bunch of tips on how to relieve migraine symptoms in addition to his most kick-ass over-the-counter painkiller. Mac was armed to the hilt when he let himself back into her room.

"Okay, how are you doing?" he asked as he stopped by her bed. She'd tangled herself in her robe and the bedsheets and was lying with her fingers pressed to her temples.

"Not good," she moaned.

"Okay, I got you some King Kong painkillers, lavender oil for your pillow and some aromatherapy massage oil," he said as he lined his purchases up on her bedside table.

She thrust a hand out blindly. "Painkillers."

He filled a tumbler with water and popped out two of the

superdrugs for her. She sat up for the few seconds it took to wash them down, then flopped onto her pillows.

"The pharmacist said they should kick in in about twenty minutes."

She grunted an acknowledgement. "This is so unfair. I haven't had a migraine since I was in college."

He felt helpless. Her face was creased with pain and he wanted to take it away for her.

"The pharmacist also said massage can be helpful," he said.

She cracked an eye and looked at him. "The pharmacist, huh?"

"I swear it," he said, holding his fingers up in classic Boy Scout mode. "You want to give it a go?"

She pressed her fingers into the bridge of her nose for a beat, then nodded. "Okay. Anything if this damned thumping will stop."

Sliding out of his shoes, Mac assessed the bed. "You need to lie in the middle more," he instructed.

Grumbling, Grace wriggled on her stomach into the center of the mattress. He arranged a pillow for her face, then climbed onto the bed beside her. Straddling her torso, he reached for the thick collar of her bathrobe.

"This needs to come off," he said. He tried to sound as impersonal as he could, like a doctor or a dentist. He figured he didn't do a very good job because Grace turned her head to squint up at him again.

"You're kidding, right?"

"Come on. There's not much under there I haven't seen already. And you're sick. What kind of a pervert takes advantage of a sick woman? Do you really think I'm that hard up?"

"You're right. Sorry," she said, levering herself up to tug her arms one at a time out of her robe. He forced himself to look away as soon as he realized she was completely naked beneath the robe, just in case he caught a glimpse of her full, creamy breasts and instantly proved himself wrong in the pervert stakes.

She resettled onto the pillows and he folded the top half of the robe down to expose her shoulders and most of her back. Reaching for the massage oil, he squeezed a generous amount onto his palms and let it warm there for a moment.

"Here we go," he warned her quietly, just in case the oil still wasn't warm enough. She shivered a little as he smoothed his hands across the velvety skin of her back. The fresh scent of lavender and rosemary filled the room.

Mac would be the first to admit that while he'd received more than his fair share of massages over the years, he was no expert at giving them. But he figured that all the time he'd put in on the other end of the equation had to give him some kind of insight into the technique.

He started by smoothing his palms up and down the whole of her back, being careful to avoid the swell of her breasts near her sides. He was only human, after all, and there was that pervert thing to consider.

The oil quickly warmed beneath his hands and he started to knead her muscles in earnest, beginning first with her shoulders and neck. She gave a low growl of relief as he found a hard knot of tension in one shoulder. Working it with his thumb until it loosened, he soothed the place again and again before moving on to the next tight spot. He worked his way slowly down her spine, lavishing attention on every part of her back.

Her skin was amazing, so clear and smooth with not a single blemish. Her vertebrae were delicate yet strong and he traced them with oil-slicked fingers. Splaying his hands wide, he dug his fingers in ever so slightly and began to work the larger muscles of her back in increasing circles.

It seemed only natural to peel the robe down as he reached the small of her back and her hips. Grabbing the bottle, he squeezed more oil onto his hands then smoothed it across her lower hips and backside.

She had the peachiest butt he'd ever seen—full and ripe and firm. Sliding his fingers around her hips, he dragged them back to the curves of her lower spine. She shifted slightly beneath him, and he moved his attention to her backside itself, kneading the rounded globe of each cheek in a rhythmic motion.

She felt so good, so sleek beneath him. Cupping her cheeks, he slid his palms up her sides, glorying in the line of her body as it raced in toward her waist, then out again as his hands slid up her rib cage. He realized he'd been wanting to do this ever since she'd first stood up from her chair in the conference room that first day. She had the kind of body men dreamed about—real breasts, real hips, soft curves, smooth skin.

Belatedly he realized that he was breathing heavily, and that his fingers were alternating between sliding around her hips to skim the sensitive skin of her belly and swooping down across her butt cheeks to skim the backs of her thighs.

Dragging his hands off her warm, welcoming flesh, he cleared his throat.

"How are you feeling?"

"Better. Headache's almost gone," she said. She sounded languorous, dreamy.

"Want me to keep going?" he asked. He wasn't sure he could handle much more—he was already hard as a rock, his erection a rigid demand against the fly of his jeans. The whole doctor/dentist thing wasn't really working for him. Probably having previously slept with his patient wasn't such a great starting point.

"Yes, please," she murmured into the pillow, wriggling her hips beneath him.

His erection twitched against the restraint of his clothing. Dear God—did he really have this much willpower?

There was only one place left to go. Moving farther down the bed, he peeled her robe down and reached for the oil bottle again. Jaw tense, he smoothed oil onto the backs of her thighs, behind her knees and down her calves to the soles of her feet. She sighed her approval and he rolled his eyes.

He was about ready to explode here. He was really kidding himself with this whole nurse Nightingale routine. She was naked, for Pete's sake. Shiny with oil, smooth and soft and incredibly feminine. Every thought he'd had of soothing and relaxing her was now turned toward stimulating and teasing, and he had to force his hands to remain flat and calming as he slid them up her thighs until they touched the lower curve of her butt again. She shifted beneath him, lifting her hips slightly. He stilled, then deliberately repeated the motion, holding his breath this time as he let his fingers stray the barest half an inch toward the dark shadow between her inner thighs. She murmured her appreciation and again lifted her hips, almost as though she was inviting him to delve deeper, to slide his fingers all the way between her thighs to find the slick, hot folds of her sex.

"I think we'd better call it quits," he grated, snatching his hands away from her before he acted on instinct and betrayed her trust.

She gave a mew of distress. "Don't stop," she said.

"Grace...I kind of have to," he admitted ruefully.

She wriggled around until she could get an elbow beneath

her body and she turned to look at him. Her eyes were heavy lidded and glittering, her cheekbones flushed.

"Don't stop," she repeated. Still he hesitated and she pulled herself higher in the bed, sliding her legs from beneath him. Flipping onto her back, her knees curled toward her chest, she held his eye very deliberately as she placed her feet flat on the sheets. Her knees tented in front of her, she slid her legs down either side of his kneeling body so that he was between her unashamedly wide-spread thighs.

"Don't. Stop."

He didn't know where to look—at her magnificent breasts, their rosy peaks already pebbled with desire, or the part of her that she'd offered up so generously to his gaze.

"Grace." He worshipped her, his oil-slicked hands sliding onto her thighs. She gasped as he raced them higher, stopping just short of touching her glistening heat.

"Tell me what you want," he said, needing to hear her say it—wanting to hear her beg, if he was honest with himself.

"I want you to kiss me. I want you to suck me. I want you to tease me," she whispered, her thighs shivering beneath his hands as she anticipated his touch.

Riding a wave of triumph, he lowered his head and gave her what they both wanted.

GRACE CURLED HER FINGERS into the bedsheets and hung on for dear life. Her migraine was a distant memory as she reveled in the hot, firm flick of Mac's tongue between her thighs. She choked back a cry as he pulled her clitoris into his mouth, the gentle suction nearly sending her over the top.

He retreated. "Not yet, baby," he murmured against her thighs.

Her hands fisted in the sheets again as he began tracing the outline of her inner lips with his fingertips while his tongue continued to tease her. Again and again he touched her and tension spiraled within her. It was too much, too hot, too wet, too wild.

He slid a finger inside her, then two.

"Oh Mac," she cried, hips arching off the bed.

He picked up the pace, his tongue firm and knowing against her as he pushed her over the edge, his fingers sliding inside her as he ensured no secret spot remained untouched.

She came with a shudder, her head whipping from side to side, hips thrusting instinctively.

She was barely able to think again when she registered the dip in the mattress as he shifted his weight. She heard the hiss and rustle of clothing being ripped off, and she smiled to herself as she heard the crinkle of a foil packet. Exactly what she'd been thinking, wanting, needing. *Exactly.*

His weight settled over her and she reveled in the heat of his skin on hers. Then his erection was probing the soft wetness between her thighs and suddenly he was inside her.

"Oh *yesssss,*" she groaned low in her throat as his body pressed down over hers and he pumped into her again and again. Her hands found the hard muscles of his perfect butt and she gripped it tightly and urged him to go faster, harder, deeper. He was only too happy to oblige, shifting his weight higher in the bed so that the shaft of his erection ground against her already sensitized clitoris with every stroke. Quickly, she began to climb again. Lowering his head, Mac licked her breasts, tonguing her nipples so firmly the pleasure was almost pain.

Panting, she met him thrust for thrust, a sob rising in her throat as she felt herself coming apart again.

"Yes, Grace, yes," he encouraged in her ear, kissing her thoroughly as her muscles clenched around him.

She felt liquid, languid, sated, and she wrapped her legs around him, locking her ankles together as she rocked her hips, wanting to help him find his own climax now.

Mac had other ideas. Slowing his thrusts, he prolonged each penetration to its fullest, sliding his hips back until his tip almost slid free of her before plunging to the hilt again. Grace bit her lip and tilted her hips to accept every inch, wanting all of him. While his mouth worked wonders on her breasts, he slid a hand between their bodies and found the swollen nub of her clitoris again.

"No, I can't…" She started to object, but he kissed her objection away and began to work her with his clever fingers.

"Oh boy," she whispered after a few seconds, feeling the tension tightening inside her once again.

He grinned and picked up his pace. Biting her lip, Grace rocked to his rhythm, her body tensing as she drew closer and closer to her peak again.

This time, he held her face between his hands, his eyes looking deeply into hers. She saw how close he was and knew he wanted them to come together. Holding his gaze, she gave him what he wanted, what he'd worked for, what he'd teased from her. As her body shattered, she stared into his eyes and saw him lose himself for a few crazy seconds. As the last shudders left both their bodies, he pressed a kiss to her lips, held it a long beat, then let his body fall boneless and heavy on top of hers.

They were both panting, their chests heaving in time with one another. After a long, long silence, Mac lifted his head.

"How's the headache?" he asked, peering down at her.

"Never been better." She smiled, feeling light and silly and frivolous.

Happy, even.

"You know, orgasm is supposed to be an excellent cure for migraine," she said.

"Yeah, the pharmacist mentioned it. Seemed a little disappointed he didn't have one in a jar I could buy," he said wryly.

"You did okay," she assured him. "More than okay."

"I counted three okays, actually," he said a little smugly.

She laughed. "What a time to be counting!"

"Trust me, it was all postcoital addition. At the time, you were too busy blowing my mind," he said, nuzzling her neck affectionately.

She ran a hand across his shoulders, exploring the dips and hollows of his muscular back. "I think you were the one blowing my mind," she corrected him. Placing a hand on his chest, she pushed him onto his back, slid a leg over his hips and straddled him. He didn't fight, just lay there, a big grin on his lips.

"Having a nice time?" he asked conversationally.

"Not yet, but I will be. I've got some catching up to do," she said, sweeping her hair over one shoulder and pressing her lips to his chest. Trailing her wet, open mouth across to first one nipple and then the other, she was pleased to feel an erection nudging her bottom.

"Start counting, math boy," she warned him as she slid farther south.

THEY HAD TO GET OUT of bed sometime, Mac knew. Technically, of course, they'd been out of bed several times. Bathroom trips, showers, baths, two expeditions all the way to the door to let room service in. But not once had they considered what lay beyond the four walls of their hotel room, beyond Hawaii, beyond this stolen time away from time.

Lifting his head, he glanced at the alarm clock on Grace's bedside table.

Six in the morning. Only another hour or two until they had to face the world. Marla and Frank were probably fit to go again today. So he and Grace wouldn't be alone.

Damn it.

He felt like a kid with a new toy—he wanted to stay in his room and play with it.

Beside him, Grace slept, her mouth pursed slightly, her cheek mushed against the pillow. Even squished she looked divine—his own personal siren, calling him onto the rocks time after time after time.

Lifting a finger, he shifted a stray strand of hair away from her face, smoothing it back into place.

Without opening her eyes, Grace spoke.

"Are you staring at me while I'm sleeping?"

"No. Maybe."

"Am I drooling?"

"A little."

"Liar. I bet I'm drooling a lot," Grace said. Then she smiled, opened her eyes and rolled onto her back. They both laughed as her stomach rumbled.

"All that exercise," she explained, pressing a hand to her stomach. "Can you remember if they have waffles on the menu?"

"A waffle lady. I should have known. When we get back to L.A., I'll take you to this little place I know," he said.

It was only when he felt her stiffen that he registered his own words. Her expression became guarded and her gaze drifted over his shoulder.

"Better shake a tail feather," she said, wriggling toward the edge of the bed.

In a moment she'd be gone and somehow he knew that if he didn't act now, he was going to let something precious slip

through his fingers. Without actually willing it, Mac reached
out to grab her arm.

"Grace, I want to see you again." The words slipped out
before he could consider them, but he meant them. Sometime
over the past week, she'd wriggled under his skin—at first in
a burr-like way, but now in a good, he-was-going-to-miss-her-
when-she-was-gone way.

"Careful there, stud, or a girl might go getting the wrong
idea," she said.

"Maybe she'd get the right idea," he said.

"What happened to Mr. No Relationship?" she said, her
tone still light.

"He met you," he said baldly.

She blinked. Then she paled.

"Not funny," she said, tugging her arm out of his grasp.

"Why would I joke about something like this? Grace, I like
you. I'm figuring the last few hours of tongue wrangling and
moaning and groaning means you like me, too. But this is
about more than sex. I want to see you again, I want to see
where this goes," he said.

God, it had been so long since he'd wanted anything. It felt
like a revolution to actually stick a stake in the sand and lay
claim to his desires. He wanted Grace—and it was more than
a sex want. He wanted to wake up with her in his arms again.
He wanted to make her laugh, to spoil her, even to spar with
her.

"I already know where this goes," she said coolly. "And
I'm not interested in going there."

Again she tried to get out of bed, but he stopped her with the
simple expedient of rolling on top of her. He was a lot heavier
than she was and she was probably feeling pretty squashed, but
he figured it was the best way to get her to stay put and listen.

"That's all you have to say?" he asked, his nose a mere inch from hers. Up close, her green eyes were clear and utterly defenseless. Even if he hadn't been able to feel the tension in her sexy body, he could see it in the sea-green of her irises.

"I told you, I'm very happy with my life," she said. "I like being in control of my own world."

"That's good, because I'm not trying to stage a coup here," he said. "I enjoy spending time with you. I think you're funny and smart and sexy. I really like doing this with you," he said, flexing his hips to press his hard-on against her belly, "and I want to do a lot more of it. I want to hang out with you, get to know you. Is that such a horrible thing? Is that asking too much?"

She stared at him and he realized she looked terrified.

"Yes," she said in a voice so quiet, so strangled that it barely qualified as a whisper.

He frowned, remembering something suddenly. Grace had been single and celibate for four years before they'd torn each other's clothes off and gone crazy. For the first time it occurred to him that something pretty profound must have happened to push a natural hedonist like her into such an unnatural, ungenerous state. And she was a hedonist. Her sensual clothes, her love of color and texture, the way she savored her food, the pleasure she took from the world around her—she was hardly a dried-up prune. So why had she backed away from the whole man-woman thing?

"Four years ago—you were in a relationship, weren't you?" he guessed, his rarely functioning male intuition signaling like crazy from a dusty corner of his brain.

She stiffened further, if that were possible. "You're getting heavy," she said, pushing ineffectually at his chest.

"Me or the conversation?" he asked, but he rolled off her. "What are you afraid of, Grace?"

"I'm not afraid of anything. God, you're as bad as Sadie and Claudia," she snapped, then she bit her lip as though she'd just blabbed a state secret.

So.

"Tell me about him, Gracie," he said, tracing the curve of her ear with his finger.

Maybe he wasn't the quickest guy off the mark when it came to emotional matters, but once he was onto something, he wasn't about to back away.

Pressing a kiss to her collarbone, he looked deep into her eyes. "Trust me. Tell me," he said.

GRACE SWALLOWED a lump of anger and irrational fear. The past few hours had been heaven on earth and now he'd gone and ruined it all with talk about the future and them seeing each other again. It was just as bad as the last time when he'd given her the brush-off so ineptly. Worse, because now he was asking her to tell him about Owen and that was the last thing she wanted to do.

"Look, contrary to current popular thinking, I'm not a big believer in the whole blab-blab, talky-talky thing," she said patiently. "Shit happens, you deal with it, you move on. End of story."

"Humor me," he said. He kissed her neck again, trailing his tongue down toward her nipple. Instantly, her body went on red alert.

He stopped, grinning at her knowingly. "Humor me and I'll make it worth your while," he said, lowering his head to pull her nipple into his mouth. She shivered with need as he ran his hot, wet tongue over and over her nipple inside his mouth, the suction and the roughness of his tongue driving her crazy.

"M-Mac," she groaned when he stopped.

He just cocked an eyebrow at her.

"My college boyfriend is much more interesting. He crashed my car then disappeared when he was afraid I'd make him pay for it," she offered.

"Fascinating. I once had a girlfriend who tried to sell my underwear on eBay. We could swap shitty ex stories all day, Grace. Tell me about the last guy. He's the one I'm interested in."

"What about the guy after car-crash sneak? He was a pathological liar. I still don't even know what his real name was," she said.

"Grace…." Mac growled.

He was getting genuinely irritated and she realized she was turning this into a big deal. And it wasn't. So…

"Be prepared to be bored into a coma," she warned.

She hadn't thought about Owen for a long time. The good times had been too good to dwell on and the bad… Well, why rake over the past? Her mind flicked over a handful of memories, most of them bad. She decided to cut to the chase and give Mac the expurgated version. Anything to get him off her back and his mouth back where it belonged.

"His name was Owen. He was an artist—a painter. He cheated on me and we broke up. Happy?"

She reached for his erection, but he batted her hand away.

"No. How long were you together?"

"Five years."

"Did you live together?"

She sighed again. "Yes. For four years. Yes, we were happy. At least I thought we were. Anything else?"

"Plenty." He was frowning. "So the cheating—was it a one-off?"

Pain lanced through her and she smiled grimly. "Wow, you want all the dirt, don't you?"

He eyed her patiently.

"No, it wasn't a one-off. They'd been sleeping together for six months before I found out."

"You must have been pretty pissed off," he said.

She forced a casual shrug. "I suppose. I understood why it happened, though. She was incredibly beautiful."

Her sister Serena's long ebony hair and pale-blue eyes still stopped men in the street.

"You must have been pretty upset," Mac said.

She shook her head. "No. It was a wake-up call. Some people might do love really well—like Sadie and Dylan, for example—but not me. It always goes pear-shaped for me so I don't go there anymore. Trust me, the past four years of my life have been great."

Mac's face was thoughtful as he reached out to touch her cheek. She stared in astonishment when his hand came away wet with tears. She was *crying?*

Mac caught her in his arms and pulled her against the comforting warmth of his body. He arranged them in the classic spoon position, his hips cradling her bottom, his arms wrapped around her body. She could feel his breath on her neck as he pressed kisses into her nape.

"It's okay, Gracie. I know it's hard to believe in something when you've convinced yourself it doesn't exist," he said quietly.

He was so solid and real and kind, his words so gentle and wise. She felt safe, cherished. What would it be like to have a tomorrow with this man, then another tomorrow after that?

She gave herself a mental slap. She didn't believe in the fantasy Mac was offering her. Because she knew, in her bones, how it would end. It always ended the same way—with her lover walking away or disappointing her in some way and Grace being left with nothing but pain. Owen had hammered that lesson home to her in no uncertain terms.

Suddenly Mac's arms felt smothering, his warm presence suffocating. Panic welled up in her and she wriggled away from him, nudging him with her elbow to get him to release his hold. He took the hint and this time she was on her feet before he could say any of the things that were written all over his gorgeous face.

She turned her back on him and went into the bathroom. Washing her mouth out, she splashed water on her face and stared at herself in the mirror. It was the same face she'd stared at all her life—the too-wide mouth, the too-big nose, the eyes that didn't match any of it.

Stepping into the shower, she turned the water on hot and stood under the rushing stream, pushing her hair back from her forehead and trying to calm the panic that was still sitting in her stomach. Then through the glass door, she saw Mac approaching. The next thing she knew he was standing under the rushing water with her, crowding her into the corner of the shower. He pressed his warm, firm body against hers, trapping her against the wall. Capturing her hands in his, he leaned close until his forehead was pressed against hers.

"I'm not going anywhere," he said, holding her eyes. "And I'm not walking away from this."

She stared at him. For a second, something flared to life inside her. She wanted to believe him, she realized. She almost laughed at her own naiveté. Maybe she hadn't learned anything after all.

Pulling him close, she kissed him, telling herself this was the last kiss, the last time they'd be together this way. Quickly, things got heated. Tongues danced and hands slid over soap-slicked skin as they discovered each other's bodies yet again. She caressed his shoulders, his back, his butt, before grasping his shaft and working him with long, firm strokes.

"Grace," he groaned. She stepped up the pace, brushing her breasts against his chest, hot water streaming down their bodies.

He caressed her breasts with his hands, then began to lick and suck each peak into trembling arousal before sliding his hand down her belly and between her thighs. She could feel how hot and steamy she was for him and she spread her legs willingly as he arrowed two fingers either side of her clitoris and began to trace a path down to her quivering entrance and back again. She murmured incoherently, writhing beneath his hands, her own still busy on his hard shaft. Kissing her deeply, he plunged a finger inside her, then two, then raced up to tease her clitoris again.

"Oh," she groaned, then she began to shudder in his arms. He took her weight as her body spasmed around his probing fingers and she pressed her face against his neck. He cupped her bottom afterward, holding her close against his still-hard erection.

Determined to make the most of this last time, she slid down his body until she was on her knees. She took him in her mouth, swirling her tongue across the head of his erection, one hand wrapping around the base of his shaft. He was so big and hard and perfect. She loved touching him, tasting him.

Between the humidity of the shower and the demanding pressure of her mouth, he didn't last long. When she'd drawn the last shudder from him, she slid back up his body and kissed him once, hard, as the water continued to pound down on them.

She purposely left the shower first, rushing through the process of drying herself and getting dressed. She needed the time to rebuild her defenses, to remember who she was and what she wanted.

Deliberately she chose one of her favorite vintage dresses, a 1960s day dress in deep maroon. She slid her feet into the highest pair of stilettos she'd brought with her and smoothed lipstick on as she heard the shower stop in the bathroom.

She'd twisted her hair into a damp chignon by the time Mac padded out of the bathroom, a towel slung low around his waist.

She turned to him. It was time to do what she was good at—sending a man packing.

"Don't say it," Mac said when she opened her mouth.

She gaped at him for a second, then recovered. "It's not going to work. I don't need a man in my life."

"You're right, you don't," he said lightly, "but would it really hurt to *want* a man in your life?"

Her mouth went dry as he whipped his towel off and slid into his boxers. Why did he have to be so fatally attractive to her?

She forced herself to stick to her line.

"I really think—" she said, but she didn't get any further than that because Mac stepped forward and captured her mouth with a kiss.

Holding her close, he looked into her eyes.

"Today's Thursday. Come to my house for dinner Sunday night and give me your answer then. If you still feel the same—fine, I'll back off. But I want you to think about it. At least give us that much of a chance. Okay?"

She stared into his too-blue eyes.

"It's not going to make any difference, Mac." He couldn't change any of the realities of life. No one could—she'd accepted that a long time ago.

He pressed another kiss to her lips.

"Sunday night," was all he said.

7

BACK IN HIS HOTEL ROOM, Mac phoned Claudia to report that they'd finished the location scout early. She told him she'd arrange to have their flights home rescheduled for that afternoon and Mac began to pack.

His mind didn't stay on work for long, even though he had about a million things he wanted to plan out. He couldn't stop thinking about Grace, about the stricken look in her eyes when she'd told him she was happy, that the past four years of her life had been great.

Owen. Mac had a feeling there was more to the Owen story than he'd been told. But he figured he had no chance of getting Grace to open up on that one again. She was so protective, so defensive—he felt as though he was trying to coax a feral cat out from beneath a Dumpster.

It occurred to him to wonder if Grace was worth it. A lot of guys would walk away, he knew. There were other women out there. Always had been, always would be. But everything in him rejected the thought.

He wanted Grace. He'd been single by choice for several years because he'd failed to connect with one special woman. He'd convinced himself she didn't exist or that his work and the crazy town he lived in made it impossible for any connection to go the distance. He'd been so defeated by his profession, by the daily reminder that his dreams were dust, that he'd been at rock bottom. Then he'd met Grace.

He remembered the thought that had blazoned itself across his mind when he'd first seen her—that she was an original. And she was. Feisty, clever, smart-mouthed, talented, funny, generous. When he was inside her, he felt complete. She made him dare to want again—and what he wanted was to take the flame that burned between them and fan it into something big and warm, something hot enough to burn for the rest of their lives.

He laughed humorlessly at his own thoughts. All those years of privately mocking his brothers' picket-fence lives and here he was, campaigning to get a woman to take a chance on him.

It wasn't going to be easy. He was going to have to coax Grace out from under the Dumpster that was her shitty romantic past. In his experience, there was only one way to retrain a scared animal—rewards and lots of patience and affection.

He smiled to himself, a new confidence surging through him as he made plans.

He might be out of practice with believing in things and going after them, but he hadn't forgotten how it was done.

EVEN THOUGH another night in Mac's arms had not dimmed his appeal for her one iota, Grace was determined to resist him and his seductive talk of seeing each other and exploring the idea of a relationship. Might as well just smack herself in the head repeatedly with a mallet as believe in some kind of shared future between them. She was confident she wouldn't have to hold firm for long, however—in her experience, men had short attention spans. Once they were back in L.A., Mac would forget about her and whatever small fascination she possessed for him would pass. She just had to resist his lures for a few days.

She hadn't counted on Mac playing dirty, however. He started his campaign midair. Somehow he maneuvered it so she was sitting next to him for the five-and-a-half-hour flight home, despite the fact that Marla had been allocated the seat next to hers. Grace eyed him warily as he settled in beside her, but he just smiled at her benignly and plucked the in-flight magazine from the seat pocket in front of him.

"I love these things," he said, running his eye down the contents page. "Check this out— 'An Epicurean's Guide to Salt.' Where else am I going to learn so much about something so simple?"

He seemed genuinely amused and she told her hormones—and her nipples—to quit sitting up and begging for attention. After nearly twelve hours of exploring one another's body, he should hold about as much interest for her as a loaf of bread. Unfortunately, what *should* be and what actually *was* were two very different things and her body didn't seem to be able to get enough of Mac.

It wasn't only his body she was attracted to, either. Even though she went through the motions of setting up her notebook computer, hoping to get in some work on the all-important wedding-special script, she was constantly distracted as he laughed to himself over something in the magazine. Occasionally, he'd share with her, paraphrasing a tidbit in pithy Mac style. Other times, he'd lean across and try to sneak peeks at her work.

After an hour, she was feeling distinctly…steamy from all of the whispering in her ear and all the casual touches as he leaned close to point out something on her screen or out the window.

It was only after their meal had been served and Mac had brushed the side of her breast three times in as many minutes as he tackled his meal that she realized there was a method to the apparently random touches and whispers and eye contacts. He was deliberately teasing her on such a subtle level that she only worked out what he was doing when she'd started contemplating dragging him into one of the tiny toilet cubicles and having her way with him.

"Stop it," she said when he reached across to snag her untouched dessert and managed to brush against both her breasts on the return journey.

"Sorry?" he said, one eyebrow cocked quizzically.

"You're deliberately touching me, trying to turn me on," she hissed, craning her head to one side to make sure Frank and Marla weren't listening. To her relief, they were both asleep, their heads lolling on their headrests.

"*Are* you turned on?" he asked, neither denying nor confirming her accusation.

She narrowed her eyes. "I know what you're doing and it won't work. I've already made up my mind. Just because you won't let me give you my answer until Sunday doesn't mean it's going to change."

"That's interesting," Mac said, nodding politely. "Now, if you don't mind, I'm going to finish reading about the Andalusian tapestry weavers."

He flashed her a bright smile and picked up the magazine again. She stared at him, then at her half-eaten meal. She was still wondering if perhaps she'd imagined the whole thing when he slid his hand onto her arm and began to absently rub the tender skin of her forearm with his thumb. She shot him a look, but he didn't so much as glance up from the magazine. For the next half-hour, in between the attendant collecting their trays and a variety of announcements, he traced delicate whorls across the pulse point at her wrist, the vulnerable skin of her forearm and the soft, hidden flesh inside her elbow.

She tried to ignore him. She didn't want to give him the satisfaction of knowing he had so much power over her. But she'd never known a thumb and a forearm could be so erotic. When had such a humble body part become so sensitive? A hot flush moved up her chest and into her face, and soon she couldn't stop herself from wriggling in her seat. When she'd recrossed her legs for the fourth time, Mac leaned toward her, his shoulder pressed close to hers.

"You have the sexiest body I've ever touched," he husked, the hush of his breath doing amazing things to her insides. "Your breasts, your thighs, your peachy backside. I can't stop thinking about being inside you. You drive me crazy. And I know it's only going to get better."

Then, he withdrew his hand and moved away from her, returning his attention to the stupid magazine again. Grace was practically panting, her thighs quivering, her nipples jutting out against the cotton of her dress. She glared at him, burning for his touch, afraid of the power he had over her.

He flicked her a sympathetic look, smiling slightly.

"Sunday night," he said, patting her hand with an avuncular air.

It only got worse.

They all went their separate ways at the airport, but Grace saw Mac first thing the next day at work. Together, they spent two hours compiling the information they'd gathered, then they met with Claudia to run it all by her.

To say that Claudia was wired was an understatement. She took copious notes, asked pointed questions and studied every image, every piece of footage, like a general assessing enemy terrain.

"This is good, I like this Lagoons location," she finally announced. "I'll get wardrobe images so they can start working on Hannah's gown. Something flowing, so we can see it trailing in the wind. And lots of tropical flowers. We'll fly them in if we have to."

She was pacing, tapping her pen into the palm of one hand. Grace and Mac exchanged amused looks.

"There are plenty of flowers on the island," Grace said, poker-faced. "I don't think we'll need to bus them in."

"Right. Of course." Claudia stopped, then smiled sheepishly. "I'm being a little anal, aren't I?"

Mac held up two fingers half an inch apart. "Only a little, and in a good way. We all want to nail this, don't worry."

"Excellent. Excellent," Claudia said.

Mac took the floor then, taking Claudia through his plan for the episode. As he pulled out rough sketches of camera angles, even storyboards of key scenes based on the story lines Sadie and Dylan had worked up, Grace realized he must have been up all night.

He was impressive. His passion, his conviction, his vision—Grace knew she wasn't the only one sitting on the edge of her seat, transfixed.

As he wound down, Mac moved to stand behind her chair, placing his hands lightly on her shoulders.

"Grace was kind enough to show me a few scenes from the script on the plane," he said. "I think we're going to blow *Heartlands* out of the water."

She forbore correcting him and telling Claudia that he'd snuck a few glances at her work while she wasn't looking; she was too distracted by the warm weight of his hands on her shoulders to do anything as complex as string two words together.

She'd had a hard time getting to sleep last night, her mind full of images of Mac, sense memories teasing for hours. She put the blame fair and square in his court—he was the one who'd spent the whole plane trip winding her up, all so he could prove some kind of point.

Now, her body was jangling with awareness again as he leaned against the back of her chair. She shot a look across the table at Claudia, sure her friend must see that something was up. But Claudia didn't seem to find anything unusual in the casual contact—she was too absorbed in discussing Mac's plans to use a helicopter for aerial shots of the wedding.

Grace almost jumped out of her chair when she felt Mac's fingers delve through the silk of her hair to find the nape of her neck with his thumbs. She swallowed a lump of pure lust as he kneaded her subtly, her mind automatically racing to the other massage he'd given her recently. Staring intently at her notes, she remembered the way his slick hands had slid over her skin, the enticing magic of his caresses, the slow build of desire as his fingers drifted closer and closer to the parts of her that had been begging for his touch.

"Great. I agree with everything you've come up with. And I'm really excited. Thanks for all your hard work, guys," Claudia said as she shut her notebook with a snap.

Grace dragged her attention back to the here and now and realized that Mac had removed his hands from her shoulders. She'd been so lost in sensual memories, she'd barely registered his withdrawal.

She waited until Claudia left the conference room before turning on him.

"You said we were about more than sex," she said, firing her first salvo.

"We are, but I'm not stupid. I told you once that a woman with a body like yours couldn't go four years without sex. Well, I'm upping the ante—I don't think you'll be able to go four days without it. But you're only getting it on my terms—and I want a relationship."

He thought she was playing a game, that she was enjoying this cat-and-mouse pursuit. Again the trapped, anxious feeling swamped her. Why couldn't he leave her alone?

"I'm giving you my answer now," she said, her voice trembling. "No. I don't want a relationship."

Grabbing her notes, she left the conference room, making a beeline for the ladies' room and privacy. She'd barely had time to set her notes on the counter when the door opened and Mac walked in. Her eyes widened as he bore down on her, walking her backward until she was pressed against the wall.

"What if someone comes in?" she squeaked as his hand slid under her skirt to cup her mound through the silk of her panties.

"I don't give a damn." Staring down into her face, a muscle ticking in his jaw, he squeezed her sex gently. Pleasure shot through her and she knew he could feel how wet she was already, just from the way he'd touched her in the meeting.

"I don't accept your answer," he said, his lips a torturous inch from hers. "Not until Sunday night."

He squeezed again and she let out a whimper of need.

"If the sex stuff bothers you, consider it gone," he said, sliding his hand away even as he said it. "No pressure, nothing until Sunday night."

He turned and exited the bathroom. Grace sagged against the wall, then abruptly straightened again when Sadie entered.

"Was that Mac Harrison I just saw leaving?" she asked suspiciously.

"He got lost," Grace fibbed weakly.

Sadie was silent for a long moment. Grace knew without looking in the mirror that she was flushed and when she glanced down she saw that part of her skirt hem was caught up.

"Okay. I'll buy that," Sadie said. There was a mischievous glint in her eye as she turned to fluff her hair in the mirror.

"You will?" Grace asked.

"No. But if you don't want to tell me what's going on between you and Mac, I can't make you," Sadie said.

Grace closed her eyes. "Nothing is going on. Not now, anyway."

Sadie frowned and Grace felt obliged to explain. "He wants more, I don't. End of story."

"Well. I guess that's your prerogative." Sadie nodded.

Grace stared at her friend. Where was Sadie's argument, her well-intentioned advice?

"You think I'm a chicken, don't you?"

Sadie soothed a hand down Grace's arm and caught Grace's fingers in her own. "I know how much Owen and Serena hurt you, even if you won't admit it to anyone," she said. "Everybody handles the shit life throws at them in different ways. You're the one who has to live with the consequences of your decisions. Just promise me you'll think about how much you'll be missing out on as well as all the usual stuff about how you don't need a man, okay?"

Grace nodded dumbly. Sadie smiled sympathetically and left. Grace stared blankly straight ahead.

She had trust issues where men were concerned. There,

she'd admitted it. Being on her own wasn't so much a choice as a defense. The problem was, she wasn't sure she was willing or able to let her defenses down.

She thought of Sadie and Dylan, remembering the yearning sensation she'd felt when she saw the open, generous love they had for each other. She hadn't been jealous of their sex lives—she'd envied their love. She could admit that now, too. She'd wanted someone to look at her the way Dylan looked at Sadie, as though she was the most desirable, precious, cherished person in the world. And didn't that make trusting Mac and believing in Mac all the scarier?

But Sadie had had the courage to declare herself to Dylan even when she knew he was determined to remain single. Even though she had as many reasons as Grace to protect herself, Sadie hadn't let the hurts of the past rule her future.

It was a thought that circled around and around Grace's mind over the following two days. She worked on the script of the wedding episode all day Saturday and into the night. Perhaps because she was feeling so raw, so torn, she found it both easier and more painful than usual to tap into the characters' emotions. As she wrote the wedding scenes, she shed tears as she gave Hannah and Gabe words of hope and love to say to one another. When they fought, she drew on her own experiences to give their words meaning and resonance.

And all the while Sadie's challenge echoed inside her heart. For four years, Grace had thought only about the negatives of being in a relationship. Now, sitting cross-legged on her bed on Sunday afternoon, she forced herself to think for the first time about the good times, the things she'd given up to be safe in her ivory tower.

She remembered the pleasure of having a large body to warm her cold feet against on a winter's night. She remembered the casual comfort of swapping sections of the Saturday paper. She remembered the joy of planning holidays, of buying presents for her love, of having someone to look after her when she was sick, and someone to come home to after a hard day at work. She thought about shared favorite movies, fighting over the blankets and the remote control, of tolerating snoring and toe-nail clippings and endless pairs of socks in the wash. She remembered the bittersweet ache of lying in a lover's arms, her heart filled with love and dreams.

She thought about the look on Dylan's face when he looked at Sadie and the softness in her friend's eyes when she looked back.

And she got off her bed and started to get ready for dinner at Mac's place.

MAC HISSED WITH PAIN as he forgot for the tenth time that the pan was hot and burned his fingers again. Swearing, he grabbed an oven mitt and returned the salt-baked fish to the oven. Eyes darting to the clock, he swore again as he pulled the vegetables from the refrigerator and consulted the recipe he was working from. He was supposed to trim the green beans and cook them with butter, salt and pepper, then sprinkle them with toasted flaked almonds. The carrots needed to be julienned and steamed, then lightly drizzled with honey just before serving. And the potatoes had to be boiled, mashed, whipped into fluffy creaminess and dolloped in perfect mounds on the plates.

Not for the first time, he regretted not organizing a caterer for the evening. It wasn't that he couldn't cook. He cooked all the time—just not impressive things such as baked fish with gourmet vegetables, followed by decadent chocolate mousse. Thank God he'd made that earlier, having scoured the whole of West Hollywood searching for the richest, most expensive chocolate he could find. The woman in the shop had assured him that ninety-percent cacao-bean content was the most concentrated kind they offered—it hadn't escaped his attention that Grace had a thing for chocolate and he wasn't ashamed of hedging his bets with a little culinary persuasion.

Finding the exact right chocolate and the freshest fish possible had taken far more time than he'd imagined and as a result he was running well behind schedule. He still hadn't tidied his bedroom and bathroom, and the living room of his Pacific Palisades house was a shambles. If all went according to plan, he'd do a quick whip around to clean up the worst of the mess after he had the vegetables sorted.

Right on cue, the phone rang. He stared at it for a beat. If it was Grace calling to chicken out… His shoulders stiff with tension, Mac scooped up the phone.

"Yeah?" he asked.

"Mac, how are you doin'," an instantly recognizable, honey-soft voice purred.

"Lisa," he said, glancing at the clock.

"Long time no speak. Or anything else," she said, laughing suggestively.

Using his shoulder to hold the phone in place, Mac wiped his hands dry on a dish towel.

"Yeah," he said, frowning.

"So…want to get together?" she asked. There was no need for either of them to be shy about things—the whole point of his relationship with Lisa was for both of them to have access to satisfying sex when and if they wanted it, no bull, no strings, no hassles.

"When were you thinking?" he hedged.

"As soon as possible, baby," Lisa said.

"The thing is… I'm kind of on the verge of something with someone," Mac heard himself say.

"Yeah?" Lisa sounded surprised. Astounded, even.

"Yeah. In fact, she's about to arrive any minute now," Mac said.

"Oh."

There was a long silence.

"She must be pretty special. Anyone I know?" Lisa finally asked.

"She's a writer," Mac said. He realized he wanted to say Grace's name, to openly stake his claim. But that would be premature, given that he had no goddamn idea whether he had a snowball's chance in hell of getting through Grace's defenses tonight.

"Well, I won't say I'm not disappointed. If things don't work out, give me a call, okay?" Lisa said. "It's been a lot of fun, Mac."

"Yeah, it has. Look after yourself, Lisa."

He didn't add that he wouldn't be calling her, even if things didn't work out with Grace. There was no reason for him not to, if he was a free agent again. He just didn't want to. He didn't want to go back to sex-to-satisfy-an-itch. He wanted Grace and the feeling he got when he was with her. He didn't want to settle anymore.

Which was why tonight was so damned important.

Glancing at the clock again, Mac swore like a trooper. He'd just lost a precious ten minutes to Lisa and brooding introspection, and the vegetables were still lying, crisp and raw, on his cutting board.

Sending up a silent prayer of forgiveness to the cooking gods, he threw all the vegetables into one saucepan and crossed his fingers. The chime of the doorbell only reinforced his decision.

Grace was here.

The house was a disaster area, the meal was still some way off and he hadn't had a chance to shower again before she arrived. Realizing that he was pointlessly shuttling piles of preparation dishes from one side of the kitchen to the other in a vain attempt to make it look tidier, he stopped to take a deep breath.

He was running around like his mother on Christmas day. He was pathetically nervous. This dinner with Grace felt a hell of a lot more important than any audition he'd ever gone for. He wanted to be a part of her life, but she was still stuck under that damned Dumpster....

The doorbell rang again and he headed for the front door. At the last minute he realized that he had a dish towel tucked into the front of his black trousers and he whipped it out and tossed it behind the umbrella stand in the hallway.

Seeing her after two days away was like getting sucker punched. He didn't know where to look first—her green eyes, that lush mouth, those stupendous breasts. He settled for a sweeping, all-encompassing head-to-toe, promising himself a more detailed inspection when she wasn't fidgeting nervously on his doorstep.

"Hi, come in," he said, stepping back.

After a small hesitation, she moved past him. He inhaled her perfume and fought his body's instinctive response to being close to her. He needed all his concentration, all his focus upstairs tonight, not downstairs.

Keeping a firm grip on his libido, he followed her up the hall.

HIS HOUSE WAS NOTHING LIKE what she'd expected. For starters, it was a lot smaller. She knew he was earning fantastic money as one of the most valued cast members and she'd imagined a lavish Hollywood home with too many rooms and too many cars, and too many swimming pools. Instead, she'd had to navigate her way up a small, poky road in the Palisades to find his driveway, nearly hidden among untamed vegetation, and she'd been more than a little surprised to find an attractive but modest two-story residence at the end of her trek. No expert on architecture, she guessed it might be classed as modern, with its strong geometric lines and angles. Inside, however, it was all space and light and warmth. Golden timber floorboards, warm-hued paintings and interesting artifacts from around the world lined the hallway, combining to create a relaxed, welcoming ambience.

The butterflies in her stomach went into overdrive as she registered that his house was as complex, warm and interesting as he was.

"I'm running a little behind schedule," he explained as he led her to the kitchen. She stopped on the threshold, taking in the litter of pots and pans and bowls spread over every surface.

He grimaced. "In a perfect parallel universe, this would have all been cleared away by the time you got here," he said.

She stared at him. He looked adorable standing there, uncertain and even a bit nervous. Her heart squeezed in her chest, and she forced herself to smile. He wasn't making her decision any easier, that was for sure.

"When I cook, half the food always ends up on the floor," she admitted.

He looked relieved. "I always cater for exactly that reason," he said.

She handed over the bottle of wine and imported chocolates she'd brought along and he busied himself with clearing a spot for her on one of the stools near his breakfast bar.

"Your house is very nice," she said, glancing through the doorway to the next room.

"This is where I'm supposed to offer you the grand tour, I know, but what I'm going to do is this instead." He poured her a glass of wine and handed it over. "I hereby give you permission to inspect every nook and cranny, open any cupboard, whatever takes your fancy—as long as it buys me an extra ten minutes alone in the kitchen to avert disaster."

She couldn't help herself—she laughed. Taking a sip of her wine, she stood.

"It's a deal. I promise not to try on any of your underwear," she said.

His gaze was suddenly smoldering. "I promise not to think about you trying on my underwear," he said.

Just like that, the sexual tension in the room rocketed from a simmer to a rolling boil.

"I'm going to go snoop," she gulped, backing away.

He let her go, but she knew he was biding his time. He was a man who was used to getting what he wanted and at the moment he wanted her.

Pushing her convoluted hopes and doubts to one side, Grace moved into the adjacent room, finding herself in a large, high-ceilinged living room furnished with squishy-looking reproduction club lounges in a dark-mocha leather. Bright cushions were jammed into the corners, evidence that Mac liked a bit of couch time. The coffee table was strewn with newspapers, travel books and half-a-dozen *Ocean Boulevard* scripts. She noted that he'd marked up the one on top, writing questions to himself in the margins, underlining certain words.

Taking a sip of wine, she wandered over to the mantelpiece where a framed family photo held pride of place. It had been taken when Mac was just a boy and seeing his bright-blue eyes smiling out of a much-younger face made her tighten her grip on her wineglass. She guessed he was maybe ten or eleven and, although there were hints of the handsome man he would become, in the picture he was all teeth and freckles and sticky-up hair, no more or less attractive than the other two boys standing on either side of him. He had his father's eyes, she noted, and his mother's mouth.

"Stop looking at the family photo," he called out from the kitchen.

She started, then smiled.

"Don't leave it lying around if you don't want people to see it," she hollered back.

She stepped into the hallway. A door was opposite, the stairs to her right. She chose the door and found herself in what was obviously Mac's study. A big slab of polished, knotted wood served as his desk and a worn-leather office chair sat behind it. The walls were lined with white-painted bookshelves, every one full to the brim. She ran her eye over historical volumes, biographies, a collection of English detective mysteries and, the biggest surprise of all, a small stash of fantasy novels.

Mac Harrison, closet *Lord of the Rings* fan. She grinned to herself.

Back in the hall once more, she eyed the stairs. She really wanted to see the rest of his home, but she wondered if she was taking him too literally at his word.

"Go upstairs. You know you want to," Mac called from the kitchen.

She snorted her amusement. The man was either psychic or she was woefully predictable. Her heels clicking on the wooden floorboards, she mounted the stairs. There were three bedrooms and two bathrooms running off a central hall. She poked her head into the two guest rooms, each nicely made up with quality linen, the decor casual but welcoming.

She saved her real attention for the master bedroom. Wide and high, it boasted a silk Persian rug in ruby-red tones, nubby golden-silk tab curtains and a big Mahogany sleigh bed. An overstuffed armchair stood in one corner with what looked like half of Mac's wardrobe strewn over or around it. Smothering a laugh with her fingers, she stepped over scrunched-up socks, boxers and T-shirts to take a look out the window. He had a view of his garden, a private oasis sheltered by tall trees.

Her gaze gravitated back to his big bed. More than anything in the world, she wanted to know what it felt like to wake up in his bed, with his arms wrapped around her.

"Okay, I think I've managed to avoid disgracing myself," Mac said, and she spun around to find him standing in the doorway.

"What are you, a ninja or something?" she asked.

He pointed to his bare feet. "Tactical advantage."

Grinning at her unease at being busted checking out his boudoir, he herded her back to the kitchen where he'd cleared off an intimate little table in the dining alcove. Candles flickered, glass glinted and snowy-white napkins garnished each place setting. He'd gone to a lot of trouble. But she'd already known that from the moment she set foot in the door.

"All right, here goes nothing," Mac said, sliding a plate before her.

"It looks great," she said, studying the long fillet of fish crusted with rock salt and the array of vegetables sprinkled with slightly over-toasted almond flakes.

"Took my eye off the damned almonds for two seconds," he explained as he sat down beside her. "But I managed to salvage the bottom layer."

She couldn't help herself; she reached out and grabbed his hand. He was too cute.

"Before we start—I really appreciate all this," she said.

"Save the thanks till after we've eaten," he said wryly, but she thought he looked pleased.

She wanted him to feel good, she realized. It had been a long time since she worried about a man's feelings above her own. Was that a good or bad sign?

"Now, I think we just brush the rock salt off," he said, frowning as he attempted to do just that and the salty crust crumbled into the fish. "As you can probably tell, I haven't made this before."

"Maybe we're supposed to eat it crust and all?" she suggested, popping a piece into her mouth. Immediately she realized she'd made a big mistake, and she struggled to stop herself from spitting out the overly salty mouthful. Grabbing her water glass, she washed it down and blinked tears away.

"I think we've answered that question," Mac said. A bemused expression on his face, he crossed to the kitchen counter and snagged a cook book. A chagrined look replaced his confusion as he read over the recipe.

"I think I see the problem," he said grimly. "I was supposed to use whole fish, not fillets. I guess the skin would make it easier to take the crust off, right?"

He looked so annoyed, so frustrated, that she couldn't help laughing. He shot her a look from under his lashes.

"Are you laughing with me or at me?" he asked.

"Definitely with," she said.

He grinned broadly and her heart did a strange sideways shuffle in her chest.

"Don't worry—we'll just eat the bottom layer, like with the almond flakes," she said.

Grumbling good-naturedly, Mac sat back down. For the next twenty minutes, they came up with increasingly elaborate strategies for getting at the fish without the surrounding salt. Grace's cheeks were aching from laughing so hard. All the tension she'd brought with her this evening had dissolved.

This was a new side to Mac. She'd seen the intense professional, the easygoing colleague, the passionate lover. This was Mac in his own territory, at ease, funny, relaxed, confident.

"I promise, dessert is foolproof," he said as he cleared the plates.

Grace inhaled the heady aroma of chocolate as he slid a decadent-looking mousse in front of her. "I love chocolate," she said, eyeing it greedily.

"I know," he said simply.

Holding her eye, he dipped his spoon into his mousse and slid the first bite into his mouth. She almost choked when she saw the stricken, disgusted expression that came over his face. Swallowing with effort, he leaned forward and snatched her mousse out from under her nose.

"Hey!" she said indignantly.

"You are not, under any circumstances, eating that mousse," he said.

"What's wrong with it?"

"You don't need to know," he said firmly.

Raising an eyebrow, Grace moved too quickly for him and snuck a spoonful from his own bowl. A gritty bitterness filled her mouth and she had to clap a hand over her mouth to stop herself from laughing and spraying her food everywhere.

Mac looked both amused and embarrassed as he shook his head.

"I swear I've made this a million times," he said. "I even

bought that fancy ninety-percent chocolate and everything. I don't get it."

She winced. "That would be your problem. The higher the ·percentage of cacao bean, the less sweet and the more bitter the chocolate is."

Mac swore, then flopped back in his chair. "Well, that's it, I'm done. I was going to impress you with the main and seduce you with dessert, but about the only thing I managed to do was turn the kitchen into a war zone and give my guest of honor a raging thirst," he said with self-disgust.

She'd come armed with a lot of rational arguments to trot out in front of him. She'd formulated a counter offer—an arrangement involving sex and no commitment, a deal she thought would protect her when, inevitably, their connection faded.

But she wasn't proof against his utter vulnerability, his desire to impress her, his uncertainty. For the first time in perhaps their entire time together, she understood that he had doubts, that he didn't know what the future held, and that he had feelings to hurt as well.

She was speaking before she could stop herself.

"Mac," she said, holding his eye. "My answer is yes."

"Sorry?" he said, clearly confused.

"To your question. Yes," she said simply.

He was very still for a moment, then he started to smile.

"Well," he said, pushing back his chair and looming over her. "Why didn't you say so earlier? I could have ordered pizza."

Then he pulled her to her feet, slung her over his shoulder and carried her up the stairs.

"You'll hurt yourself," she laughed as he groaned near the top step. "You'll wear yourself out."

He dropped her onto his bed and flopped on top of her. "Then it will be up to you to do all the work."

Smiling, she proceeded to do just that.

8

GRACE STIRRED, SHIVERING a little in the cool morning air. She reached for the blanket, finding nothing but thin air. Craving warmth, she curved her body more closely into the warm male back in front of her. Half awake, she pressed her face into the nape of Owen's neck, seeking the comforting scent of his skin. Memory flickered on the edge of her awareness as she inhaled deeply and her body stiffened as she fully realized where she was—in *Mac's* bed, her body curved against *his* back, her face pressed into *his* nape.

Mac. Not Owen.

Abruptly she rolled away from Mac, her stomach churning with old memories. God, how could she confuse Mac and Owen like that? They were so different, in personality as well as physically. So why had her waking mind gone there?

She felt faintly nauseous. Sliding out of bed, she made her way to Mac's ensuite and poured herself a glass of water. She had a serious case of bed head, but she was too busy reliving the painful memory to really notice.

She could almost feel the roughness of the wood of Owen's studio door beneath her fingers as she pushed it open. She could almost smell the pungent tang of oil paint and turpentine, almost see the dust dancing in the streaming sunlight that poured through the studio's skylight as she walked into that wide, open space.

She'd seen the paintings first—so many of them, their power en mass overwhelming. And then she'd seen them, their bodies gilded by sunlight. Owen had been on his back on the ancient paint-mottled rug, her sister Serena astride him, her dark hair flowing over her shoulders as she rode him. Her head had been thrown back, her spine arched, her pert breasts thrust forward. Owen had been gazing up at her with adoration.

"You're so beautiful," he'd groaned.

And then he'd realized Grace was there. She must have made a sound. Maybe she gasped. Owen's head had come up and he had stared at her in horror.

"Grace!" he'd said, a world of dismay and shock in his voice.

Then she'd turned away, broken into a run as she passed all those paintings of her sister, image after image, each one a work of art, all of them bold, dynamic, riveting nudes. The sunlight outside had seemed blinding after the darkness of the studio, she remembered. She hadn't known where to go, what to do with her pain.

She came out of the memory and registered her pale reflection in the mirror in front of her.

God, how could she have said yes last night?

She saw panic in her own eyes. What crazy woman had been in charge of her brain and her tongue when she said those fateful words? Sure, Mac was pretty much irresistible—extensively easy on the eyes, funny, charming, intelligent—but that was no excuse for not resisting him.

Had she been on crack last night?

Turning back to the bedroom, her first thought was to get

out of there. Retreat to her apartment, rebuild her defenses, remind herself of all the reasons why the last four years had been so great. As if she needed a reminder, after waking with the illusion that she was lying beside Owen again.

She could see her clothes, a piece here, a piece there. She started to collect them, darting nervous glances toward Mac. He lay sprawled on his stomach, one fist jammed into the pillow beneath his head, the blankets a messy tangle around him, his mouth slightly open. He looked adorable and sexy in equal measure, and a surge of pure tenderness pulsed through her as she automatically moved to the edge of the bed.

She didn't want to sneak away from him.

She hadn't wanted to say no to him last night, either. Somewhere in between meeting her fantasy lover in the flesh and scraping rock salt off her fish fillet, she'd grown awfully fond of Mac Harrison—*fond* being the only word she was prepared to acknowledge at this point in time. She stood holding her clothes, torn. Suppose—hypothetically speaking—she chose to play along with the whole let's-see-what-happens arrangement. What was the worst thing that could happen?

Her stomach clenched and she squeezed her eyes shut tightly as the searing loss of her memories washed back over her.

Okay, point taken. She didn't want to go there again.

She ran her eyes over Mac again, unable to hold back a smile when his mouth worked and he screwed up his face, on the verge of waking up.

She wanted him; she wanted this. Was she insane? Maybe. But something in him drew her so powerfully. She couldn't walk away.

But she had to protect herself. The thought resonated inside her. This time, she had to be prepared. If she was going to do this, she would go in with her eyes open, with no illusions.

She was not a beautiful woman, like her sisters or Claudia or Sadie, but she had a body that some men seemed to admire and she had a sharp mind and a good sense of humor. She could write. She had great taste in clothes and cars. She liked sex.

All of that should be enough to hold Mac for a while. And she would be prepared this time for the inevitable fading of attraction. This time, she wouldn't be caught off guard when he stopped wanting her. She would protect herself. She would be smart.

She took a deep breath. She felt a little dizzy, as though she were standing on top of the world's tallest building, looking down, down, down. She was going to do this.

She was going to try for a relationship with Mac. On her terms.

She let her breath out, and her tense body softened and relaxed. She allowed herself at last to remember last night: Mac poised above her, hard and demanding, on the brink of plunging inside her. Mac suckling her breasts, his attentions so thorough and so sensual that she'd been begging for release. Mac watching her through half-closed eyelids as she rode astride him, her hips finding their own instinctive rhythm as she chased paradise for them both.

It had been a long, hot, sweaty, glorious night.

Giving in to the need to touch him again, to prove to herself that he was real, she climbed back into bed, burrowing beneath his stash of blankets and smoothing the arch of her foot down the length of his long, muscular calf. His back felt hot and hard against her breasts as she pressed herself against him and rested her cheek on the broad plane of his shoulder blade.

"Mmmph," he said approvingly.

"Good morning, blanket hog," she whispered in his ear.

He smiled into the pillow.

"Did I steal the covers?" he murmured.

"Yep." She pressed a kiss to the nape of his neck.

"Maybe you were too hot and, like a gentleman, I relieved you of the burden of all those blankets," he suggested, his voice husky with early-morning lack of use.

"It's an interesting, if self-serving, theory. Sadly, however, it's wrong," she said, sliding on top of him fully now so that the front of her was pressed to the back of him. He felt amazing, warm and smooth and hard and muscular and incredibly, arousingly sexy.

"You must have been cold," he said.

"Freezing. Lucky I didn't get hypothermia," she said, raining kisses onto the expanse of his shoulders.

"It's a miracle you survived, in fact."

"Definitely. Someone should call *60 Minutes.*"

He laughed, and she was so distracted by the rumble of his amusement vibrating through his body that she was taken completely by surprise when he rolled out from beneath her, swiftly reversing their positions so that he was the one pressed to the back of her while she lay face down on the bed.

She could feel his arousal against the softness of her backside and she smiled into the pillow.

"You're squashing me," she said, wriggling her hips suggestively.

"Am I?" he asked idly, nudging a knee between her legs and encouraging one thigh to the side, leaving the heart of her exposed to his touch.

She bit her lip as his fingers slid between her thighs from behind. She could feel his hard-on pulse against her backside as he discovered how ready she was for him. She groaned her approval as he stroked her, then slid a finger inside her.

"You want me to get off?" he asked, all innocence.

She laughed. "What do you think?"

"I think you don't feel very cold to me. In fact, you're about the hottest thing I can think of right now," he said in between pressing wet, open-mouthed kisses into the sensitive curve of her shoulder and neck.

She felt the nudge of his erection at her entrance and she tilted her hips to encourage his penetration. He slid in slowly, inch by inch, and they both shuddered with pleasure.

"This just gets better and better," he said near her ear.

She could only agree as he picked up the rhythm. Before long, she couldn't bear simply being a passive receiver and she arched her back and pushed up with her knees and then they were both on their knees, her head pillowed on her folded arms as Mac thrust inside her. The exquisite slide of his body inside hers was too, too fine. Within a handful of minutes she was tightening around him as she climbed toward her climax. Mac encouraged her toward her goal, his hands soothing along her back, cupping her buttocks and swooping around her torso to pluck at her nipples. She came powerfully, her hips bucking, and she felt him soar over the edge behind her, his body shuddering into hers even as her orgasm began to dissipate.

They collapsed on the mattress, legs and arms intertwined, his face pressed into the back of her neck.

"That is the best wake-up call I've ever had," he said after a short silence.

She started to laugh and so did he, and soon they both had tears in their eyes from laughing too much. It wasn't that funny. At best it was only mildly amusing. But the anxiety and jubilation were still battling within her and there was no other way to express the feelings percolating inside her.

"Shit!" Mac said suddenly, sitting bolt upright and squinting at his alarm clock. "Shit. We must have slept through the alarm."

Grace shot up beside him and groaned when she saw the time. It was nine o'clock on a Monday morning.

"What time were you due on set?" she asked, wincing in anticipation of his answer.

He looked guilty. "Eight."

She grimaced. "Sorry."

The chagrined expression on his handsome face was immediately replaced with a smile.

"Don't be. I'm not. I wouldn't swap this morning or last night for anything in the world."

The way he waggled his eyebrows and injected a lascivious note into his voice kept his words light and meaningless, but Grace still felt a distinct rush of emotion in response to his silly declaration.

Don't! she ordered herself sharply. Next she'd be looking for fairies and unicorns at the bottom of the garden.

She rolled to the edge of the bed.

"Come on, stud, better get that million-dollar heiny of yours on set," she said, serving up a brisk spank to the asset in question.

"Yow!" he complained, shooting her a mock-annoyed look. "Be careful you don't go buying yourself a whole world full of trouble there, lady," he warned her.

The ring of the phone stopped him from exacting revenge, and she watched guiltily as he responded with a crisp assurance that he was on his way, pronto, before ending the call.

She pushed herself off the bed.

"Time to hustle?" she said, trying to keep the relief out of her voice. She needed time to regroup.

"Yep," he said ruefully. "What I wouldn't give for a sick day right now."

He was eyeing her greedily as she once again tried to find her clothes in the mass of his laundry spreading from the corner of the room.

"Your fault for being the big star," she said.

He frowned a little as he pushed himself off the bed, but he didn't say anything until he had drawn her with him beneath the warm spray of the shower.

"You don't really think I'm a big star, do you?" he asked uncomfortably.

His words and his tone pulled her out of her own convoluted thoughts and feelings. She stopped in the middle of soaping his chest and stared up at him.

"Hello? You *were* voted the sexiest man in daytime just last month."

"Yeah, in *daytime,*" he said dismissively. "And what does sexiest man mean, anyway? It has nothing to do with what I do, whether I'm good at it, nothing. It's about the fact that I stay away from carbs and do a shitload of sit-ups, that's all," he said disparagingly.

Suddenly she had a flash of insight. Mac doubted himself. This amazing, gifted man worried about being good enough.

"Mac, you're the best actor on the show," she said earnestly, unable to stem the impulse to reassure him. "And that's not just me talking—I've heard the same thing said in directors' meetings, script meetings, you name it."

He smiled slightly, then reached out to run a thumb along her cheekbone.

"You're good for my ego, you know that?" he said.

"I'm not bullshitting you," she said, annoyed at his ridiculously self-effacing response. "You're incredibly talented."

"Yeah, well, pity the rest of the industry didn't agree with you," he said flatly.

"What do you mean?"

He looked as though he wanted to change the subject, but he knew her well enough by now to know she wouldn't just let this go.

"Why do you think I came back to the show, Grace? I spent six years trying to hock my box around Hollywood, trying to prove to people that I could be something other than Kirk Young, daytime beefcake. I left the show when I was twenty-six to do *Blood Honor,* and it was all downhill from there. I was lining up to wear the chicken suit in Campbell's soup ads when *Ocean* called me."

She punched him on the arm, knowing he was exaggerating about the chicken suit but understanding the disappointment in his tone.

"You're still young, Mac. You're better now than you've ever been. The *Boulevard* isn't the sum of your talents as an actor."

He reached for the shampoo.

"I don't care anymore, Gracie," he said. Squeezing shampoo into his palm, he hauled her close and began to massage the liquid into her hair.

She closed her eyes as his fingers worked magic against her scalp and had to force herself to concentrate on what he was saying.

"Then what do you care about?" she couldn't resist asking.

She still had her eyes closed to avoid the sting of the lather and his hesitation seemed to last forever.

"World peace. The ozone layer. I care deeply about the way your nipples stand to attention when I do this," he said, tweaking her nipples lightly.

He was deflecting and they both knew it. She'd just had a glimpse into the dark side of Mac. But she wasn't going to push him any further. She had an idea about what Mac cared about, where his ambitions lay. But if he wasn't ready to say it out loud yet, who was she to force him? After all, she understood more than anyone that sometimes a person simply didn't want to talk about stuff.

When it was safe to open her eyes again, she stood on tiptoes and kissed him. Mac's arms came around her and he stared down into her eyes. She pulled away from him as unbidden, unexpected words rose to the back of her throat—important, heavy, emotional words. She swallowed them back down.

Way to protect yourself, lady. Why not just rip your heart out right now and throw it at his feet, save both of you a bit of time and effort?

"Do you think this was what they meant when they said they wanted you at the studio ASAP?" she asked lightly, avoiding his eye.

A flicker of awareness crossed his face and she held her breath, waiting for him to call her on her withdrawal. Then he smiled, looking boyishly caught out.

"I'm probably in big trouble," he admitted sheepishly.

"So am I. I'll be just as late as you by the time I get into the office."

They smiled at each other, everything light and easy again.

She wasn't smiling when she crept across the open-plan office an hour and a half later, hoping to slip into her office unobserved by her work colleagues. If anyone asked, she'd decided, she'd say she had a doctor's appointment. Or that she'd locked herself out of her car. Or something equally innocuous.

She wasn't quite ready to be out and proud about her relationship with Mac yet. She had to find a way to present it to her friends. She knew Sadie and Claudia would read a whole bunch of things into her and Mac sleeping with each other and she had to find a way to head them off at the pass. First, however, she needed coffee.

"Grace. Nice of you to join us."

Grace froze mid-creep and winced when she saw that Claudia was standing in her office doorway, arms crossed over her chest and a distinctly wicked gleam in her eye.

Claudia knew. Grace didn't know how she knew, but she did.

Diverting from her original course to face Claudia, Grace smiled lamely.

"Hi. Sorry I'm late, I'll make the time up this evening," she promised.

Claudia wave a hand dismissively. "I know that. Why don't you come into my office for a quick chat, though?"

Grace opened her mouth to protest, fully aware that she'd be letting herself in for the Greek version of the Spanish inquisition, but Claudia just grabbed her upper arm and pulled her forward. Once they were inside, she shoved Grace into a chair and punched up the internal intercom mode on the phone on her desk.

"Sadie? The eagle has landed," she said cryptically.

Grace heard the squawk of excitement from Sadie on the other end and rolled her eyes.

"I'm not telling you guys anything," she said repressively.

"We'll see about that," Claudia said, just as Sadie strode into the room, shutting the door behind her and leaning against it, her eyes shining with excitement.

"So. How was it? Your first sex in four years. Did the earth move? God, did everything still work?" Sadie asked.

"First of all, I want to know how you know," Grace said.

"Duh. You've just had a week in Hawaii together, now Mac is late on set and you're late in. I'm no rocket scientist, but I can add two and two together and get sixty nine," Claudia said.

Grace choked out a laugh despite herself. "I might have had a doctor's appointment. Or car trouble. The Corvette has been known to act up on occasion," she said.

"Yeah, yeah, sure. So, how was it?" Sadie asked, sliding into the second visitor's chair.

"It was private, is how it was," Grace said firmly.

"We don't want details. Okay, not itty-bitty details, anyway. Just broad strokes. Like…did you have a good time? Are you seeing him again? Or does this mean you're officially off the celibacy wagon and I can start setting you up with some of the great guys I know?" Claudia asked.

Grace counted off her answers rapidly. "Yes, yes, no. Anything else?"

Claudia looked perplexed. "Hang on, I can't remember what order I asked my questions in," she wailed.

"I do. Yes, she had a good time. As if we need to ask her to know that, with that big goofy smile on her face. And yes, she's seeing him again. Hence the big goofy smile, I guess. And no, she doesn't want to meet anyone else. Which means it's serious," Sadie interpreted.

They both fixed questioning gazes on her. Grace threw her hands in the air.

"How am I supposed to answer that? It's less than twenty-four-hours old, give or take a few nights here and there. We're *seeing* each other," she said.

"A few nights?" Sadie gasped, eyes wide. "I knew something was happening when he turned up at your place that time."

Grace blushed and Claudia shook her head.

"You dirty, dirty dog. You've been playing bed-time pogo with Mac Harrison for weeks and you haven't spilled," Claudia guessed.

"Gracie, I'm so happy for you," Sadie said, leaning forward to rub Grace's arm.

"And I'm impressed. Here I was, wondering how we were ever going to coax you out of your celibate's castle and you've quietly gone and landed Mac Harrison," Claudia said.

Grace held up a hand. "Um, guys—not getting married here. Just dating, seeing how it goes. So let's not get all misty-eyed about it."

Her friends were treating this like it meant something, like it was going to last more than a few weeks or a handful of months at the most.

"Too late," Sadie said, blinking rapidly.

Claudia laughed. "Too sooky even for a women in love, Sadie. Please tell me you're not pregnant."

Sadie looked as though she'd been struck by lightning for a second, and Grace and Claudia held their breath as their friend did a mental calendar check, then shook her head.

"No. At least, not yet."

"Thank God. I want all my team onboard so we can kick *Heartlands* into the gutter and jump on its rotting carcass," Claudia said with gusto.

"Am I free to go now? Is the interrogation over? You don't want to know anything else, like penis size or what kind of stamina he has?" Grace asked, rising to her feet.

"Well, of course we want to know those things but we would never be so uncouth as to ask." Claudia grinned.

"*You* might like to know, but I can survive without knowing the size of Mac's equipment," Sadie said primly.

"Okay. You block your ears and I'll just whisper it to Claudia," Grace said, calling her friend's bluff.

For a moment, Sadie looked so torn between outrage and curiosity that Grace and Claudia broke into laughter again.

"As if, Sadie," Grace said.

Sadie looked sheepish. "You might have."

"Seriously, though, Gracie—I'm really proud of you," Claudia said, her near-black eyes shining with warmth. "I know how hard it must be for you to trust someone again. I've got a good feeling about this, too. Remember, I'm the one who threw Sadie and Dylan together. I have an excellent track record with these things."

"Guys, please don't make too big a deal out of this," Grace said.

"Of course not," Sadie said innocently.

"Would we do that to you?" Claudia asked.

Grace rolled her eyes and was about to extract a promise from both of them when her cell phone buzzed in her handbag. Shooting her friends both admonitory glances, she managed to answer it on the fourth ring.

"Grace speaking," she said.

"Gracie, it's Felicity. I just wanted to let you know I'm going to be in town in two weeks' time and I though it would be a great chance to catch up with everyone on the Saturday night. Hope is still staying out with Mom and Dad in Pasadena, and it's been so long since I saw you all together. What do you think?"

Grace blinked. What did she think about seeing her sisters again, all together as in the old days? As Felicity said, it had been ages. One or the other of them had always been away at Christmas or birthdays for the last few years.

"That sounds great," she said.

"Serena is going to organize a restaurant. She'll text you the details. Oh—and it's partners, too. I've got Brad with me and Hope will be bringing Zane."

"Right," Grace said.

"Are you seeing anyone at the moment? Serena wasn't sure…." Felicity fished awkwardly.

"No, I'm not seeing anyone at the moment," Grace said automatically. "I'll see you soon, Flick."

"Great. Really looking forward to it," Felicity said before killing the line.

Sadie and Claudia were glaring at her when she put the phone down.

"What?" Grace said.

"Why did you just lie about Mac to your sister?" Sadie asked.

"I didn't," Grace said defensively. "I just…forgot for a minute. God, it's barely happened, give me a chance to adjust here."

"You're worried about them meeting him, aren't you?" Claudia asked.

As usual, Claudia didn't pull her punches. Grace blinked, then straightened her shoulders.

"Read my lips—I just forgot. I'll ask Mac if he wants to be bored to death by my family, but I bet he'll be thrilled to be let off the hook." Grace shrugged.

Neither Sadie nor Claudia looked convinced. Not being able to get away with self-deceiving bullshit was the one drawback of having such close friends, Grace mused later in her office as she sorted through her e-mail. Sometimes, it was nice to hide behind a white lie. Even for a little while. But Sadie and Claudia weren't buying, which meant Grace couldn't fool herself, either. The truth was, the odds of her asking Mac to have dinner with her family were very slim. Practically nonexistent. And she could tell herself that she was trying to save him from boredom, but that wasn't true, either. She didn't want him to meet her beautiful sisters.

A great start.

Grace rested her forehead on her hands and stared at her desk. She'd always had self-esteem issues around her sisters. She'd have been a poster child for freakishly self-sufficient kids if she hadn't been affected by all those years of living in their perfect, beautiful shadows. But she wasn't a kid anymore—she was a grown, adult woman. And the prospect of seeing her sisters and introducing them to the man she was dating should not have triggered an automatic Pinocchio response.

She sighed, fondly recalling the simplicity of pre-Mac days. Her feelings about herself and men were inextricably tangled up with those surrounding her relationship with her sisters. And she so didn't want to think about untangling them. Was denial really that bad a coping mechanism? She didn't think so.

Her cell rang again and the screen display told her it was Mac. Time to choose—did she invite Mac to meet her family next weekend or did she play it safe and put off the inevitable?

There was no decision, really. She'd already made her choice that morning, staring at his sleeping body on the bed, trying to negotiate her way through the panic and anxiety she'd been feeling.

She was protecting herself every step of the way. And that meant she was flying solo with her family.

ALMOST TWO WEEKS later, she was glad of her decision as she applied a last coat of lipstick and ran a comb through her hair.

She was feeling strangely nervous about seeing her sisters. Which was stupid and silly and childish. Lord only knew what was going on in the Freudian soup that was her subconscious—she could only thank her lucky stars that she hadn't dragged Mac into the whole arrangement.

Her gaze flicked to the mirror where she could see him lying sprawled across his bed behind her, script pages and contracts and storyboards creating a sea of paper around him. He was utterly absorbed in the pre-production planning for the wedding special, had been all day.

Looking at him made her body go crazy. He was such a good lover. And such good company. She'd had to exert some major self-control over the past few weeks.

So far, she'd managed to limit herself to spending every second night in Mac's arms and she knew he was becoming frustrated. But she had to keep her limits, no matter how much she wanted to give in and let things happen. Already the situation felt as though it had taken on a life of its own— he had a toothbrush at her place, she had one at his. She'd left earrings, makeup, perfume in his bathroom, while she was accruing a tidy collection of his boxers at her apartment. Sadie and Dylan had invited them over for dinner next week—a cozy couples dinner, a real version of the one they'd inadvertently faked at her place just a few short weeks ago.

On one hand, she was deliriously happy, sated, turned on, content. But she was also constantly looking over her shoulder, waiting for the rug to be pulled from beneath her feet. It would be so easy to relax into the heat of their mutual desire. Too easy. She had to keep reminding herself to hold back, to bite her tongue on words of affection, to abstain from buying him the aftershave/book/CD she'd seen that she knew he'd like.

She was being sensible. She'd learned her lesson.

Sliding her glasses on, she turned to face him.

"Right, I'm off," she said.

He looked up from the script page he was marking up and her thighs trembled as his gaze went from distant and preoccupied to instantly hungry.

"I like that dress," he said, his voice very low. "Come here."

She looked at her watch. She'd been late getting out of the shower and she was supposed to be meeting her family in twenty minutes at a restaurant that was at least a fifteen minutes' drive away. Somehow, however, she was already moving toward the bed.

She stopped in front of where he sat on the edge of the mattress and he reached out to rest his hands on her hips, his fingers fanning out to span her waistline.

"Have I told you how much I love your hips?" he asked.

"Yes." He'd sung their praises often, but she'd never get sick of him telling her how much he wanted her.

She shivered as he slid his hands over the fine cotton of her skirt and down toward her hem. In a flash his hands were beneath her dress, smoothing up her silk-stocking-clad legs. She bit her lip as his hand slid onto the bare flesh at the top of her stockings and he growled low in his throat.

"God. How am I supposed to sit here and concentrate on work when I know you're walking around out there dressed like this?" he muttered.

Impatient, he rucked her skirt up out of the way so he could see her. Her heart began to slam against her rib cage as he drank in the sight of her black-lace panties and red-silk garter belt.

His eyes flicked up to her face briefly as he leaned toward her, his hands firmly guiding her hips forward, and then she gave a moan of pure pleasure as his mouth fastened over her sex and she felt the wet heat of his tongue through her panties. His hands massaged her butt cheeks as he nibbled at her through the lace and she had to hold onto his shoulders as he hooked a finger beneath the elastic and pushed it to one side.

The firm, wet pressure of his tongue sliding into her folds almost did her in. She widened her stance, inviting him closer, deeper. He grunted his approval and began to tease her inner lips with his fingers even as he zeroed in on her clitoris with his mouth.

Liquid heat pooled between her thighs and quickly she began to climb toward her climax. He knew what she liked, how to tease her, when to go hard, when to back off. He played her like a virtuoso and within minutes she was sobbing out his name, her body pulsing around his fingers as his mouth coaxed the last shred of pleasure from her body.

He lifted his head so that he could lay his face against her stomach for a beat afterward, his hands cradling her backside gently. Then he pressed a kiss to her belly button and sat back, letting her dress fall into place.

"What time were you supposed to meet them?" he asked wickedly, and Grace's eyes flew to the clock.

She was late. Surprise surprise.

"You did that on purpose," she said.

"Serves you right for not inviting me," he said.

"I told you, it's just my sisters and my folks. We haven't seen each other for ages. You'd be bored rigid. You can meet them another time," she fibbed.

Of all the men she'd ever gone out with, why did Mac have to be the only one who was actually keen to meet her family?

"Come back here afterward," he said, wagging his eyebrows suggestively. "I'll give you dessert."

Her eyes lowered to the significant bulge tenting the front of his boxers.

"It'll probably be too late," she said noncommittally, tearing her eyes away from his erection.

"Come anyway," he said.

She tried to avoid answering by kissing him goodbye, but he caught her hand.

"Okay?"

"Sure," she said. They both knew it was a lie and she saw his face settle into the frustrated lines that were becoming all-too-familiar.

"I really have to go," she said, grateful as all hell that she had an excuse to get out of there.

Hopefully, by the next time she saw him he'd be so horny he'd forget her broken promise.

As luck would have it, she had trouble finding a parking spot and she was well and truly the last to arrive at the table. It had been so long since she'd seen her sisters en masse that she actually stopped in her tracks and blinked when she entered the restaurant.

Like three different artists' impressions of perfection, they sat ranged around the end of the table. On the left, Felicity, her blond hair sleek and straight and perfect. She shared Grace's tilted eyes, although hers were a vibrant aquamarine. Her nose was snubbed and she had a neater, less generous version of Grace's mouth. Serena sat on the end, the perfect foil for Felicity's fair beauty with her long dark hair. She had Grace's nose with the addition of a strong jawline to balance it and pale-blue eyes with long dark lashes. The youngest sister, Hope, sat on the right, her full, bee-stung lips arranged in a pout. She was pure runway model—all cheekbones, sharp planes and dead-straight ash-blond hair. Her pale-gray eyes flicked over Grace dismissively as Grace greeted her and Grace smiled grimly to herself. It had been nearly two months, but Hope was obviously still angry that Grace had given her her marching orders when Hope had taken advantage of her hospitality too long.

As befitted such attractive women, Felicity and Hope both sat next to handsome men—Brad, Felicity's on-again, off-again boyfriend, and Zane, Hope's equally transient partner. Brad's greeting was friendly enough, but Zane offered her a limp handshake that was designed to let her know that he, too, hadn't forgiven Grace for ejecting Hope from her apartment. For a wild moment, Grace was tempted to call both Zane and Hope on their sulkiness. She wondered what they would say if she told them she'd overheard them talking about her, referring to her as "the family mascot." Would they drop the wounded air and scramble to apologize or would they simply suggest Grace had misheard them?

She decided it wasn't worth the fuss. Her parents were sitting there, smiling at having their brood of children all together, and Grace let the thought go. She sank into the remaining seat at the foot of the table. It didn't escape her notice that she was as far from Serena as possible. She wondered vaguely if it had been planned that way, or if it had just happened naturally. She didn't know what they were worried about—it wasn't as though there had ever been any ugliness between her and Serena over what had happened. The two of them had an unspoken agreement—Grace had offered absolution and in return Serena kept her distance. Since family gatherings were few and far between, it didn't stretch either of them too much.

Because they lived out on the fringes of Pasadena, she hadn't seen her parents for a while and she spent a few minutes catching up with them. Her mother was dressed in pale-pink and brown to complement her fair skin and carefully styled blond hair, and her former-beauty-queen's face was holding up well to the rigors of aging.

Grace waited patiently as her mother inspected her latest vintage find, a 1960s-era red-chiffon cocktail dress with a high neck and no sleeves.

"Gracie, you look lovely. You know, I never looked that good in those dresses," her mom said affectionately.

"I've seen the pictures, Mom," Grace said dryly. "You did okay."

Her mother had been just as stunning as her sisters when she was a younger woman.

"So you've been across to Oahu, have you? Don't suppose you got a chance to play a few holes at the Moanalua Golf Club?" her father asked a tad wistfully.

Despite the fact that Grace had never set foot on a golf course in her life, David Wellington persisted in hoping that one of his children might share his passion for golf.

"Ah, no, Dad. It was a working trip," Grace said, exchanging amused looks with her mother.

For some reason, Grace was preternaturally aware of Serena that evening, even though her sister was sitting at the other end of the table. She kept catching a word here and there as Serena told a story in her sexy, husky voice, or being distracted by Serena's throaty laugh. She looked well, Grace noted during a lull in the conversation. She'd cut her hair a little shorter, although it still fell past her shoulder blades, and her wide blue eyes were clear and worry free.

Grace pulled her gaze away, surprised to catch herself wondering how someone who had betrayed a loved one so foully could sit so comfortably, so easily, within the circle of her family, with not a blush or a guilty flicker to show for it.

It wasn't the last dark thought to cross her mind as the evening progressed. Her sisters became more raucous as the wine bottles emptied, while Grace became more and more quiet as she watched them interact with each other and the world. It was more than just a family dinner she was observing—it was a command performance. The whole restaurant was fascinated by the table with the three stunning women at it. Eyes—particularly male eyes—constantly drifted their way, the waiters and waitresses fawned, the host kept stopping by their table to check that their meals were up to standard.

Grace had seen it before. She'd seen it all her life, in fact. But for the first time she noticed how much her sisters played up to the situation—the overloud laughter, the knowing looks if they happened to catch a man ogling them, the flirtatious giggles between themselves. They were like a floor show, the fabulous Wellington sisters, showcasing their attractiveness to the world. And God forbid that anyone not be dazzled by their beauty.

This last sour thought brought Grace up sharp and she pushed her wineglass away. For starters, she was driving. And she didn't particularly feel like descending into a pit of black self-pity. It had been the coping mechanism—if she could call it that—of her teen years, before she'd become her own woman. Reaching for her water glass, she took a long swallow and swept her hair over her shoulder.

It was just dinner, nothing special. And they were her sisters, not the enemy.

All went well until they neared the end of their meal. Desserts were on the way, and Grace found herself sitting between Hope and Serena when Felicity asked her to swap places so she could chat with their parents at the other end of the table.

Having discovered that Serena was single at present, Hope was going through the address book in her cell phone, trying to hook her older sister up with one of her model friends.

"You'll like this guy—he's so sexy," Hope said. "He rides a motorbike and he's desperate to fall in love."

"Where's the challenge in that?" Serena joked. "It's no fun if they roll over and play dead right from the start."

Instantly Grace's thoughts went to Owen. Had he been a challenge? Had that been part of the attraction for Serena?

She'd never asked—because she'd told herself it didn't matter. But now Serena was making jokes about seducing men. Was it just Grace, or was the whole conversation in pretty bad taste?

"Oooh, here's one who should be a worthy opponent," Hope said, her gray eyes sparkling with interest as she keyed up another entry. "A confirmed bachelor—sworn off women for good he said last time I saw him."

Serena cocked her head. "Now I'm interested," she said in a sultry purr, wriggling in her seat suggestively. "I love a man who's hard to get."

Grace was speaking before she could help herself, four years of bile suddenly surging up her throat and out her mouth.

"But is being a committed bachelor really enough, Serena?" she drawled. "Surely you want someone a little more challenging. Haven't you got a married guy in there, Hope? Preferably one with kids. That's more up Serena's alley, don't you think?"

As luck would have it, she'd spoken during a pause in her parents' conversation, and her words carried clearly. Her mother paled, and Felicity's gaze widened in shock. Serena sucked in an audible breath and Hope's mouth puckered into a bemused pout. For what seemed a long, long heartbeat, all eyes were on Grace. Very cool, she pushed her chair back.

"I really have to be going. Great to see you all," she said, scooping up her handbag and keys. Tossing some money onto the table, she headed for the exit.

She was furious, she realized. She couldn't understand where so much anger had come from so fast. Her hands were shaking as she tried to open the Corvette, and she took a deep breath to steady herself. She'd never spoken to one of her sisters that way before. Sure, she'd been mildly provoked, but she'd practically called Serena a whore in front of the whole family.

Slowly Grace's pulse slowed and she felt calmer. For some reason, she'd been more sensitive to the situation with Serena tonight. She'd been edgy with Mac, too. If she was the kind of woman who liked to pull her innards out and analyze them, she might draw some conclusions about those two circumstances. But she wasn't, so she was going to opt for denial, her favorite religion.

But just for a moment as Grace started her car and prepared to drive away from the whole shitty evening, the lump of anger in her belly threatened to rebel and coalesce into something bigger, more untameable. Grace pushed it down—way down, back where it belonged. In the past where it couldn't hurt her.

Starting the car, she signaled and pulled out into the traffic. She was halfway to Mac's place before she registered what she was doing—obeying her subconscious wish to be with him, to seek comfort and reassurance in his arms.

A slippery slope.

Pulling into the nearest driveway, she turned around and headed for her apartment, where she should have been going in the first place.

9

_____

MAC WOKE the next morning alone in his bed. Grace hadn't come over to his place after her family dinner, as she'd agreed she would.

But he'd kind of known she wouldn't, hadn't he?

Staring up at the ceiling, he admitted the truth to himself at last. Grace was eking out their time together as though they were on rations and it was beginning to seriously grate on him. She never committed to spending two nights in a row with him, even if she had to come up with some outlandish excuse to put him off. So far, she'd had a hair appointment, a massage and a dinner with old school friends. And, of course, last night, the family reunion. He was waiting for her to use washing the cat as an excuse.

She had trust issues. He didn't need to be too quick on the uptake to get that about her. But short of laying his feelings on the line and telling her in no uncertain terms where he thought they were going, he didn't know what else he could do. He'd been holding off, but maybe it was time to push a little. They were never going to get where he wanted to go if Grace was constantly pulling in the other direction.

After a quick shower, he dressed and stopped by his favorite deli to grab a selection of walnut bread, free-range eggs, smoked paprika, fresh herbs. By ten he was on her doorstep, a man on a mission.

She opened the door looking puffy and half asleep. He liked that her eyes lit up the moment she saw him, despite the fact that she did her best to seem nonchalant.

"You're up early," she said.

"Yep. Came to cook you breakfast in return for making use of your delectable body," he said, dropping a kiss on her lips on the way inside.

"I probably have dragon breath," she said apologetically.

He pulled a face to confirm this and she swatted his backside as they made their way up the hall and into the kitchen.

"Why don't you go shower while I whip us up some Eggs Baghdad?"

"Why am I sensing an ulterior motive?" she asked suspiciously. "There's not some *Lord of the Rings* marathon playing somewhere, is there?"

He stopped in his tracks. "I was wondering if you saw my secret stash."

"Oh yeah," she said, looking smug.

"I swear I have no ulterior motive except sex. Lots of it." He checked his watch. "In about five minutes' time. And counting."

She accepted this at face value and disappeared in the general direction of the shower.

Ten minutes later, they faced each other across her small dining table. Grace was wearing her black-silk robe and, as far as he could tell, precious little else. He was finding it difficult to concentrate on his real ulterior motive.

"So, how was dinner last night?" he asked.

She shrugged. "Good. Same old, same old. Dad wants someone to be interested in golf as much as he is and Mom still worries about eating dessert in case it ruins her figure."

Her gaze slid away from him and Mac found himself getting annoyed. This was exactly the kind of thing he'd been thinking about—she was lying to him about something. It made him feel shut out, like an outsider looking in.

"What happened?" he asked bluntly, annoyance making him sharper than he'd intended.

She looked a little startled. "Sorry?"

"Something happened to upset you last night. I want to know what it was," he said. He held up a hand before she could respond. "And before you give me the inevitable brush-off, I'm asking because as well as being your lover, I'm your friend and I want to know when you're upset about something."

She looked even more startled and started collecting their empty plates. "I'll do the dishes since you cooked," she said.

He caught her with an arm about her waist, pulling her onto his lap.

"You asked me the other day what I cared about and I wanted to say this then, but I didn't because I knew you'd freak. I care about *you*, Grace," he said.

For a moment he saw something soften and unfold behind her eyes. A smile curled her lips. He found himself smiling back.

Then Grace's ever-present self-editor stepped in and she wriggled off his lap.

"Thank you," she said carefully. "That was a nice thing to say."

He let her go into the kitchen before he followed her.

"You could send me a polite little note, if you like," he said testily as he watched her rinse the plates.

She stopped what she was doing and put a hand on her hip. "Pardon?"

"'Dear Mac, thank you for your kind words on Sunday regarding your feelings. I was most flattered. Unfortunately I am unable to return your sentiments. Have a nice life. Yours, Grace'," he recited mockingly.

He was angry again, sick of being held at arm's length by a woman he was beginning to realize he wanted to cherish and worship and adore.

She looked stricken and the carefully composed expression dropped from her face.

"Mac, don't. It's not that I don't feel the same," she said. He could tell the words were torn from her by the way she immediately pressed her lips shut firmly, as though she were trying to prevent more truths from escaping.

He moved closer, pulling her into his arms and looking down into her face.

"We said we'd see where this went, but you're not with me all the way, Grace," he said. "I am not Owen, okay? And I can't make a relationship work between us on my own. You need to share the heavy lifting. You need to talk to me. I need to know what's going on in your head, because, believe it or not, I am not psychic."

She leaned forward and put her head on his chest so that he was looking down at the top of her head.

"I'm trying," she said, her voice muffled. "I just don't want to be the one left behind again."

"It's not going to happen," he said, feeling an intense, burning need to hunt Owen down and make it impossible for him to ever screw a woman over again.

"You don't know that," she said.

"Yeah, I do. I will never hurt you, Grace," he vowed.

She was silent for a long moment, then she looked up at him.

"I had a fight with one of my sisters last night. I had to

leave the dinner because I didn't trust myself not to say anything else," she said.

He nodded, understanding that she was offering up this information to him in return for his declaration. Not quite the reciprocation a man falling in love longs for, but he'd take what he could get from his prickly Grace.

"She must have provoked you," he said. "I've never seen you lose your temper without cause. Well, except with me, but that was because you were longing for my hot body," he said.

To his utter astonishment, Grace blushed a fiery, beet red. She was so embarrassed he could feel her body burn with it.

"Whoa, something just struck a nerve," he said.

Grace bit her lip, then closed her eyes. "I used to fantasize about you," she blurted in a rush. "Before Claudia made us work together, I used to bring home the episodes from work and watch you and think about you and me and… you know."

Suddenly it all made sense to him—her ball-breaking attitude on that first day, the way she'd torn his clothes off like there was no tomorrow. His Gracie had had a crush on him! A wave of intense satisfaction washed over him. Closely followed by a surge of pure, unadulterated lust.

"You used to fantasize about me," he repeated. "How often?"

"A lot. I hadn't had sex for four years, remember," she said a little defiantly.

"What did I do in these fantasies?" he asked, growing harder by the second.

"Everything," she said boldly. Her eyes had dilated and he dropped his gaze to where her nipples were jutting against the silk of her robe.

"Anything in particular that you remember?" he asked, reaching for the tie on her robe.

They'd been in the middle of an important discussion, and he knew he should capitalize on her willingness to be frank with him. But he was hard and hot for her and her robe was already sliding to the ground.

She licked her lips and reached for the buckle on his belt.

"There was this one fantasy with chocolate sauce," she said.

"Sounds messy."

"It was. Very, very messy."

Her hand was inside his pants now, stroking him.

"You, ah, you got any chocolate sauce?" he asked, reaching for her breasts.

"In the cupboard," she said, shuddering as he thumbed her nipples then squeezed them firmly.

"Excellent. Did I ever tell you how much I like to finger paint?"

AFTERWARD, GRACE LAY sticky and sated in Mac's arms. She'd broken her own rules today, telling him about her fantasies and her fight with Serena. Surely it was crazy to give him so much power over her? But just telling Mac those two small things had felt so good, so right. She remembered what he'd said about them being friends as well as lovers. It had touched her more than she dared to admit even to herself.

"Does chocolate stain?" Mac asked, eyeing her chocolate-smeared sheets.

"I don't care," she murmured, pressing a kiss to his chest.

"These fantasies of yours—you've probably got quite a few up your sleeve, yeah?" he asked.

She smiled. "Hundreds."

"Hundreds. Dear God, I am the luckiest man on the planet," he said.

No, she couldn't regret what had happened this morning.

For good or for bad, Mac was whittling away the last of her defenses. And as much as it terrified her, she didn't want to stop him. Was it crazy to let herself feel this way about a man again? Or was she kidding herself that she had any control over any of it at all? She'd been magnetically attracted to Mac from the moment she met him and every minute with him only reinforced that attraction. Perhaps she should give in and let this happen—whatever it was.

For the next ten days, she proceeded to do just that. They spent every night with each other, mostly at his place since it was larger and more private. Each morning she woke feeling a little safer, a little braver. The words that she'd been biting back didn't seem so stupid or unfeasible anymore. Maybe, one day soon, she'd even allow herself to say them out loud.

She'd fallen in love with Mac. Irretrievably, head over heels, lock, stock and barrel in love. And she suspected—no, she knew—he felt the same.

Not bad for two cynics who claimed they didn't believe in love..

She was still luxuriating in the new contentment and certainty that was growing between them when Mac came home from work on Wednesday night, his blue eyes shining with excitement. She knew he'd been grappling with casting problems and other production issues to do with the special and she recognized his excitement with relief.

He'd been so stressed-out, she'd been rubbing the knots from his shoulders on a nightly basis. Now, he grabbed her and kissed her soundly.

"What are we celebrating?" she asked.

He waved a DVD case under her nose.

"Guess who this is?" he asked triumphantly.

"You cast Tania," she guessed, knowing that finding the

right actress to play the part of the seductive troublemaker in Gabe and Hannah's story had been his biggest bugbear.

"Oh yeah, baby," he said. "Wait till you see her."

He crossed to Grace's entertainment unit, pressing buttons until the screen came to life. A dark-haired beauty filled the screen and Grace's hands curled into fists instinctively, even as her world seemed to tilt on its axis.

"Isn't she perfect?" Mac said. "Her name's Serena Watts. Great look, a really mature sexiness. And she looks uncannily like Gabe's first wife. She's exactly right to make the audience think that Gabe might actually cheat on Hannah."

Grace summoned a nod from somewhere as she marvelled at how quickly a person's world could fall apart.

"What do you think?" Mac asked after they'd watched the two-minute audition scene from beginning to end. "Perfect, right?"

Grace opened her mouth, but no words came out. She cleared her throat, her eyes glued to the television screen where Serena's beautiful face was paused.

"She's my sister," she said. Not quite the bright, casual revelation she'd imagined in her mind, but passable.

"What? No way," Mac said, his face alight with amazement. "Really?"

"I told you that one of my sisters is an actress. Watts is her stage name," Grace said. Even to her own ears her voice sounded flat and she twisted her stiff lips into what she hoped was a pleased smile.

Mac was studying Serena's face on-screen, his head cocked to one side.

"I can kind of see it. She's got your nose, right?" he said.

Grace suddenly couldn't stand it for another second. She wanted to scream—maybe break something—not discuss the finer points of her sister's facial features. She stood abruptly and turned toward her bedroom.

"Hey—are you okay?" Mac asked. He was looking at her intently, clearly registering her odd reaction.

"Yeah. I just realized I forgot something," Grace said vaguely.

He frowned, but she was out of the room before he could push for more.

In her bedroom, Grace sat on the bed and stared at her hands, tightly clenched into fists in her lap.

Of all the actresses in Hollywood, Mac had cast her sister. Her cheating, lying, boyfriend-stealing, gorgeous siren of a sister.

She'd choked down a lot over the past four years. She'd sat opposite Serena at family dinners, smiled as she unwrapped Serena's Christmas gifts, listened to tales of Serena's exploits without revealing even by the flicker of an eyelid that she had any residual feelings over what had happened. Apart from her recent blowup at the family dinner, she'd personified the adage forgive and forget. But she had no idea how she was going to stomach the idea of Serena working daily with Mac, acting out the lines of dialogue that Grace had so painstakingly written. The alternative—telling Mac the full story of her break up with Owen—made her stomach churn with anxiety, however. More than anything, she didn't want him to see her as a victim.

Confused and angry and very aware that Mac would be wondering what was keeping her, Grace stood and smoothed her skirt. Taking a deep breath, she stepped out into the living room, ready to do what she'd always done where Serena was concerned—suck it up.

THE NEXT MORNING, Claudia and Sadie converged on Grace's office the moment they heard.

"I can't believe Mac would do this to you. What a butt head. I thought he was one of the good guys," Sadie said as she strode in the door.

Claudia eyed Grace narrowly and shook her head.

"I think you might be slandering Mac in vain there, Sadie. What do you think, Grace?"

Grace acknowledged Claudia's hit.

"He doesn't know. I haven't told him about Serena and Owen," she admitted. She felt as though she was dragging her voice up from the soles of her feet. She'd been feeling oddly detached ever since she'd seen her sister larger than life on her television screen last night. She felt… on hold. As though some vital part of herself had withdrawn from play.

"What?" Sadie almost screamed. "You and Mac spend practically every nonwork moment in each other's pockets and you haven't told him about the most important thing that's ever happened in your life?"

That got Grace snapping to attention, odd feeling or not.

"Owen cheating on me was not the most important thing in my life," she said.

"Yeah? Then why haven't you told Mac about it if it's so damn everyday?" Claudia asked.

Grace glared at them both mutinously. She didn't want to agree with them. To do so felt as though she'd be admitting a whole bunch of other things, too—such as that the last four years had been a fraud, that she'd been hiding out rather than being her own woman and that, far from being over Owen, she was still flailing in the debris of their breakup all these years later.

She was over him. Wasn't she? She must be—she was with Mac now. They were happy. Claudia and Sadie were wrong.

"I didn't want him to see me as a victim," Grace justified. It was a legitimate reason for withholding the story—except Claudia just put her hands on her hips and shook her head.

"You're such a bad liar, Grace. At least be honest with yourself—before you screw things up with Mac," Claudia said.

Grace flinched.

"Tell him what she did to you," Sadie said.

"I'm going to," Grace said with dignity, eyeing Claudia coolly. "I'd already decided that before you guys came in here."

"Good. That'll be the end of that nasty little skank," Sadie said, dusting her hands together as though she'd just thrown out the trash. Grace's friends had always wanted to punish Serena for her betrayal. "I still can't believe she had the gall to audition."

"She needs the work. She hasn't had anything for months now," Grace explained.

"She should have thought about that before she stuck her tongue down Owen's throat all those years ago. I wouldn't hire her if my life depended on it," Claudia said.

"Mac thinks she's great. Perfect for the part. She did a great audition," Grace said. She still felt oddly detached and spacey.

"This is Hollywood. Women like Serena really are a dime a dozen. He'll find someone else," Claudia said dismissively.

"Now we've got that settled—tell me what's going on inside that head of yours, Gracie," Sadie said, leaning forward intently. "You must be steaming that she would do this."

Grace stared over Sadie's shoulder, trying to articulate the emotions churning in her stomach.

"I think I'm just…surprised. After everything. I forgave her. And Owen. And I don't understand why she has to come into my world like this. I mean, we have an understanding—we're polite at family gatherings, but we keep our distance. Now I feel like she's invaded my backyard. Hasn't she taken enough already?"

She knew what she was saying wasn't entirely rational, but the essence of it was right. She'd made a new life for herself after Serena had destroyed her old one. But now Serena wanted to be part of that, too. It was too much. Too greedy.

Claudia nodded with approval.

"Gracie's getting angry," she said. "About time."

"I was mean to her at dinner the other night," Grace confessed.

"Yeah?" Sadie asked expectantly. "What did you say?"

Grace reported the incident and Claudia clapped her hands together with approval.

"Yay, Gracie. How did the rest of them take it?" she asked.

"Like I'd said I was having a sex-change operation."

"They're not used to you rocking the boat," Sadie said.

"Mom hates it when we fight," Grace said, suddenly feeling angry all over again. "She's called twice since dinner, wondering whether I've spoken to Serena yet. I think I'm supposed to apologize."

"No freakin' way. Serena deserves to have her ass kicked, not kissed. I think it's sick the way your family all pretend that nothing ever happened," Claudia said.

"It was the way I wanted it. I didn't want to make a fuss," Grace said.

"You're worth making a fuss over, Gracie. And what happened needs to be acknowledged—by everyone," Sadie said firmly.

It was a hard concept for Grace to get her head around. She knew her parents loved her, that her sisters loved her. But somehow, over the years, she'd gotten used to being the "other" sister, the odd one out. She never made a fuss or demanded attention or caused a drama—apart from one recent notable exception.

But maybe her friends were right. Maybe it was time to start letting her feelings be known, to actively mark her turf and defend it.

Starting with *Ocean Boulevard,* and Mac.

MAC SAT BACK in the crappy, under-padded chair in the crappy, under-decorated temporary office they'd given him out at the studio and massaged his temples. Thank God he had casting sorted out was all he could say. The latest delightful hiccup he'd had to deal with was the news that their wedding location on the Ko Olina Lagoons was out of the question thanks to the local council's decision to have the beach regraded during the week they needed to shoot. Mac had been wrangling with local bureaucrats all day, trying to talk them into rescheduling. The closest he'd come to a solution was their suggestion that the production company pay for the contractor's fees for the week he'd be stood down. Since Mac was already right on budget, that idea wasn't about to fly. Running a hand through his hair in exasperation, he clicked open the footage file on his computer. There were a number of other beaches that they'd scouted in Hawaii. There had to be somewhere else that was up to scratch.

But he couldn't stop thinking about the Lagoons as he trawled through the other footage. The location was perfect and he wanted the episode to be perfect. No—he wanted it to be more than that. He wanted it to be his second chance.

Sitting in his shoe-box office, his ass protesting the lack of padding on the seat beneath him, Mac knew it was time to come clean with himself. He wasn't dabbling in directing. He wasn't killing time or finding some way to keep himself sane while his acting contract spun itself out.

He wanted to direct. He wanted to tell stories from behind the camera instead of in front of it.

He knew the chances of him transitioning from a role as a beefcake heartthrob on a daytime soap to the role of respected director were slim, if not non-existent. And for a long time, that cynical, realistic piece of knowledge had held him back from being honest with himself. But lately, he'd found himself daring to hope again. Daring to dream the impossible dream.

Why the hell not, after all? He'd tried and failed before. He'd been lying around licking his wounds for the last little while, true—but it hadn't killed him. It might even have made him stronger.

Admitting the full truth to himself was like standing in the sunshine after months of rain. First Grace and now this. Things were looking up.

Grace. Just thinking her name made him smile. Among other things. Adjusting his jeans, he allowed himself a moment of indulgence at the end of a frustrating day.

He was crazy about her. Probably in love with her, if he was going to carry this honesty jag through to the end. He'd started dreaming things where she was concerned, too. Things that included not having separate addresses and spare toothbrushes at each other's houses.

The past week or so had been great. The distance he'd always felt between them was gone. She'd opened up, put her trust in him. And he was determined not to abuse it. Grinning like an idiot, he wondered how long he'd have to wait before he tried to talk her into moving in with him. There was plenty of room at his place. He'd already earmarked one of the upstairs bedrooms for conversion into her study. He'd even covertly scouted a cherrywood desk that would be the perfect place for Grace to work from. He loved the idea of knowing she would be there when he came home, of waking with her every morning. Very quickly—scarily quickly—she'd become central to his life.

A knock on the office door drew him out of his reverie.

"Come in," he called.

The door opened and he hid his surprise when he saw Serena Watts standing there.

"Hi," she said uncertainly. "Have you got a moment?"

He gestured for her to come in, then realized he didn't have another chair to offer her.

"Sorry, this office is a little low on home comforts," he apologized, wondering why she was here. He'd contacted her agent and offered her the part that morning.

He hoped like hell she wasn't going to try to pressure him for more money. Grace's sister or not, he had a budget to consider.

"My agent called and said you'd offered me the part," Serena said, her voice husky.

He couldn't help feeling a little thrill of satisfaction—that sexy voice was exactly what he'd been looking for for the part of Tania. He'd seen hundreds of beautiful women during the casting process, but sexy was a whole other ball game from beautiful. Grace had sexy in spades and so did Serena. Must run in the family.

"Yep. Did you have some questions? If it's about the contract, I should confess up front that I'm a complete legal dufus," he said.

Serena shook her head, then bit her lip. It was odd seeing

someone who looked so much like Grace use one of Grace's little habits. Not that Serena and Grace looked that much alike or he wouldn't have been fooled by Serena's stage name. But the resemblance was there, now that he knew to look for it. They had the same amazing, creamy skin. The same nose. Grace's eyes were green to Serena's pale-blue, however, and he much preferred their exotic tilt. Grace's mouth was more generous, too—wider and fuller. Judging by conventional standards, Serena was the more beautiful. But Grace had her sister beat in his book. She was the whole package, a gorgeous face and a hot body, all of it powered by a mind like a steel trap. It might not float some guys' boats, but it did a lot for him. He was figuring it would do enough for him to last a lifetime, in fact.

"Have I got spinach in my teeth?" Serena asked self-consciously.

He realized he'd been staring, and he laughed guiltily.

"Sorry, I was just looking for the family resemblance. I took your audition over to Grace's last night to celebrate—you have no idea how long we've been looking for Tania—and I was pretty thrown when she told me you were her sister. You should have said something at the audition," he said. "Not that it would have made a difference to the outcome, but it would have made up for not being invited to that family dinner you guys had a few weeks' back."

It was a joke, but Serena didn't laugh. Instead, she looked sick.

"God, this is just getting worse," she said. She looked around the office as though she was searching for something to throw up in. Since there wasn't anything, Mac fervently hoped he was wrong.

"Hey. Um, maybe you ought to sit down," he said, jumping up to offer her his own chair.

She shook her head. "I'm okay. I just didn't know you and Grace were…seeing each other."

He shrugged philosophically. "Why doesn't that surprise me? Grace is the best keeper of secrets I've ever met. But you must know that."

Serena swallowed noisily. "She didn't always used to be like that. She used to be the most open person in the world."

Okay, now she was going to cry, he was fairly certain. Not only did he not have a sick bucket, he didn't have a box of tissues, either.

But Serena was blinking rapidly and taking a deep breath.

"I'll just say what I need to say, and then I'll leave," she said with determination. "I can't take the part. I wanted to tell you in person because I didn't want you to get the wrong idea. But I guess you must know why I'm here, since you know Grace so well."

She looked utterly miserable and the tears that had been threatening finally welled up.

"I'm so sorry. I'll get out of your hair," Serena said.

"Don't be silly. Couple of tears won't kill me—have you seen how many women work on this show?" he joked.

"I hope it doesn't muck you around too much, me not taking the part. I should never have gone to the audition. It was stupid, but my car broke down and I really needed the money…."

Since she'd refused his offer of his chair, Mac sank back into it and Serena parked her butt on the corner of his desk. In the calculating budding-director's part of his brain, he hoped it was because she wanted him to talk her into taking the part. The last thing he needed was to have to recast when he'd already found the perfect actress.

"Sounds like a pretty good reason for taking the part to me," he said lightly, testing the waters.

Serena stared at him, her blue eyes wide and luminous with tears. She was one of those rare women who could cry and remain beautiful and she looked the picture of tragedy.

"How can you even say that, now you know who I am?" she said. She sounded a little annoyed, as if Mac had just put his hand on her knee or something.

That was the second time she'd referred to some knowledge he was supposed to have, something to do with her identity. He frowned, suddenly remembering last night and the way Grace had reacted when she'd seen her sister's face on her television screen. For a second he'd got the old feeling from her as she smiled and explained who Serena was. Then she'd left the room for a few minutes before returning to ask all the right questions. The feeling that she had withdrawn from him had faded and he'd let the moment go.

"You know that thing I was talking about before, about Grace being a good keeper of secrets? I think we might be stumbling through the middle of one right now," he said. "You want to tell me what it is you think I already know, Serena?"

If it was possible, Serena's face got even paler.

"God, you *don't* know any of it? Shit," she said.

The sick look was back, and more tears. Mac stood and put his hand on her shoulder, stooping to make eye contact with her.

"What the hell is going on?" he asked gently but firmly.

GRACE HAD WAITED till the end of the day to drive out to the studio to confess all to Mac. She'd almost convinced herself that he wouldn't be fazed, that she wouldn't see a return of that frustrated look that had been such a frequent feature of the early days of their relationship. She should have told him ages ago. Claudia was right. Damn her.

Why hadn't she? Part of it was genuinely that she hadn't wanted him to look at her with pity. She didn't need his sympathy. Perhaps it was as simple as the fact that she didn't want to acknowledge it. Sadie had called the Owen-Serena thing the most important thing in her life. She hated to think of it that way. It was part of the reason she'd moved on when she'd found out about Owen—she hadn't wanted to acknowledge how hurt she'd been, how devastated. If she never talked about it, it hadn't happened. Her reasoning had almost been that simple.

But now it was all unraveling. She'd snapped at Serena at the family dinner, despite having told herself and the world for four years that she'd forgiven her sister. And now she was filled with rage that her sister had dared to step onto her turf at the *Boulevard*. Grace was only just now beginning to realize that she hadn't forgiven her sister—not by a long shot. Ever since she'd seen Serena's face staring at her from her own TV last night, anger had been percolating inside her.

Her sister had crept into her life and stolen her lover. She had destroyed the world that Grace had created with Owen, the future they'd imagined with each other. Serena had seen something—someone—that she wanted and she'd taken it, with no thought to the consequences for Grace, her own sister.

Because they were the closest in age, she and Serena had played together the most when they were children. They'd plaited each other's hair, jumped rope, had Barbie doll adventures together using homemade miniature furniture and mommade clothes. Then puberty had intervened and boys had become the most important thing, and the world had been divided into the beautiful and the not-so-beautiful for Grace.

She'd started staying home from the beauty pageants, working on articles for the school newspaper or going thrift-shop trawling with her beloved Nana Wellington. Naturally, she and Serena had drifted apart, but they'd still been sisters. Grace had still agonized over getting the perfect Christmas or birthday gift for her sister and looked forward to the occasional dinner or movie with Serena.

And Serena had abused that trust. She had chosen her own comfort and desire over that of a loved one.

Grace was trembling as she negotiated her way through the warren of corridors, on the lookout for Mac's temporary office. She realized all of a sudden that she didn't just *need* to tell Mac about it all—she *wanted* to tell him. And not only because of the situation they were in, but because she knew he loved her and that somehow, by sharing her pain, she could somehow move through it, rather than pushing it aside and pretending it didn't exist.

She'd tried that for four years, and it hadn't worked worth a damn—witness the merry dance she'd led Mac on and her ongoing battle with intimacy.

Spotting the door she was looking for, Grace took a deep breath, rapped once sharply and opened the door.

What she saw sent bile bubbling up the back of her throat and pure, unadulterated rage ricocheting around her body.

Mac was standing in front of Serena, who was seated on the corner of his desk in a classic come-on pose. His hand was on Serena's shoulder, his head lowered toward hers. They looked cozy. Close. Like two people on the verge of something.

Grace's lip curled even as her hands found her hips and she slipped into Bette Davis mode instinctively.

"Didn't take you two long, did it?" she drawled.

Mac dropped his hand, a frown creasing his forehead as

he instinctively stepped away from her sister. Too late—Grace had already caught him red-handed.

Images from another long-ago scene flashed across Grace's mind—Owen's contrite face, Serena scrabbling desperately for something to cover herself as Grace stood, aghast, trying to comprehend what she'd walked into. And all around them, leaning against the walls of Owen's studio, hanging from the walls, dozens of portraits of Serena. Serena laughing. Serena crying. Serena in ecstasy. All nudes, all amazing, Owen's best work. A damning, graphic homage to her sister's beauty and evidence that the man that Grace loved had been betraying her systematically with her sister for months on end.

Serena had a hand pressed to her mouth and was shaking her head, but Grace had nothing to say to her. She fixed her gaze on Mac, the man she'd thought she was in love with.

"All the talk, all the big promises. But when it came down to it it's always the same, isn't it? Little head rules big head. I hope she's worth it, Mac. Owen thought so—he spent six months screwing her behind my back," she said, turning away before her anger deserted her and the hurt lapping at her ankles rose up to engulf her.

She'd believed in Mac. Stupid stupid stupid.

Mac lunged forward and grabbed her arm before she could get to the door.

"Wait—this isn't what you think," he said.

Maybe it was the feel of his hand on her skin when she knew he'd just been touching Serena. Maybe it was the ridiculous leap her heart made, wanting to believe him. Whatever the reason, the outcome was the same: she lost it.

Spectacularly. Wrenching her arm free from his gasp, she swung her open palm at his face and slapped him so hard his head rocked.

"Don't you ever lay a finger on me again. I don't want to hear your voice, see your face, nothing. You have lied to me over and over and you've thrown away everything that we had. You make me sick, you bastard, sick to my stomach with your bullshit about trust and friendship and the future," she screamed. "Go screw yourself, and take that faithless slut with you. You deserve each other."

Then she was out the door, her hand stinging from its impact with his face, her body vibrating with rage.

10

GRACE HAD NO RECOLLECTION of the drive back to her apartment. She slammed her way inside, still trembling with anger, but there was no one to scream and yell at so she wound up pacing, her hands clenched into fists.

She kept seeing the red imprint of her hand on Mac's shocked face, wishing that she'd punched him and kicked him in the balls and really hurt him, the way he'd really hurt her.

Because it was useless to pretend he hadn't. He'd cut her to the bone.

The sound of someone pounding on her front door broke her feverish pacing and she made a bet with herself that it would be Mac. She was reaching for the phone, ready to call the police and have him charged with whatever they could come up with when she heard her sister's voice.

"If you don't let me in, Grace, I'm going to kick this goddamn door down," Serena hollered. "I'll get a rock and smash this little window and open the lock or I'll go to the nearest Home Depot and get an axe and hack my way in."

Grace put the phone down and resumed pacing. She felt sick with reaction as her adrenaline ebbed and she rushed to the bathroom to retch into the basin. She was washing her mouth out when she heard the unmistakable sound of glass shattering and she realized her sister hadn't been making empty threats.

Outrage welled up inside her and she stalked through her apartment to the front hallway just as Serena was letting herself in.

"How *dare* you come in here," Grace said, her voice low and venomous. She felt as though her body would split open with anger, as though mere flesh and bone could not contain her white-hot rage.

To her utter astonishment, Serena's chin came up and she lunged forward, shoving Grace hard in the chest, just like a frustrated child at the end of her tether. Grace staggered backward, lost her balance and fell flat on her butt.

Serena loomed over her, her face ugly with emotion.

"Just shut up and listen for five seconds! You could have killed yourself driving like that on the freeway. I thought you were going to die when you cut in front of that truck. And all for nothing. Nothing happened between me and Mac just now. I went to see him to tell him I couldn't take the part. Then he told me you two were in a relationship and I figured he must know about me and Owen and I got emotional. But he didn't know and I was just about to explain to him when you walked in."

Grace glared mutinously at her sister.

"I don't have to listen to this," she said, trying to get to her feet again.

Serena pushed her down again and held her there, her face just inches from Grace's as she made her case.

"Do you really think I would do that to you again?" she asked, her voice breaking. "Do you really think I would hurt you like that again?"

Her face crumpled and she began to cry. Letting go of Grace's shoulders, she sank to the ground until she was huddled in an abject squat.

"I know I deserve every bad thing you've ever thought about me, but you have to believe me, Gracie, there is not a day that goes by when I don't regret what happened with Owen.

"I hate myself for what I did to you. I know I am a horrible, horrible person. But I have learned from that mistake and I would never, ever do that to you or anyone ever again," Serena said.

Looking at her sister's huddled form, hearing the sincerity in her voice, Grace knew she was speaking the truth. Nothing had happened with Mac. Somehow, though, it didn't seem to make a difference to the maelstrom of feelings swirling inside her. She'd had four years to think about Serena's betrayal. They'd never really talked about it, except for one awkward conversation when Serena had offered up a bunch of feeble excuses and Grace had assured her she forgave her.

The first of many lies that Grace had told herself.

She'd never been able to understand why her sister did what she did or forgive her her actions. Owen, too. How could the man who had slept beside her every night for five years—who had been inside her body, who'd dried her tears and cheered her victories—throw away everything that had happened between them so readily? It was unfathomable to Grace, who prized her friendships and family above all else. She would rather die than hurt Sadie or Claudia or any of her sisters the way Owen and Serena had hurt her.

"Why?" she demanded suddenly, needing to know after four years of silence.

Serena didn't seem to hear her and Grace stretched out a foot and none too gently nudged her sister with it.

"Why? Why did you sleep with him?" she yelled, unable to contain the anger inside herself.

Serena lost her balance and rocked back onto her ass. Her face was a wet mask of running makeup and tears and she sniffed mightily as she nodded.

"Okay, okay. This conversation has been a long time coming, I know," she said.

She swiped at her tears with her hands, wiped them dry inelegantly on her jeans. "Four years ago I had just turned thirty," Serena began.

"I know how goddamn old you are. I'm your sister!" Grace said belligerently.

Serena grabbed her handbag from the floor nearby and threw it at Grace, narrowly missing her head.

"Just listen. You want to know and I'm telling you. This is the only way I know how," Serena yelled.

Grace glared at her, but didn't say anything else and Serena started talking again.

"I'd just turned thirty and I'd been going to auditions for nearly ten years. And I still hadn't scored a break. Every week I was out at auditions, being told I was too tall, too short, too brunette, too skinny, too fat, too whatever that made me unsuitable for the parts I wanted. You don't know what it's like wanting something you can't have, Grace. You've succeeded at everything you've ever put your hand to. You got great marks in school, you edited the school paper, you got a scholarship to UCLA and you walked out of university and straight into a job with a production company."

"This isn't about me. This is about why you threw away twenty-eight years of being my sister so you could hop into bed with my boyfriend," Grace said contemptuously.

Serena's jaw tightened and she looked as if she might cry again, but she stuck to her guns.

"When I turned thirty and I was still a waitress and not an

actress, I made a deal with myself. I was going to quit, give up and do something else. Except I couldn't do it. Every time I tried to think of another life to live, I came up blank. I wasn't smart enough to go back to college and qualify for anything, and I'm hopeless at all things admin-related. I realized that if I stopped trying to be an actress, then I had to accept what I was—a thirty-year-old waitress who was going to become a forty-year-old waitress and then a fifty-year-old waitress.

"That scared the crap out of me, Grace. And I was still freaking out when I saw Owen again at Mom's fiftieth birthday party. I always thought he was a nice guy. Then he called me a few weeks later and asked me to sit for him. He explained that he had an exhibition coming up, and he needed a model, and he wanted that person to be me.

"I was so flattered. For the first time in what felt like forever, someone was choosing *me,* not one of the hundreds of other hopefuls. Then I sat for him and he was so charming and flattering. He told me I had perfect features, that I was a portrait artist's dream. He told me that just capturing the texture of my skin on canvas was going to take months. He told me… It doesn't really matter what he told me, actually, because it was all crap, really. He just wanted to screw me. And I let him, because he made me feel special again. He made me feel like I wasn't just a waitress. I didn't think about you, Grace. I didn't let myself. I kept telling myself that I needed something to keep me going."

Serena had been studying her hands as she spoke, twisting her fingers together, grasping them tightly then releasing them. Now she looked at Grace, her blue eyes clear and honest.

"None of it's an excuse. And I know I can never make it up to you. But it's how I felt. It's why it happened. I hated myself afterward when I realized what I'd done. But I was a coward. I couldn't end it because it felt like the only thing I had and I was too scared to face reality. And I wound up hurting one of the people who means more to me than anything else in the world."

Grace broke eye contact, focusing her gaze beyond her sister's shoulder as she mulled over the past.

"I should never have even thought about auditioning for *Ocean Boulevard,*" Serena said. "I knew it was wrong, but I needed the money and… Again, I was being selfish. I fooled myself into believing that you didn't care. That you really had forgiven me. But deep inside I knew that you hadn't. That maybe you never would."

"Why should I? What's in it for me?" Grace said coldly. It had taken her so long to find her rage, she wasn't letting it go without a fight.

Serena nodded as though she accepted this, as though it was only her due.

"I want you to go," Grace said, pushing herself to her feet. She didn't want to look at her sister's huddled miserableness anymore. She wanted to feel pure in her anger, righteous and justified. She didn't want there to be consequences or feelings at the other end of the equation. Serena didn't deserve her understanding or her consideration or her compassion.

"I'll send you the bill for the window," Grace said.

Serena stood and walked past Grace to fetch her handbag.

"Thank you for listening. If you have any questions, if there's anything else you want to know—even if you just want to scream at me—you know where to find me," Serena said.

Grace crossed her arms over her chest and locked her jaw, willing her sister to go. Serena nodded, then headed for the door. At last.

Serena had disappeared down the outside staircase before Grace registered that the phone had not rung once while they had been talking. And that no one else had pulled up with a screech of tires in front of her apartment. She hustled to the top of the stairs.

"Hey!" she hollered down to Serena.

Her sister turned back, a ridiculous expression of hope on her face. Grace almost snorted with disbelief. Did her sister really think it was going to be that easy? That Grace would just open her arms and forgive her after a bit of crying and self-recrimination?

"Did Mac say anything?" she called down.

Serena stared at Grace for a beat, then shook her head.

"I explained more about me and Owen before I came after you. But he didn't say anything," Serena called back.

Grace frowned. In her heart of hearts, ever since she'd calmed down enough to accept that Serena was telling her the truth, that she'd misinterpreted what she'd seen, she'd expected Mac to be hot on her heels the way Serena had been. Grace had expected him to see past her furious slap and insults to the pain and fear she'd been feeling. She'd expected him to understand. He always had before. He'd taken everything she threw at him and bounced back. He'd been patient. He'd been caring and kind.

Grace bit her lip as her sister got into her car and drove away.

Surely Mac hadn't taken to heart the things she'd said to him? She tried to remember exactly *what* she had said. Something about never wanting to see him again.

But he'd know that wasn't true. Right?

And something else about him having lied to her again and again and again.

Grace winced. She'd been so angry, she hadn't really been

rational. Owen was the one who had lied to her, not Mac. But, again, Mac knew he hadn't lied to her.

Then she'd told him to go fornicate with himself and various other insults that were neither here nor there. If you weren't on the receiving end of them.

The soft patter of rain on her face prompted her to return to her apartment.

Shutting the door behind her, she stared at the crushed glass beneath her feet with a complete lack of comprehension, her mind occupied elsewhere.

Mac wasn't coming. He wasn't calling. He'd had enough.

And why wouldn't he have?

She remembered the conversation they'd had in her apartment that Sunday after her family dinner. Mac had challenged her to be honest about her feelings, to stop holding back with him. He'd told her he couldn't make their relationship work on his own.

He wasn't angry because she'd insulted him or because she'd slapped him. He was angry because she hadn't told him the truth. Because she'd withheld herself and her past from him. The past ten days of increased intimacy had shown both of them that what they had together was real, lasting.

But it all had been based on a lie. Her lie. She'd kept her most painful secret hidden, locked away. And now he knew what she'd done.

And he'd given up.

The magnitude of what she'd done hit her like a freight train. She'd fallen in love with Mac and he had fallen in love with her—and she'd pushed him away because she was a coward, because she hadn't dealt with the pain from her past.

She was already crying by the time she got to the phone. Claudia answered on the second ring.

"I'm such an idiot," Grace sobbed.

"Where are you?" Claudia asked.

"Home."

"Sadie and I will be there as soon as we can," Claudia promised.

Grace ended the call and sank down onto the couch.

She occupied the time before her friends' arrival mentally reviewing all the times Mac had reached out to her and she had pushed him away.

She felt as though she'd woken from a deep, dreamless sleep. She'd been so paralyzed by fear of rejection, so busy repressing the pain and anger from her breakup with Owen, that she had pushed away the sexiest, funniest, most clever man she'd ever known.

By the time Claudia and Sadie were enfolding her in their arms, she'd worked herself into a hiccupping state. She was so disgusted with herself that she couldn't accept her friends' comfort for long and she struggled out of their embraces to pace the space between her couches and her dining table.

"I've ruined everything," she said. "He has been so generous, so patient, and I slapped him in the face and told him I never wanted to see him again. I'm such a coward. I never even told him I loved him—I never told him half of what I was feeling. I was always too scared. All this time I've been walking around doing Bette Davis and tearing men apart limb from limb—and it's all a big joke. I'm not tough. I'm the biggest yellow belly out there. I'm a gutless wonder."

Claudia and Sadie took up positions on the couch and Sadie nudged the box of tissues forward.

"Just in case you want to blow your nose or anything," she hinted. Grace guessed that meant she had more than tears on her face. She grabbed a fistful of tissues and blew her nose with a noisy honk.

"I take it things didn't go so great with telling Mac about Serena and Owen?" Claudia asked.

Quickly Grace filled them in, dropping onto the other couch halfway through and pressing her head into her hands.

"Wow, you really hit him?" Claudia said.

"I nearly took his head off."

"A slap four years in the making. What a pity you wasted it on Mac instead of that rat Owen," Sadie said.

Grace's head came up and she bared her teeth in a growl.

"Don't even say his name. How I wish I had hit him all those years ago. I should have hit him and kicked him and punched him. I should have shredded his clothes and keyed his car and given his favorite possessions away to the homeless."

"Now you're talking. You know, Gracie, it's never too late to pay Owen a little visit. Sadie and I will be your wingmen. Any man who diddles a woman's sister for six months behind her back deserves a bit of harassment."

Grace managed a watery smile. "You guys are so good to me. And I'm such a selfish cow," she said, dissolving into tears once more as she was again hit with the big mess she'd made of things.

"I want to hear more about Serena. She was really upset, huh?" Sadie asked, exhibiting a not entirely humane interest in Serena's misery. "You really gave it to her, right?"

"I made her squirm," Grace said dully. "But you know what? I get the feeling she's pretty miserable anyway. Her career's in the toilet. She's essentially a full-time waitress these days. She's thirty-four now. Not many actresses get their big breaks after thirty."

"Boo hoo," Claudia said unsympathetically.

Grace's tears had slowed, and she took a deep, shuddering breath.

"I need to make this right, guys. I may have blown it with Mac for good. I may have pushed him away once too often. But I have to try to make it right," she said.

Claudia shook her head.

"You have to sort *you* out first, Gracie," she said firmly. "You've been sitting on a powder keg of emotion for four years, pretending that none of it mattered. But we all know it matters a lot. At the risk of sounding like a complete wanker, you need to honor the hurt you felt when Owen and Serena betrayed you. No more sweeping it under the rug."

"It's been four years, Gracie. Talk to us," Sadie said.

Grace stared at her two dear friends. Inside her, the old hurt was rising to the surface. There was nowhere for it to go but out. And she realized she wanted it out, wanted it gone.

"Do you know the thing that got me the most?" she said, her voice low with intensity. "He never painted me. Not once in five years. But he couldn't get enough of Serena. All those paintings. And they were so good. Because she was beautiful."

The tears started again, and out it all came—how she'd felt when she walked in the door of Owen's studio and found him entangled with her sister. How she'd stared, unable to comprehend what she was seeing.

She started to get angry as she remembered Owen's apologies, his pleas for understanding. But she saved the worst anger for herself as she recalled how much she'd wanted to believe in Owen, to accept and understand because she was so afraid of losing him.

"And then the little shit went and used all those nudes in his show after you'd taken him back," Sadie remembered with a disgusted shake of her head.

"I will never forget walking into that gallery with you, Gracie, and seeing all those paintings of your sister staring back at us. I wanted to kill him for what he'd done to you," Claudia said. She was crying, too, and she crossed to Grace's couch and took her in her arms.

"I love you so much, babe. It was one of the worst moments in my life seeing you hurt so much," she said, her voice muffled as she hugged Grace tight.

Grace held on for dear life and pressed her face into Claudia's shoulder. Sadie and Claudia had been the best of friends that night. They'd hustled her out the door and offered to visit hellfire and damnation on Owen on her behalf. But Grace had only wanted to do one thing—go home and pack. She'd spent two hours collecting her clothes and books from the apartment she'd shared with Owen for so long and then she'd walked out the door.

And after that moment, she'd never cried or spoken about what had happened. Owen had taken so much from her, she'd reasoned. She didn't want to give him any more of her time or energy or emotion. Sadie and Claudia had tried to get her to talk, to rant, to rage, but Grace had refused. She'd lied and said she was over it. She'd moved on. It was dust already, gone.

But really, Grace acknowledged to herself now, she'd been unable to face the depth of her feelings. The breadth of her anger. The width of hurt. She'd stuffed the monster down deep inside and pretended that she didn't care. And she'd taken steps to ensure she would never, ever be vulnerable like that again.

And poor Mac had inherited all that grief, all that anger. He'd put his hand out to offer her love and friendship and companionship, and she'd acted as though he were offering her hemlock.

Why had he bothered? But she knew. All the time that she'd been falling in love with him despite herself, he'd been falling in love with her. She remembered the conversation they'd had about love the day after their first night together, how they'd both claimed not to believe in it for themselves anymore. They'd both been lying. But Mac had been so much braver than her. He'd been willing to take a chance on love when he recognized it.

He'd cajoled her into delaying her decision and cooked her that silly, disastrous meal to impress her. Then he'd laid himself on the line when she'd tried to have her cake and eat it too, having a relationship with him but keeping him at a distance.

But today she'd pushed him too far.

They talked long into the night, Claudia and Sadie offering their wisdom, jokes, love and support. They drank innumerable cups of tea and coffee and, finally, at three in the morning her friends tucked her into her bed. She was puffy-faced and slit-eyed from crying so much, and utterly exhausted. But she felt at peace. Four years of solid emotion had dissolved inside her. She wasn't naive enough to think that she'd exorcised all her ghosts in one night—but she'd made a good start. She'd been honest with herself for the first time in years. And she knew what she wanted.

She wanted Mac. She was going to try to get him, too.

She just hoped he had it in him to believe in her one more time.

MAC WOKE WITH GRITTY EYES and a frown on his face. For a few seconds he had no idea what was wrong and then memory returned. Grace. The scene in his office. The revelation about her sister. The knowledge was like a weight landing on his chest.

He'd been so angry last night. He couldn't understand why

she hadn't told him about Serena and her ex from the beginning. He had been building some pretty substantial castles in the sky where she was concerned. He'd been thinking kids, a bigger house, shared projects, shared forever. And she'd been keeping a pretty damn substantial truth to herself.

He'd known she'd been hurt, that she was vulnerable. Right from the start he'd sensed that about her. And he'd been patient. But he was beginning to suspect that Grace had been speaking the truth when she'd said that she didn't want a man in her life. Maybe she was just too damaged. Maybe that shit Owen had snapped her heart and her trust in two and it would never be the same again.

As he stared blindly at the sunlight speckling the ceiling, he made the decision he'd put off making last night, knowing that he was too angry, too reactive to think clearly. Maybe it was time to give up on the dream of him and Grace and acknowledge to himself that she was unable to meet him halfway.

God, what a miserable conclusion. He dropped his forearm across his eyes and took a deep, rib-cracking breath.

Feeling distinctly grim, he showered and dressed for work and drove out to the studio. He threw himself into work all morning, narrowing his thoughts to just the matter at hand. It didn't stop him from thinking about her entirely. He wasn't completely reconciled to the decision his rational self wanted to make. He was aware in the back of his mind that he was disappointed she hadn't called. Just like she hadn't called him last night, either.

Was she waiting for him to run to her again?

He was all run out.

Which meant that his gut was right—it was over between them.

He spent the morning wrangling with a local council

official in Hawaii and by the time he put the phone down he'd successfully negotiated for the sand regrading to be delayed a few weeks. He had his star location back. He felt a warm glow of satisfaction and anticipation, closely followed by the realization that he had no one to share his good news with.

Damn Grace and her ironclad fortress of a heart. Double damn her sister and her faithless ex for making her that way.

"Mac."

His head shot up as he recognized Claudia's voice. He'd been so absorbed in his thoughts that he hadn't heard her knock on his door.

"How are you doing?" she asked neutrally, her dark eyes scanning his face searchingly.

"Good. Managed to sort out the problem with Ko Olina Lagoons, so we're back on there."

"That's great, but I meant how are *you* doing?" she asked, propping her butt on the edge of his desk.

He shrugged. Obviously Sadie and Claudia knew what had gone down last night.

"How is she?" he asked neutrally.

"Getting there, I think. I gave her the day off work," she said.

"Good."

"Mac, I think you're a nice man. And I think you're good for Grace and I know she feels very strongly for you, so even though I hate people who interfere in other people's love lives, I'm going to break my own rule for Grace," Claudia said.

She made sure she had his attention before continuing.

"The thing with Grace is she's the most generous person in the world with her time and attention and love, but she refuses to share her hurts. Sadie and I have been trying to train her out of the habit, but as you've probably realized, she's pretty damned stubborn," Claudia said. There was a break in her voice and a suspicious sheen to her eyes. She blinked rapidly a few times.

"Grace has always had to fight long and hard to feel good about herself. She grew up in a house where beauty was the ultimate commodity. You've seen Serena—Hope and Felicity are just as gorgeous. Grace has always felt like the ugly duckling. She's always tried to fight on her own terms, her own ground. None of it was helped by the fact that she never had a lot of luck with men. She really thought Owen was different. But when Owen chose Serena over her, I think something inside her just couldn't fight anymore."

She held his eye, then reached out and put a hand on his shoulder.

"I guess what I'm trying to say, Mac, is don't give up on her," she said.

Mac stared at his desk for a long time after Claudia left. What she'd told him made sense, confirmed so many of his half-formed ideas about Grace.

But he shouldn't have to rely on Grace's friends to give him insights into the woman he loved. As much as he wanted to make the world right for her, the next move was Grace's. Judging by the lack of phone calls, she'd made it.

It was over.

11

GRACE DRESSED VERY CAREFULLY. She'd had all day to recover from her crying marathon. She'd slept in, taken a calming bath, drunk lots of water. She'd also made an appointment with a counselor that Sadie had recommended. There was still old stuff to excavate. She wanted it all out in the open. She didn't want to be ruled by the past anymore.

It was late afternoon when she stepped back to survey herself in the full-length mirror inside her wardrobe door.

She was wearing her most elegant outfit—a princess-line sleeveless dress with a cream bodice and a black flared skirt. The high neck featured a black collar and the armholes were similarly trimmed with black. It hugged her curves faithfully and paired with a pair of black pumps and a cream clutch purse, she looked damned fine.

She wanted to look great. She wanted to feel utterly sure of herself. Turning to her dressing table, she automatically reached for her glasses. Somehow, though, her hand ended up hovering over them as she stared down at their heavy black frames.

Sadie and Claudia hated her glasses. Her mother did, too. Mac had never said anything, but he always removed them at the first opportunity. Grace considered them briefly. They *were* thick and dark and chunky. She'd always felt safe behind them, armored.

But it was time to stop hiding.

Before she could rethink her decision, she dropped the frames to the floor and pressed the ball of her stiletto-clad foot against a lens. The crack of vintage plastic snapping sounded in her apartment. Stooping, she scooped the fragments into the garbage. Then she scouted out the contact lenses Sadie had insisted she wear for the wedding-that-never-was to Greg. It took several attempts to get them in but, five minutes later, Grace was sweeping out the door.

It was mid-afternoon and the traffic was reasonably light. She made good time as she traveled to the freeway and got on the ramp to take her south.

Just over two hours later, she exited the 405 and wound her way through the streets of La Jolla. The gleaming towers of the Mormon temple were like a beacon ahead of her as she followed the instructions she'd written down.

Finally, she pulled up in a quiet suburban street in front of an unpretentious weatherboard house. She removed her head scarf, checked her lipstick and hair, then exited the Corvette. Her heels clicked quietly on the paving stones as she made her way to a faded-blue door. A piece of cardboard that had obviously been ripped from a box was wedged in the door frame. She read it in a glance: Johnny, come around the back.

She wasn't Johnny, but she figured the invitation was good enough for her as well.

She rounded the house to find a large shed sprawling across most of the backyard. Two huge double doors opened onto the small lawn. Inside the shed, she could see canvases piled against the walls, standing in easels and stacked in piles. One easel stood in the center of the sunlight spilling in the doorway and in front of it stood a man with paint-splotched clothes and long, flowing dark hair.

Owen.

He turned his head slightly as he heard her approach, his eyes not leaving his work, his brush busy on the canvas.

"Hi. I'll be with you in a minute—unless you're selling something and then I don't want to know," he said.

Her heels sank into the lawn as she moved closer. Her stomach was turning flip-flops and her fingers were tingling with adrenaline and unease. Her denial had made him far more important in her life than he should have been. She was here to kick the skeleton out of the closet.

He looked shorter than she remembered, a little thicker around the waist. His arms were tanned a deep brown, probably from working in the sun as he was now.

She stopped just a few feet behind him.

"Hello, Owen," she said.

He froze for a beat.

"Grace?" he said, pivoting on one foot. His face was twisted in disbelief.

They stared at each other for a long moment, each taking in the changes in the other. His hair had receded a little, but his brown eyes were just as compelling and lively, his lips still as ready to smile. She wondered if he would notice that her hair was longer and darker than when he'd known her and that she'd lost a bit of weight.

"You look exactly how I remember you," he said after a long silence. "You look great."

His words and his half smile tugged on a raft of memories, some good, some bad. She took her sunglasses off so she could look him in the eye.

"I came to tell you some things that I should have told you four years ago," she said.

He nodded, then widened his stance as though he was bracing himself.

"All right," he said.

She took a deep breath and called to mind the things she wanted to say.

"You hurt me," she said. "I loved you so much. I believed in you and I couldn't imagine my world without you. And you betrayed me with my sister. You broke my family as well as my heart, Owen. I want to know why. Why would you be so cruel to someone who had only ever loved you?"

It was hard to get it out without crying, but she'd shed her tears last night. She was proud of the fact that her voice didn't break and that she held his eye throughout.

He swallowed noisily and went to run a hand through his hair, only remembering at the last minute that he was still holding a paint brush.

"Good questions," he said, nodding as he dumped his brush in a jar full of turpentine nearby. "You want to go inside to talk? Have a coffee?"

She shook her head. She didn't want to see what kind of life he'd made for himself, whether he was living with another woman. She wanted closure, then she wanted out.

"At least come inside the shed. That fair skin of yours will burn in seconds," he said.

Wordlessly she followed him into the shady interior of the shed. He unfolded a deck chair for her and one for himself, then gestured for her to take a seat. She did, sitting with her knees tightly together, her eyes fixed on his face.

"Okay," Owen said, clearing his throat. "First up, Gracie, I want you to know that I have regretted what I did to you every day since you walked into that studio and saw me and

Serena. I loved you too, believe it or not. It was only when I'd trashed it all that I realized how much."

"Then why…?" she asked. She didn't know if she would be able to understand. But she had to ask.

"You were working on that kids' TV show, remember?" he said. "Man, I was so proud of you when you were nominated for that award. You were doing so well. I knew you were going to get where you wanted to be. You've got that thing, Gracie, that thing that some people have—like you've been sprinkled with fairy dust. Gorgeous, smart as a whip, talented. You were always going to get whatever you went after."

"I only ever wanted you," she said.

"Yeah. That's how dumb I am, eh? I looked at you, with your award nomination and all those screen credits piling up and I looked at me and all I saw was shit. Dross. Old ideas, no originality, nothing. I had that show booked and I didn't have a freakin' clue how I was going to fill a gallery with the whole load of nothing I had in my head.

"Then I saw Serena at your mom's place and there was a sadness in her, a kind of desperation that I understood. I asked her to sit for me. And we got talking, as you do when you're sharing the same space for hours on end. She told me about her work, about how much she hated waiting tables. How she was getting varicose veins in her legs from standing all day, how sick she was of guys hitting on her because they thought she'd be grateful for any kind of attention with such a shit job. She knew she was going nowhere. And I knew how that felt. One afternoon, we both hit rock bottom at the same time.

"We were just looking for some comfort, I guess. And once we'd started, it seemed pointless to stop. The damage was done, right? I felt so low and guilty, going home to you at night, but it was like all the dark stuff turned on something inside me and I could paint again. So I started doing those nudes of Serena. The best work I ever did. And then you walked in and found us."

Owen placed his hands palm down on his knees and met her eye.

"I didn't plan it, Grace. I didn't seduce her. I didn't intend for anything to happen. It just did. And every time I saw her I knew I was a shit—that I was hurting you, that we had to stop. But I couldn't give up the painting," he admitted.

Grace nodded. She could remember how restless he'd been when he'd been given the show, all the nights he'd paced and drunk too much and ranted about having no ideas, no talent, no future. She'd rubbed his shoulders and pulled out his folio and shown him his work, pointing out his strengths, encouraging his ideas. She'd thought that the period of dark intensity following that time had been about his creative process. But it had been guilt. Guilt because he was betraying her and guilt because he knew he should stop but couldn't, because the painting meant so much to him.

She closed her eyes for a second, reliving that last awful day when she'd walked into the gallery with Sadie and Claudia and seen that despite the fact that she'd decided to stay, to give him another chance, he'd chosen to use his nudes of Serena for his show. Everyone had known, instantly, that he'd been screwing his model. It was in every brushstroke, every shadow, every smudge. Her family had been there. Her friends. Her work colleagues. She'd felt betrayed all over again.

"You're so selfish," she said now, shaking her head in wonder. "You knew how I would feel when I walked into that gallery opening, but you chose the work over me. Just like you chose to keep sleeping with Serena so you could keep painting."

"Yes. If it's any consolation, I haven't had a girlfriend since you left me, Gracie. I figured if the work is what's important, if I can't put anyone else before it, I've got no business getting involved with someone."

She shrugged. She didn't care whether he was alone or not. Standing, she brushed off her skirt. His gaze dropped as he scanned her from head to toe.

"You look so good, Gracie. That dress—no one has style like you," he said admiringly.

She eyed him coolly. She'd come here expecting to yell at him. She'd wanted to. She'd given herself permission to say or do anything, no matter how revealing or embarrassing when she looked back on it in retrospect. But the heat she'd felt last night hadn't translated to the reality of this meeting. Owen was a man, a friend, a lover who had let her down. But he didn't define her, she realized. His approval—his betrayal—was not a judgment on her. It was about his failure, not hers. She hadn't been not funny enough or not sexy enough or not beautiful enough or not loving enough. *He* had been lacking. *He* had felt inadequate and reached for the nearest comfort.

"Before you go, I've got something for you," Owen said, jumping to his feet. "I was always going to send it to you, but I could never quite let it go."

He disappeared into the shadows at the back of the shed. She heard him scuffling around, then he returned holding a small twelve-by-fourteen-inch canvas. He looked at it assessingly for a moment before handing it to her.

"I never could quite get the color of your eyes right," he said.

She took it automatically. Her own face gazed back at her from a boldly colored portrait. He'd captured the tilt of her eyes, the curve of her cheek, the pout of her lips. She was smiling, a far-off expression on her face. She looked happy. And beautiful.

"Thank you," she said.

"I'm sorry I hurt you. It was the last thing I ever wanted," he said.

The sound of approaching footsteps announced another arrival, and a tall, gangly man entered the yard.

"Owen, you prick, have you got that portrait done yet?" he asked jovially.

"Be with you in a minute, Johnny," Owen said.

Her cue to leave. She was ready to go, anyway. She eyed Owen steadily.

"Goodbye."

"Goodbye, Grace."

She made her way down the driveway and lay the painting on the backseat of her car. She supposed she ought to hate it, because Owen had painted it. But she didn't. The woman in the painting was the old Grace, the woman she'd been before she'd isolated herself. The painting was her map back. She wanted to be that woman again.

Pulling out from the curb, she turned for home. She'd started the healing process. She was ready to talk to Mac, to apologize, to explain. To tell him she loved him. To hope.

Sliding her sunglasses on, she stepped on the gas.

IT WAS DARK by the time Mac turned into his driveway on Saturday night. He'd spent most of the day in the house, but Claudia had called him out to the studio in the late afternoon so he could go over his plans for the wedding episode. The studio shoot started on Monday and he was confident he had all his ducks in a row, but that hadn't stopped Claudia from asking him to parade each and every one of them in front of her. He'd figured she was nervous and had humored her, but he was glad that she'd finally announced herself satisfied.

He frowned as he pulled up in front of his house. Every light was on, the windows glowing with golden auras. He might have left one light on, or two, but not the whole damn house.

Then his headlights picked up the dull glint of the not-so-pristine fender of Grace's Corvette in his carport.

So.

No phone call for the past two days, but now she was here.

Locking the Corvette, he strode toward the house. He'd shown her where he kept a spare key hidden in the garden for emergencies and she'd obviously made free use of it.

Opening the front door, he stepped into the foyer.

"Grace?" he called when she didn't appear to greet him.

He waited a moment, but still she didn't appear. His frown deepening, he ducked his head into the living room. No Grace. She wasn't in the kitchen, either. It wasn't until he reached the staircase that he saw the sheet of paper taped to the wall.

It had an arrow on it pointing upwards and an old photograph was glued in the center of the page.

He tugged it free and studied it. Grace stared back at him, a toddler in denim pants and a bright-purple top. Her eyes were wide and guileless, her grinning mouth displaying a mouthful of baby teeth.

He glanced up along the stairwell and saw that a new sheet of paper beckoned him onward every second step or so. He stepped up.

The second sheet was just a note: *Things you should know about me: I snore when I've had too much to drink.*

He tugged it free and shuffled it beneath the first sheet.

Another step, then another.

A photo this time. Grace was probably ten or eleven. She

was standing with her three sisters, all of whom were sporting finalist's ribbons for a shopping-mall beauty pageant. Grace's gaze was tortured as she stared at the camera and hunched her shoulders.

He tucked it beneath the others and took another two steps.

A note: *I sometimes drink the milk straight from the carton. And I put the juice back when there's only an inch left.*

He added it to his growing pile and moved to the next sheet.

Grace at a Halloween party, age maybe fifteen. She was wearing a ridiculous pumpkin costume and bobbing for apples, and the photographer had captured her in a moment of pure joy, her mouth open wide with laughter, her eyes squeezed tightly shut.

The next note read: *I need to learn to love myself more and to trust other people.*

He was at the top of the stairs.

He turned into the corridor and found another photo of Grace, this one from her university days. She had adopted the big black glasses and retro fashion, but hadn't quite perfected the look yet. She posed with younger versions of Sadie and Claudia, both of whom sported their own embarrassing fashion faux pas.

There was one last note before he reached his bedroom doorway.

I am afraid to love, but even more afraid of what will happen if I don't take the risk. I want to be brave. I want to be worthy of you.

He stepped into his bedroom.

She was standing in the middle of the room, naked. She met his eyes bravely.

"This is me. No more secrets. No more hiding. I want to know you and I want you to know me. I love you, Mac. And I hope you still love me," she said.

Words crowded his throat, but they weren't even close to being adequate and there was something he had to do first. He closed the space between them and pulled her into his arms. It had been way too long since he'd held her. He cupped the back of her head and pressed his cheek against her hair, just absorbing the fact that she was there.

"I love you, Grace," he said. "It would take a lot more than what happened the other day to stop me loving you—but I knew you had to want to be here as much as I wanted you to."

She lifted her head so that he could see her eyes.

"I do. I want it more than anything," she said. "I'm sorry I've been such hard work. But the bad old shit is on the way out and I want to replace it with good stuff."

His reached out to rub a thumb along her cheekbone. She smiled at him. Then, as if they had a mind of their own, his eyes dropped to her breasts.

Man, was he the luckiest guy in the world or what? He got to spend the rest of his life making love to Grace.

"Hey, up here," she said wryly, clicking his fingers to get his attention. "I'm making a heartfelt declaration."

"You know what would really help with that?" he said, reaching for his belt buckle.

"What?"

"If we were both naked. I think you might get your message across much more clearly then," he said, dragging his T-shirt over his head.

"You think so?" she said, her eyes dropping to his straining erection as he stepped out of his jeans.

"I know so," he said.

Pulling her into his arms again, he kissed her deeply and walked her toward the bed. Like a good girl, she flopped backward when she felt the mattress hit the back of her knees, and he fell on top of her. He wanted everything at once and didn't know where to start, so he took a bit of everything—he nibbled her ear and plucked at her breasts, and kneed her thighs apart and sucked her nipples and slid a hand between her legs and groaned at how wet and ready she was.

"Grace, I love you," he whispered in her ear as he slid inside her.

"I love you, too," she whispered back, then neither of them spoke except to urge the other on or to issue a panting instruction.

"Harder."

"Now."

"Yesssss."

"Please."

Mac's climax rocketed through him at the exact moment that he felt Grace's body tighten around his. He rode the last waves home, relishing the rightness, the glory of it.

Afterward, he lay pressed against her, breathing in her scent and running her silky hair through his fingers.

"I missed you," he said.

"I thought you might have had more than enough of me," she said.

"No."

"I pushed you pretty far," she said.

"Yeah. But I'm a stubborn guy."

"Thank you for being stubborn."

After they'd made love for the second time, he took her through to the largest of the spare bedrooms and showed her what he'd been working on for the bulk of the day. He'd cleared the room out and started painting the walls a soft, warm yellow. If he hadn't been called into the studio, he would have finished the first coat. He grunted with amusement as he belatedly realized that Claudia's pointless meeting might have had a point after all—to give Grace the opportunity to break into his house.

"I thought you'd prefer this room for your study because the view is better and it's bigger, but it's your choice," he said.

The cherrywood desk he'd been coveting for her was in one corner covered with a drop cloth, but he whisked it off to show her.

She spread her hands flat on the desk and turned to him with wide, tear-filled eyes.

"Mac. You did this for me after I slapped you? After I pushed you away so many times?"

"What can I say? I'm a glutton for punishment," he said. She smiled ruefully and he pulled her close. "And I know a good thing when I'm onto it. So, will you?"

"What?"

"Move in?"

"I might be stupid, but I know when I'm onto a good thing, too," she said.

"Is that a yes?"

"Yes, that's a yes."

Mac felt a surge of emotion as he looked into her eyes and saw happiness and love and not a trace of doubt.

Finally, they were dreaming the same dream.

* * * * *

Don't miss the conclusion of
The Secret Lives of Daytime Divas *miniseries.*
Look for Claudia's story,
HOT FOR HIM
by Sarah Mayberry.
Available May 2007 from Harlequin Blaze.

Set in darkness beyond the ordinary world.
Passionate tales of life and death.
With characters' lives ruled by laws the everyday world
can't begin to imagine.

n o c t u r n e

It's time to discover the Raintree trilogy...

New York Times *bestselling author*
LINDA HOWARD
brings you the dramatic first book
RAINTREE: INFERNO

The Ansara Wizards are rising and the Raintree clan
must rejoin the battle against their foes,
testing their powers, relationships and forcing
upon them lives they never could
have imagined before...

Turn the page for a sneak preview
of the captivating first book
in the Raintree trilogy,
RAINTREE: INFERNO
by LINDA HOWARD
On sale April 25

Dante Raintree stood with his arms crossed as he watched the woman on the monitor. The image was in black and white to better show details; color distracted the brain. He focused on her hands, watching every move she made, but what struck him most was how uncommonly *still* she was. She didn't fidget or play with her chips, or look around at the other players. She peeked once at her down card, then didn't touch it again, signaling for another hit by tapping a fingernail on the table. Just because she didn't seem to be paying attention to the other players, though, didn't mean she was as unaware as she seemed.

"What's her name?" Dante asked.

"Lorna Clay," replied his chief of security, Al Rayburn.

"At first I thought she was counting, but she doesn't pay enough attention."

"She's paying attention, all right," Dante murmured. "You just don't see her doing it." A card counter had to remember every card played. Supposedly counting cards was impossible with the number of decks used by the casinos, but there were those rare individuals who could calculate the odds even with multiple decks.

"I thought that, too," said Al. "But look at this piece of tape coming up. Someone she knows comes up to her and speaks, she looks around and starts chatting, completely misses the play of the people to her left—and doesn't look around even when the deal comes back to her, just taps that finger. And damn if she didn't win. Again."

Dante watched the tape, rewound it, watched it again. Then he watched it a third time. There had to be something he was missing, because he couldn't pick out a single giveaway.

"If she's cheating," Al said with something like respect, "she's the best I've ever seen."

"What does your gut say?"

Al scratched the side of his jaw, considering. Finally, he said, "If she isn't cheating, she's the luckiest person walking. She wins. Week in, week out, she wins. Never a huge amount, but I ran the numbers and she's into us for about five grand a week. Hell, boss, on her way out of the casino she'll stop by a slot machine, feed a dollar in and walk away with at least fifty. It's never the same machine, either. I've had her watched, I've had her followed, I've even looked for the same faces in the casino every time she's in here, and I can't find a common denominator."

"Is she here now?"

"She came in about half an hour ago. She's playing black-jack, as usual."

"Bring her to my office," Dante said, making a swift decision. "Don't make a scene."

"Got it," said Al, turning on his heel and leaving the security center.

Dante left, too, going up to his office. His face was calm. Normally he would leave it to Al to deal with a cheater, but he was curious. How was she doing it? There were a lot of bad cheaters, a few good ones, and every so often one would come along who was the stuff of which legends were made:

the cheater who didn't get caught, even when people were alert and the camera was on him—or, in this case, her.

It was possible to simply be lucky, as most people understood luck. Chance could turn a habitual loser into a big-time winner. Casinos, in fact, thrived on that hope. But luck itself wasn't habitual, and he knew that what passed for luck was often something else: cheating. And there was the other kind of luck, the kind he himself possessed, but it depended not on chance but on who and what he was. He knew it was an innate power and not Dame Fortune's erratic smile. Since power like his was rare, the odds made it likely the woman he'd been watching was merely a very clever cheat.

Her skill could provide her with a very good living, he thought, doing some swift calculations in his head. Five grand a week equaled $260,000 a year, and that was just from his casino. She probably hit them all, careful to keep the numbers relatively low so she stayed under the radar.

He wondered how long she'd been taking him, how long she'd been winning a little here, a little there, before Al noticed.

The curtains were open on the wall-to-wall window in his office, giving the impression, when one first opened the door, of stepping out on to a covered balcony. The glazed window faced west, so he could catch the sunsets. The sun was low now, the sky painted in purple and gold. At his home in the mountains, most of the windows faced east, affording him views of the sunrise. Something in him needed both the greeting and the goodbye of the sun. He'd always been drawn to sunlight, maybe because fire was his element to call, to control.

He checked his internal time: four minutes until sundown. Without checking the sunrise tables every day, he knew exactly when the sun would slide behind the mountains. He didn't own an alarm clock. He didn't need one.

He was so acutely attuned to the sun's position that he had only to check within himself to know the time. As for waking at a particular time, he was one of those people who could tell himself to wake at a certain time, and he did. That talent had nothing to do with being Raintree, so he didn't have to hide it; a lot of perfectly ordinary people had the same ability.

He had other talents and abilities, however, that did require careful shielding. The long days of summer instilled in him an almost sexual high, when he could feel contained power buzzing just beneath his skin. He had to be doubly careful not to cause candles to leap into flame just by his presence, or to start wildfires with a glance in the dry-as-tinder brush. He loved Reno; he didn't want to burn it down. He just felt so damn *alive* with all the sunshine pouring down that he wanted to let the energy pour through him instead of holding it inside.

This must be how his brother Gideon felt while pulling lightning, all that hot power searing through his muscles, his veins. They had this in common, the connection with raw power. All the members of the far-flung Raintree clan had some power, some heightened ability, but only members of the royal family could channel and control the earth's natural energies.

Dante wasn't just of the royal family, he was the Dranir, the leader of the entire clan. "Dranir" was synonymous with king, but the position he held wasn't ceremonial, it was one of sheer power. He was the oldest son of the previous Dranir, but he would have been passed over for the position if he hadn't also inherited the power to hold it.

Behind him came Al's distinctive knock on the door. The outer office was empty, Dante's secretary having gone home hours before. "Come in," he called, not turning from his view of the sunset.

The door opened, and Al said, "Mr. Raintree, this is Lorna Clay."

Dante turned and looked at the woman, all his senses on alert. The first thing he noticed was the vibrant color of her hair, a rich, dark red that encompassed a multitude of shades from copper to burgundy. The warm amber light danced along the iridescent strands, and he felt a hard tug of sheer lust in his gut. Looking at her hair was almost like looking at fire, and he had the same reaction.

The second thing he noticed was that she was spitting mad.

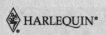

EVERLASTING LOVE™

Every great love has a story to tell™

If you're a romantic at heart, you'll definitely want to read this new series.

Available April 24

The Marriage Bed by Judith Arnold

An emotional story about a couple's love that is put to the test when the shocking truth of a long-buried secret comes to the surface.

&

Family Stories by Tessa McDermid

A couple's epic love story is pieced together by their granddaughter in time for their seventy-fifth anniversary.

And look for

The Scrapbook by Lynnette Kent

&

When Love Is True by Joan Kilby

from Harlequin® Everlasting Love™ this June.

Pick up a book today!

www.eHarlequin.com

REQUEST YOUR FREE BOOKS!

2 FREE NOVELS PLUS 2 FREE GIFTS!

HARLEQUIN®

Blaze®

Red-hot reads!

YES! Please send me 2 FREE Harlequin® Blaze® novels and my 2 FREE gifts. After receiving them, if I don't wish to receive any more books, I can return the shipping statement marked "cancel." If I don't cancel, I will receive 6 brand-new novels every month and be billed just $3.99 per book in the U.S., or $4.47 per book in Canada, plus 25¢ shipping and handling per book and applicable taxes, if any*. That's a savings of at least 15% off the cover price! I understand that accepting the 2 free books and gifts places me under no obligation to buy anything. I can always return a shipment and cancel at any time. Even if I never buy another book from Harlequin, the two free books and gifts are mine to keep forever.

151 HDN EF3W   351 HDN EF3X

Name	(PLEASE PRINT)
Address	Apt.
City	State/Prov.	Zip/Postal Code

Signature (if under 18, a parent or guardian must sign)

Mail to the **Harlequin Reader Service**®:
IN U.S.A.: P.O. Box 1867, Buffalo, NY 14240-1867
IN CANADA: P.O. Box 609, Fort Erie, Ontario L2A 5X3

Not valid to current Harlequin Blaze subscribers.

Want to try two free books from another line?
Call 1-800-873-8635 or visit www.morefreebooks.com.

* Terms and prices subject to change without notice. NY residents add applicable sales tax. Canadian residents will be charged applicable provincial taxes and GST. This offer is limited to one order per household. All orders subject to approval. Credit or debit balances in a customer's account(s) may be offset by any other outstanding balance owed by or to the customer. Please allow 4 to 6 weeks for delivery.

Your Privacy: Harlequin is committed to protecting your privacy. Our Privacy Policy is available online at www.eHarlequin.com or upon request from the Reader Service. From time to time we make our lists of customers available to reputable firms who may have a product or service of interest to you. If you would prefer we not share your name and address, please check here. ☐

HARLEQUIN®

Blaze™

COMING NEXT MONTH

#321 BEYOND SEDUCTION Kathleen O'Reilly
The Red Choo Diaries, Bk. 3
The last thing respected talk-show host Sam Porter wants is to be the subject of a sex blog—but that's exactly what happens when up-and-coming writer Mercedes Brooks gets hold of him…and never wants to let him go!

#322 THE EX-GIRLFRIENDS' CLUB Rhonda Nelson
Ben Wilder is stunned when he discovers a Web site dedicated to bashing him. Sure, he's a little wild. So what? Then he learns Eden Rutherford, his first love, is behind the site, and decides some payback is in order. And he's going to start by showing Eden *exactly* what she's been missing….

#323 THE MAN TAMER Cindi Myers
It's All About Attitude…
Can't get your man to behave? Columnist Rachel Westover has the answer: man taming, aka behavior modification. Too bad she can't get Garret Kelly to obey. Sure, he's hers to command between the sheets, but outside…well, there might be something to be said for going wild!

#324 DOUBLE DARE Tawny Weber
Audra Walker is the ultimate bad girl. And to prove it, she takes a friend's dare—to hit on the next guy who comes through the door of the bar. Lucky for her, the guy's a definite hottie. Too bad he's also a cop….

#325 KISS AND DWELL Kelley St. John
The Sexth Sense, Bk. 1
Monique Vicknair has a secret—she and her family are mediums, charged with the job of helping lost souls cross over. But when Monique discovers her next assignment is sexy Ryan Chappelle, the last thing she wants to do is send him away. Because Ryan is way too much man to be a ghost….

#326 HOT FOR HIM Sarah Mayberry
Secret Lives of Daytime Divas, Bk. 3
Beating her rival for a coveted award has put Claudia Dostis on top. But when Leandro Mandalor challenges her to address the sizzle between them, her pride won't let her back down. In this battle for supremacy the gloves—and a lot of other clothes—are coming off!

www.eHarlequin.com

HBCNM0407